I0714491

Other books by Joe Taylor:

NOVELS
Pineapple, a novel in verse
Back to the Wine Jog, a novel in verse
Bad Form
Oldcat & Ms. Puss: A book of days for you and me
Persephone's Escalator (forthcoming)
The Alleged Woman
Highway 28 West
Silent Bob
Let There Be Lite, OR, How I Came To Know and Love Godel's Incompleteness Proof
The Theoretics of Love
Don't Be Lonely, Lone Ranger (forthcoming)
Eric and the Anti-Tankers (forthcoming)

STORY COLLECTIONS
Some Heroes, Some Heroines, Some Others
Ghostly Demasrcations
Masques for the Fields of Time

EDITOR
Belles' Letters: stories by Alabama Women
        co-editor with Tina Jones, Livingston Press
Tartts 1-9

The World's Thinnest Fat Man

stories by

Joe Taylor

Swallow's Tale Press
at Livingston Press
The University of West Alabama

Typesetting and page layout: David Smith
Cover design: Joe Taylor
Cover photo: Tricia Taylor
Proofreading: Margaret Walburn, Ariane Godfrey,
Chris Hawkins, Danielle Hornsby, Tricia Taylor
Jason Sheehan

Grateful acknowledgment is made to Shapiro Bernstein & Co. for

permission to reprint portions of "A Walk on the Wild Side,"

@1961, 1962, music by Elmer Bernstein, lyrics by Mack David.

These stories appeared in earlier versions in the following:

"The Woman Who Wouldn't Talk" *The Southern Review*

"Angels on a Pinhead" *Cimarron Review*

"Faithful Companion" *cleansheets.com*

"My Life as an Imaginary Number" *GW Review*

"Alpha and Omega" *Alabama Bound*

"The Phantom Tipper" *honeydii*

"The Odds Against Going to Heaven" *Beloit Fiction Journal*

"Judas" in the first edition of Janet Burroway's *Writing Fiction*

"My Ode to Sylvia Plath" *A State of Laughter*

This is a work of fiction.
You know the rest: any resemblance
to persons living or dead is coincidental.

Swallow's Tale Press is distributed by Livingston Press,
part of The University of West Alabama.
Livingston Press has non-profit status.
Donations are tax-deductible

Table of Contents

*For the folks at Lexington's Paddock Club
and the Mexican High on Rose,
especially Joe Stearns, Fred Moore and Rita Gatton;
and for the folks at West Palm's Red Lion Lounge, especially
Harry (in memoriam), Melanie and Melody. Thanks to all for
your support.*

The World's Thinnest Fat Man

The Woman Who Wouldn't Talk, The Man Who Wouldn't Listen

"I LIVED WITH HER for one year and one month. A funny thing: she never talked. I thought her silence meant love. Typical male ego, huh?" The woman I was telling this to shrugged sleepily, since she had barely opened her shop. Mid-morning in the French Quarter hovers like fog on a predawn riverbank. The only other movement came as a black cat behind the counter rubbed against the stub of an old water or gas pipe jutting from the plaster wall. The cat's golden eyes saw through me.

"When Sally did finally talk, we were at our favorite Italian restaurant, and—you're not going to believe this—she told me she was running away to Maine with a lesbian lover." I waited for a reaction, but the woman turned to stare at a young couple in the back of her shop, near the shriveled voodoo chicken feet and Louisiana Love Spice. Sassafras root, the ingredients read—you slip it in a wayward lover's hot drink. Minutes before I'd read those ingredients through the shop's filmy display window and thought: *Maybe ten kilos will do me.*

"Lesbian. I mean, I didn't know how to handle that. I just clammed up." The woman's breasts rose and fell under her black, tasselled dress. She had beautiful butterscotch eyes and *café au lait* skin. The combination prompted me onward. " 'Josey, either get a new girl or get out of town,' all my friends told me. So I was going for the

"

latter, I was going to chase Sally to Maine. But she panicked over the phone when I called, and promised she'd try things with me again in two weeks." I caught my breath, just as the *au lait* woman once more inhaled deeply. "So meanwhile," I continued, "I came here to New Orleans, to see you, for when she comes back, I mean. I want to be prepared."

Her nod was brief, for her butterscotch eyes regarded the young couple congregated in the rear, fingering bleached chicken claws. Then she turned to me and smiled, her teeth a fluorescent contrast with her skin. "Je will *faites vous un* potion at midnight tonight," she said, "and you must think of your lover—*quelle est*—what is her name?"

"Sally," I answered, eyeing the young couple myself, fully expecting them to slip their hands and a chicken's foot apiece into one another's jeans and rotate with gravelly Mediterranean sex. It was New Orleans after all, and such was my Kentucky idea of the place.

"S-sall-ee," the woman repeated, hissing the name and taking a pad and writing it down. "You must think of S-sall-ee at exactly midnight *ce soir.* You must think of her for fifteen full minutes, *le temps* it take me to *faire* un doll. *Avez-vous*—do you have a photo?"

I was prepared for this and pulled out a B&W photo taken of Sally when her hair fell to her waist, pre-lesbian. She was standing in front of a barn where a mutual friend was playing at milking a goat—for the cheese, he'd explained. We'd gone to visit and I envisioned Sally and myself on a similar farm, in a similar home, with a similar barn and wood-burning stove and goats hopping outside. I'd constantly be smoking my pipe and watching her brown ribbon of hair swaying like the pendulum of a happy grandfather clock. But then she cut her ponytail to butch length, and . . .

The *au lait* woman behind the counter looked at the photo, then at me. This woman was four or five years older than me and a rare beauty, from her sculptured cherry nails to her shock of long raven hair, braided then swirled into a bun. I momentarily felt embarrassed for Sally, so small in that photograph, so tomboyish with her repressed bosoms—more than tomboyish, more masculine looking than I am, should I ever shave my beard.

"Fifty dollars," the woman said, rubbing her fingertips over the photo.

I'd come prepared to pay up to three hundred cash, and charge three hundred more. Anything to get the woman who never talked back. As I slid over a single bill, both the shopkeeper and I saw the girl slip a chicken claw into her purse as her boyfriend clumsily tried to block our view. The *au lait* shopkeeper bent to scratch her black cat's ears and its gold eyes glowed fiercely, like something you'd stumble on in a deep Louisiana swamp. She then reached into a nearby box and tossed a pinch of dried, nasty-yellow herbs at the boy and girl. At least that looked like what she tossed, since seeds fell on the glass counter with pop-pop-pops. The couple started for the door and the *au lait* woman said, "*S'il vous plaît*. The rooster mojo costs $18.50."

"We ain't buying nothing, we decided against it," the boy answered.

He put his hand in his pocket. The kid was nineteen or twenty and looked like every hayseed from eastern Kentucky I'd ever met. I put my own hand in my pocket, and feeling the steel of my knife, opened its blade halfway. There was a click and we all looked to the front door, which had an electric deadbolt.

"No one steal from Madame LaBonne. The rooster mojo cost $18.50."

"Lady, you accusing my girl of stealing?"

"*J'accuse* her of stealing *et vous* of lying," Madame LaBonne answered evenly. "*Vous êtes* young. For $18.50, no police and no curse."

"Curse?" the girl asked.

Madame LaBonne's cat jumped onto the counter and arched its back. Maybe it jumped because she was tapping her nails there, prompting like an expert trainer. Maybe not. The girl inhaled at the cat's glossy blackness, and her painted rosy cheeks puffed a stupidity matching her lime-green polka dot blouse. A prom queen if ever. The cat stared, slinging its tail like a whip. A mystery if ever.

"That cat comes near me or her either one, I'll cut it up," the boy said, pulling out a knife. I was glad to see his was no longer than my own, maybe even a tad shorter. And since mine was expensive Damascus steel, his was all the less impressive.

"Open the damned door and let me out." He reached for peach fuzz on his chin but stopped himself.

"Eighteen-fifty," Madame LaBonne said.

The boy raised the knife to his waist and took a step forward. The cat jumped off the counter and he jerked back.

"Danny," his girl whined.

"It's self-defense. She's locked us in and's threatening us." He turned full to the shopkeeper, who remained remarkably cool, considering. "You want that cat alive you better—"

I love cats. I pulled my knife out and held it at waist level. My pants felt cold and I wondered if I'd peed myself. My legs were probably visibly shivering, but so were the boy's, and his girlfriend, wide-eyed before, became absolutely polka-dot-eyed at the sight of two knives.

"Don't get involved with Madame LaBonne's problems, *cheri*," the *au lait* woman said.

I crab-stepped toward the counter, away from the door, allowing the boy and girl a clean route of escape.

"Here! Here's twenty dollars!" The girl threw a bill toward the counter, but it fell on the floor, in front of the cat. "Let us out now—please. We don't want trouble, we were just playing, making a dare."

The front door clicked and seemed to spring inward.

The girl grabbed her boyfriend's arm and tugged. He walked sideways, sneering at me.

"Screw both of you!" he yelled once out on the concrete steps. He tried to slam the door but its spring was too heavy. Madame LaBonne flicked more herbs, and more seeds popped on the black linoleum floor. Through the shop's filmy window we watched the two of them run off. Madame LaBonne's black cat sprang through the still open door. Madame LaBonne smiled and pinched my shoulder.

"That was sweet of you, *cheri*."

"Do you want me to get your cat?" I folded my knife and replaced it in my pocket.

She smiled wryly. One of her canines was solid gold. Why didn't

I notice it before? "Chocolat *cherchera* his own way back. He has business to attend." She said "Shock-o-la" and I loved her for it. She glanced out the window at three college kids in their University Of Wherever tee shirts. Drunk already, and it wasn't even noon.

I bent for the twenty the girl had thrown, and Madame LaBonne handed my fifty-dollar bill back in exchange, brushing the tips of my fingers with her nail or something that shocked—as in high amperage. Straightening, I stared into her eyes, thinking of caramel candied apples. "*Tu viens* back here at midnight, *cheri*. Be sober and be ready, and you will have back your *cherie*."

Another slice of her nail on my palm. Another zap of alternating current straight from the 200 amp service box. A customer walked in, or the phone rang, or both. I left, as much in puppy love as any young man can be who's at the same time struggling in the throes of unrequited amor.

Once outside, I heard yelling and scuffling two blocks down. It was the three college boys and the couple. Two of the college boys had backed the hick into a brick wall and were pounding him. The girl screamed and the other college boy picked up a can of garbage and dumped it over her head. It dripped yellow and green chunks to match her polka dots. Garbage around the French Quarter can be pretty oozy, I noticed. Then the college boys ran off.

The clop-clop of two mounted police horses sounded from behind. The cops ignored the retreating college kids to encircle the couple, evidently thinking the boy had been fighting with his girl. One horse bumped the boy and knocked him down into what was left of the goopy garbage. Madame LaBonne's black cat sauntered back along the sidewalk, licking its whiskers and watching me. I nodded in what I hoped was a respectful manner and quickly crossed the street.

To remain sober I'd have to spend the rest of the morning, afternoon, and night walking other streets, eating pizza slices and drinking coffee. How come no one sold chicory coffee, I wondered after a couple of hours. Then I realized it was amazing anyone near Bourbon Street sold *any* coffee: tourists take the street's name very seriously.

At two there was a brief but heavy storm, so I stopped in a used book store. I browsed the occult section until my fingers skittered over a bumpy, ugly green binding with black lettering. Inset in the middle was a picture of a woman I first thought was Madame LaBonne, but this woman lived in the Quarter at the turn of the century. No identifying name underneath, simply a legend that read, "Young Creole works charms on New Orleans street." Two splotched snakes wound about her wrists and several young men gathered about. What charms she was working remained uncertain. Thunder boomed outside.

The bookstore's shelving reached well over my head and I'd had to stand on a rickety wooden stool to fetch this book. As I balanced on the stool and thumbed through the book I thought I saw someone staring from an aisle to my left, through dust-laden spaces between the shelves. I shifted but spotted no one, though a black man was browsing in the aisle to my right. "POETRY," a faded, hand-inked sign read through what seemed an infinity of refracting motes and floating spores.

The book I held was entitled *Charms and Potions*. A chapter called "Love" contained recipes for cookies (which required a single drop of blood from the forsaken); hidden sachets (which required hair and nail clippings dipped in used bath water from the beloved); candle-burning (which needed to be practiced twice daily and worked best when used in conjunction with other charms); and voodoo (which depended on dolls, though the author, a turn-of-the century sorceress hep on technology, argued practitioners had effectively employed daguerreotypes and even photographs).

The room brightened and I could see sunlight outside. My nose itched as I stepped off the stool. Once more I had an uneasy feeling that someone was watching. The black man was making a purchase near the front of the store, several couples and a young leftover hippie relic were browsing. The leftover hippie had been loudly trying to make a swap with the owner—skin books the hippie'd "found," for a first issue comic book the owner was selling. A comic book? Why not *Das Kapital* in the original German, or the little red firebook of

Chairman Mao? Where were the idealists of yesteryear? Vacationing in Maine?

Something moved on the other side of the shelving. What looked like a black cat's tail slid underneath the lowest shelf and disappeared. "Shock-o-la?" I called. Four more rows of books lay ahead, ending in a brick wall painted mint green, all dimly lit by two bare, low-wattage bulbs floating over a placid sea of motes and spores. I inhaled deeply and dove into "TRAVEL," "SHIPS & PLANES," "GLASSWARE & ANTIQUES." The mint green wall was damp from seepage, and mustiness pervaded the area. I'd be sneezing for a week.

"Kitty, kitty," I called. Only the silence of once-read books answered. Retreating to brighter lighting and clicking my fingers, I tried again. "Shock-o-la?" An older, well-groomed couple eyed me. The man had a barbed white beard and was nearly a walking advertisement for Kentucky Fried Chicken, though his suit was powder blue, not the Colonel's snow white. I smiled stupidly, tucked *Charms and Potions* under my arm and stolled to the cash register.

Outside in the steam, walking, walking, and all the strip-tease joints reminded me of Sally. I guess that's not put right. I mean that when I looked in at the fleshy women slinking under glaring violet lights, they naturally aroused me, and that arousal naturally made me think of what I was missing—Sally. Her announcement of newfound lesbianism seemed to fit—to my untutored Kentucky mind—Bourbon Street's debauchery. So my final reaction to the strippers was to hunch my shoulders and slink too. It's a wonder I wasn't frisked by the vice squad.

Things probably would have been easier if I'd just burst out and cried or shouted or stomped, but axons and neurons kept crisscrossing inside my skull. Every time I spotted some woman's long hair or vaguely tomboyish face passing in the street I would stare: *It's Sally! Sure, why not. She's had a change of heart and has heard from mutual friends that I've driven down here to forget.* But it never was her, of course. And when I noticed all the male and female homosexuals peppering the French Quarter, I wanted to talk with them, see if they knew my Sally, who'd run off to be a lesbian in Maine. Instead of asking, I drank more coffee, with no chicory.

Finally, one hundred and eleven Sally look-alikes later, at ten minutes to midnight, I was nearing Madame LaBonne's. Her shop lay off the main drag by a block, which may as well have been a mile at that time of night. A bar was open two doors down, though only four or five customers, all hunched like they'd heard the same sad Sally-went-to-Maine news, were visible through its swinging Western saloon doors. I stood outside Madame LaBonne's. A single lamp lit her back room, one of those green banker lamps. What looked like a small skull lounged on a bare worktable, its red eyes lit too. When the eyes flickered I started, but realized the skull must be a candle. The front part of the shop loomed so darkly that I couldn't discern anything in it past the display window and the good old sassafrass potion. I raised my hand to tap on the door, then felt rubbing against my leg. Shock-o-la.

"We're friends, right?" I hesitated, and when the cat rubbed again, I stooped to scratch his ears. He purred and stood on his back legs to sniff the book I held, then hopped the last step to slap at a low-hung bell painted black, invisible from the night street.

"*Chocolat?*" a voice called from within the store.

Shock-o-la. It sounded scary now, foreign. I looked around; the entire block was barren of movement. Had someone cleaned up the sodden garbage from this afternoon? Since all the cans stood grayly upright, I supposed so.

"It's me too," I called. The electric bolt slid back and the yellow wood door sprung inward while steamy heat—I don't know how else to describe the perfume-laden air—rushed out.

"*Cheri.* Just in time." Heavy beads slapped her thighs (flesh, or flesh-colored tights?) as she held the door open and peered down from the top step. Her face glowed from something silvery—the moon or a street lamp, maybe. Realizing the black cat had already run inside, I started in too, but Madame LaBonne bent and sniffed, then lit a cigarette lighter and looked into my eyes. "Sober," she announced, in a tone of surprise.

"You said not to drink, or the magic wouldn't work as well."

"Yes, but this is New Orleans," she answered, cozily bedding that city's last 'N' in the back of her nasal passage. "Oh-la, la, *cheri, tu* must have it *très mal. Très, très mal.*" She shook her head and swung the door open. Once I was in she pocketed the lighter and the click of the closed door's electric lock hit home.

Movement somewhere in the shop. Chocolat.

"*Je*, ah, I, have been, ah, es-tood-ay-ing *le photo de ta* Sally, *cheri,*" Madame LaBonne said, taking my elbow and leading me toward the back room and the skull candle. I stumbled over something heavy and soft; I didn't want to know what. The farther we walked the more her perfume oozed into my pores, while her nails bit through my short sleeve like safety pins. When we neared the worktable I could see that the small skull was real, not a candle, and that she really had been studying Sally's picture, for it was surrounded by three half-burned black candles.

"*Assieds-toi.* Sit, sit," she told me.

I did and she sat too. "Do you smoke?" she asked. Once more her skin glowed in the candlelight and I realized she must have been wearing oil, maybe musk mixed with olive, it smelled so weird.

"No. Just a pipe. The other makes me cough."

"Not *les* cigarettes." She laughed and pulled out a brown, rolled joint that glowed like an autumn leaf in the candlelight.

"Marijuana makes me stupid."

"So does love, *oui*? But who refuse to fall *en amour* because of that?" She lit the joint and inhaled. I watched her cleavage deepen; then I took the joint and concentrated on inhaling, still seeing on either side of the glowing tip her breasts wrinkling with age marks upon her exhaling. The age marks surprised me. She tapped the photo. Her nails were now painted a glow-in-the-dark ivory. "And do you talk with this one often?"

"She never talks. Just listens." I handed her the joint.

"Ah. *Cheri, tu aussi*, you should listen to silence. It is always telling you something, guaranteed."

We breathed for a moment. There was no sound—well yes, there was: Chocolat purred underneath the worktable. Madame LaBonne passed the joint back. I first shook my head, then took it as her nails brushed my fingertips. It was New Orleans, right?

She lit the three other candles surrounding the photo of Sally. These weren't black, but violet.

"Tell me about this S-sall-ee."

So I told her how Sally and I had lived together for a year and a month. How we'd planned to go to France, me to chef school, her to get a master's in archaeology. How that had fallen through for both of us. How Sally'd met some lesbian women at a party on a horse farm outside of Paris, Kentucky. How she'd left for Maine with one of them.

"Paree? Kentucky?" Madame LaBonne asked, as if amazed.

I nodded then laughed at the ridiculous metropolitan fall our, my, dreams had taken. I felt like I was writing a smoky country song, one that would never be sung.

"She didn't even really tell me where she was going. I found out through her lover's lover. We were both jilted, you see."

"*Cheri*, you should be writing this down for *les* Soaps on tel-e-vee-see-on." She crowded more syllables into that last word than I'd ever heard it given.

I told her where the photo had been taken, how that farm too was one of my dreams for Sally and me. *My* dream, for Sally and me.

A single chime sounded. I turned to a grandfather clock. It showed twelve-thirty. What had happened to the midnight chime? As I turned to ask this, her ankle touched mine and she leaned forward after a grand inhalation.

When we kissed, she blew smoke from the marijuana into my mouth. My eyes bulged and I could feel the artery on my throat pump. She touched my thigh where I kept my wallet safe from big city pickpockets. Time, did it pass? I looked into her eyes, which glowed liquidly from the guttering candles. Her hand stayed on my thigh, warm.

"*Tu* can *prends* your money up and down this city to every practitioner, gypsy and witch you can find, *cheri. Quienne le sait*? Maybe enough magic would finally get S-sall-ee back. But *le grand* question: Do you want back this lady who does not talk? *Les filles* give you that."

"*Les filles?*"

"Hookers, *cheri.*"

I must have already been high, or I would have gotten mad, it seems, at her comparing Sally to a hooker. She removed her hand from my thigh to take another toke from the marijuana, and then she smiled, passing it. After I inhaled, the joint reached roach size, so she snuffed it, then held my hand.

"Close your eyes and *je toi donne la magie.*" Seeing my hesitation, she once more kissed me. My eyes closed on autopilot. "Now keep them closed and I'll show you the future *si tu as la magie comme* you want." I could hear her stand. She reached for something, her nipples tickling my cheek, and she began combing my hair.

"Five months from now—Christmas—she *vient* back and you think how *joli* everything be. Does she talk with you then? No, she hang *le* mistletoe in some dark corner. One year from now, say Mardi Gras or Easter, *elle engrosse avec ton* baby. Does she tell you? No, she talk with some girlfriend and find *le docteur* to make her thin again." My head was twisted to the side as Madame LaBonne tugged something from my hair. My hair is very fine for a man's—plenty of women tell me they wish they had it—still, it doesn't usually tangle. I jerked and could feel Madame LaBonne's breasts cushion my neck: "Keep your eyes closed, *cheri*, or I cannot show your future or untangle this love knot." I inhaled her warm breath and nodded.

"Her girlfriend from the Paree farm, or some other girlfriend, *parle avec elle: 'Vous pauvre jeune fille.* That man make you go to doctor and get sick and feel so hurt. Come *chez moi* for dinner *ce soir*. We will have *le coq et le vin* and you will forget his bad.'" I could feel her fingertips scratching and running along my scalp with that same voltage I'd felt earlier when she'd handed back my fifty. "Ah la-la," she exclaimed softly into my ear on pulling out another tangle. "So many, so many." She kept combing, I could smell her body, feel it touching my cheeks, my nose, my eyes. Then she began to talk again:

"And S-sall-ee *va* to this horse farm woman friend or that horse farm woman friend and they drink *le vin* and talk mal of *toi*." Madame LaBonne was whispering in my other ear now, I could feel her teeth nibbling.

"Ouch!"

"*Tais-toi. Tais-toi.* Hush, hush. Soon, what do you think your man-woman friend she do? *Elle* begin to weep and say 'He magic me.' Her friend shake her head—hold still now, *cheri, c'est un grand* tangle *ici*." Madame pulled so hard I had to grab the arms of the chair. She pulled again. "Her friend shake her head and *dite*, 'Drink this, do this, burn this, wear that; then you find freedom to leave him and come back to me.'"

I bit my lip as she pulled a dense clump from my hair. Then she combed and combed and combed, singing softly while I thought about what she'd said. She had a tiny, fairy-tale voice when she sang, as opposed to her sultry foreign chitchat.

The clock struck and she covered my eyes, evidently knowing I'd open them to look. "Twelve-thirty, *cheri*. We have half an hour of witching left."

I started to speak, to correct her and say it must be one, because . . .

"*Tais-toi.* Hush." She licked the artery along my neck and brushed smoothly through my hair and beard. "All the love-tangles put witchy-like in your hair vanish now. Now you must think about what I told you." She licked the vein on the other side of my neck and I shivered, envisioning Sally in that farmhouse, at the large wooden table, drinking wine and listening to her girlfriend. I saw her friend rubbing her shoulders—I became Sally and I felt her friend's comforting hands and I felt Sally's face swell with tears. I felt her mouth move happily, rapidly, as she talked and talked and talked and the girlfriend nodded and nodded and nodded. I felt the clicking of Sally's small square teeth that always reminded me of a child's—but wait: The woman who never talked was talking. I pulled back and watched her square teeth chattering and laughing. I realized that even if I should get her back through magic, I'd do neither of us a favor. Something dropped onto my hand. A feather, a piece of paper?

"Open your eyes."

I did and saw four tangles of hair in the candlelight, resting in my palm.

"The love knots come all out, *cheri*." She plucked them up and dropped each into separate candles. They sputtered and popped onto Sally's photo, hitting her eyes and giving her an unearthly look.

"I could see her. I could feel her. She was talking. It was magic. She was talking," I said. My voice croaked.

"But not to you, not to you. She has her world, and *tu* have yours."

Odors mixed: cinnamon, swampland marijuana, incense, musk. I placed my hand on Madame LaBonne's hip. Underneath heavy beads I could feel warm flesh and I massaged it as the last love knot burned. She bent to kiss my forehead. For some reason I kept my eyes open and could once more see age lines in her cleavage. As my other hand moved to embrace her she slipped away to sit across from me.

"*Bien. Les* love knots are no more. But you must always be careful that *qui tu* sleep *avec* live in your same world. Talk, talk, *cheri*. Lovemaking without talk is *mal magie*. Sorcery. It is flesh without spirit, and that can *finit tres mal*. End very bad, you understand?"

"Could we—you and me—"

"Too young. *Tu es trop, trop jeune. Je suis* old *comme les* bricks *dans les* streets, *oui?*"

Chocolat meowed and Madame walked into the front showroom to feed him. She momentarily turned on a light. I held my breath, for she appeared to be in her nineties. The light went out and she returned to the back room and its candles. She smiled and her gold canine glinted. "Your book," she said, handing me the package I thought I'd held all along. I thanked her, my mouth dry.

"*C'est Nouveau Orleans, cheri*. New Orleans. Go have a drink. Go meet someone."

I nodded and walked out, hearing the doorbell ting once, then again. Was Chocolat following me? Looking back I saw only the dark street and upright garbage cans. Looking ahead I saw that the bar two doors down was still open. Acoustic music floated out, a relief from the Dixieland bombarding me all sober night. I walked in and took a stool at a very old and smoke-stained cherry bar. A threesome of two women and a man sat to my left. The woman nearest me was blonde, mid-twenties, and very feminine—unlike Sally. I ordered a gin and tonic to fight the heat. The woman smiled at me while the bartender mixed the drink. I smiled back. The book gave a tug, so I opened the sack, despite that I've always felt that reading in a bar is the height of either pretension or lunacy, one or both. The book I pulled out wasn't *Charms and Potions* that I'd bought, but *Kama Sutra: For Western Ears.* There was a leather marker, so I opened to it and read this inscription: "Leave the charms to me. Talk, and above all, listen; that's all the magic you need. *Avec* affection from another world, Madame LaBonne."

"Whatcha reading in the middle of New Orleans for?"

I looked up at her smile. "It's a long story," I said.

"Not as long as mine, I bet. Anyway, it's Bourbon Street. We've got all night."

My ears actually tingled. The Man Who Wouldn't Listen was listening. It was a start, a real start.

Angels on a Pinhead

IT WAS DURING THE Enlightenment, I believe. Rousseau and Hobbes, or Locke. Voltaire. One of the bunch, all of them. Their running argument, when they and their dandy compatriots weren't burning witches, went like this: Say if two humans were truly isolated, if they'd lived out their entire existence as gatherers or carnivores or some in-between aboriginal mixture; say these two strangers were thrown upon one another, say by happenstance reining in for a drink under the same walnut tree; if this were to occur, would the pair hurl walnuts and tangle unto death, or would they French kiss and become asshole buddies? So the argument went and so the sides gathered, just as if everyone had donned regalia to line up in a medieval university hall and debate how many angels might dance on a pinhead.—And we label that "Enlightenment"? Humanity's wick hadn't really brightened one watt beyond the Darkling Middle Ages.

SOUTH FLORIDA—you needn't be reminded that it's hot, and you'd allow that this minimal information had filtered to the majority of human intelligence encountered there. But one crumpled, graying woman in West Palm Beach never seemed to notice the fish-smelling heat. *Crumpled* might not be the exact word. Short at one point in her life, she grew to shrivel. Not hump-backed like old watchmakers or professors, but compressed like ancient mud-brick dwellings enduring the weight of shifting African sand. And as she shriveled, the long green raincoat she wore year-round in that fish-smelling heat sagged, perilously closing upon the patient ground.

Her face was creased like a lizard's hide around the leg joints. Her face was scorched by the sun until it resembled whiskey stains on some discarded napkin in some dirty dive. Her face, ah, like the dreaded Iron Maiden, held her eyes motionless prisoners, never allowing them to focus on anyone in the sidewalk ahead or on the street nearby—rather, forcing those eyes to search elusive memories amid baking concrete cracks.

The sidewalk was her worldly domain. I'd heard her variously nicknamed "the Sea Hag of West Palm," "Mrs. Bag Lady," or simply "Sidewalk Momma." Once, two black teenage girls raced their Buick by and yelled out, "Step along, Witch Woman!" She did, for that was her primary occupation: walking from one end of West Palm Beach to the other. But never alongside the intra-coastal, where water channeled a sweet breeze. No, perhaps feeling unworthy of that landscape, she strayed only the diabolically hot inner streets. Or perhaps she'd lost a sailor boy and couldn't stand the sight of the sea. Or perhaps . . . hell, she might not have even realized the intra-coastal existed, for all I knew. So she walked those nasty, bleached, inner flat streets of West Palm Beach with their same-same semi-semi-Spanish haciendas of pink, yellow, and blue; with their rushing traffic that mimicked Miami all too well by rolling lugubriously nowhere. She walked in her army green, her seaweed green raincoat and its polka-dot grease slicks that floated as offensively as any off-shore oil spill, should you pass close enough to smell. She existed as Gassendi's counter-argument to Descartes' *Cogito. Ambulo ergo sum.* Not I *think*, but I *walk* therefore I am. This woman was living proof.

While children yelled, adults remained infinitely kinder—they shunned her. Of course, being the polite gentleman from Kentucky, I always empathized and nodded. She was, after all, alone and walking withering streets.

I worked at night, so I saw her quite often in the day when I strolled out for a paper, a cup of coffee, or a beer. She was always walking. Coffee, beer, newspapers, lunch, park—they all lay near, so I walked too. Sometimes I walked so much that my journey's purpose faded into cofbeerparknews—bleached into meaninglessness by an angry, blistering sun.

There came one exceptionally long-walk day to cofbeerparknews when I spotted her ahead, swaying like a plastic Disney Pluto toy that wobbles four steps before falling. I passed her, and we exchanged a few words. Her eyes, those previous prisoners, focused briefly—I could see that she recognized me as a co-walker. She smelled incredibly stale as I rushed forward, my own eyes bulging as if they might shout out before my mouth could even open, "She recognized me! She recognized me! She recognized me!"

As a cohort, she recognized me.

Within the week, I made plans to leave West Palm, its seaweed hag, and its non-existent beach.

Had a Kentucky friend who once told me that everyone needed to hang around someone who'd lift him from the blues, someone who was so bad off that a mere peripheral glance at said person's dour face and spindly physique would convince the onlooker that life could yet turn worse. It was a peculiar time for me, and I wasn't quite sure what role I was fulfilling with this same friend; that is, if I weren't role modeling that dour and spindly someone. Divorce, job-change, age— all combined to stir my unease.

The bar I worked at during that time closed early, seven o'clock in the evening. It had metamorphosed from a wino den called the Rosebud Tavern to a hopeful downtown-uptown spot. It was an overnight miracle for the owners, with some few exceptions, some few customers who had to be coaxed or bounced out. Not being an owner, don't you see, I was elected to do both.

Understand that the Rosebud Tavern had previously served cheap draft, made book, and hustled women. Four dollar and fifty cent mushroomburgers as a substitute to affordable vices was enough to anger any street bum. So when the decor of the bar—early American tobacco stain—shifted from quagmire to quaint, the bums thinned but turned belligerent. One morning when I arrived, lambent light blended the interior walnut walls and nicotine stains into a cancerous splotch.

This was because the front door's glass had been shattered by a late-night wino unappreciative of mushroomburgers on asparagus buns. Blood pooled outside the door, so the drunk had probably rammed his head or fist through. By mid-morn the owners replaced the window with Plexiglas. *There, beat whatever part of your body you want against that, you damned winos.*

I was closing a few nights later when a head literally did crash against the Plexiglas. Despite the sound, the heavy door barely budged—sure sign of an empty skull, I quipped to myself. Sliding down the Plexiglas a rubbery face resembling a brontosaurus lost under a great cabbage leaf for eons drooled. This brontosaurus could not only drool but talk too, as it happened. A shoo-in for Ringling Brothers.

"Drink!"

"We're closed!"

"Drink!"

"We're closed!"

Our breaths condensed on either side of the Plexiglas. I took advantage of the conversation's lull to press the door and lock it. The face remained caught on the lower window dressing—so I shook my head and mouthed "No," then walked back to check lights, bolt doors, hide cash. Joni Mitchell was still simpering on the jukebox from just minutes before when I'd been feeling sorry for myself. But I didn't need Joni anymore—not after the talking brontosaurus. In sudden inspiration I snapped my fingers and turned to shout, "Hey, wait!" I rushed back, but it was too late. He'd left. Only his grease stain remained. No matter how hard I stared, that Plexiglas stain obscured my reflection.

Yeah, if I just could've snagged that guy in, bought him a beer and convinced him to follow me around town, things would have been great. I'd never-ever-never have to feel lousy about myself again.

Kentucky, it didn't have much snow when I was growing up. That all came later. I've heard it's because of the nuclear testing. That there's a new Ice Age coming. The reverse Greenhouse Effect. That Jesus, the

Lord, is pissed. Taking the Republicans into account, it could even be a top-secret C. I. A. stress test on the American public. I don't know; there just wasn't much snow there when I was a kid.

But something infinitely better visited every winter to take the bite out of the cold. A reddish old man used to make the trek from Lawrenceburg (which lay across the river, which lay beyond Versailles, which lay off a good way in itself) to Lexington. Actually, for us kids that long trek was the least remarkable thing about this old fellow. He sported a yellow-white beard which fluffed all the way down to his chest; he stood stout, hardly fat, but large enough to please a child's imagination during Christmas season; he carried a Friar John staff which could easily transform into a Saint Nicholas crosier; and he invariably walked barefooted and red-faced, as I mentioned.

Yes, Virginia, there is a Santa. . . .

This wasn't a one-time fling, this trek from Lawrenceburg. It was a seasonal necessity, for whatever reason the old gentleman had, be it relatives or savings bonds.

He was barefoot in sleet. I was riding on a bus.

He was barefoot across the street. My spring breath fogged a car's window.

Once, shopping for records downtown, I followed him three blocks, but there was no way short of running that my stubby legs could catch up, especially on the ice.

For years, I enjoyed my private Santa Claus, as I suspect did every youngster in Lexington. Then I moved to Bardstown, home of fine Kentucky bourbon, an apocryphal bullet hole left by Jesse James, and a nearly defunct Catholic prep school. Certainly in that properly descending order.

So it wasn't until after college that I saw the old guy again. Winters had become an annoyance, a danger, then a memory. Ah, life in Florida, where a man could bass fish on Christmas Day. I saw him because I was visiting Kentucky during the dead of an Ohio Valley summer, humid enough without being near the river, oppressing as Dante's inferno then. I saw him resting on a bench before an old folks' home in Lawrenceburg. I shouted, pointing him out to my two companions, but they didn't recognize him, having grown up outside Lexington. As we drove by, he waved.

My mouth fell. Could it? Could it be? Yes, Virginia, I was still child enough to believe in camaraderie through the ages, still child enough to think he recognized me from sleety years before.

HER FLAMING HAIR arrives first. It always has.

I shamble by on the sidewalk, unseen by her, rather, unnoticed. Instead, she scrutinizes her clanking, trundled load of empty Pepsi bottles, the big kind worth a quarter, lest any jump off the cart to creep away, for *ensemble* they'll garner a pint of whiskey and a six pack of beer.

She comes to the down and out where I work. She knows me well enough then.

"Falls City," she demands.

And she buys one for Momma and the other girls who are with her. "Girls," they call one another. I suppose she's the youngest; yes, she must be. She speaks with a slight accent, unidentifiable over the jukebox and the beer. I guess that it's Austrian or German. Others guess it's Norwegian. Bulgarian. Even English, one woman claims. Perhaps, we whisper, she's a gypsy who escaped Hitler.

She used to be in the circus, she says. I overhear. In the circus, traveling through Europe. I think of her, high-breasted in those glittery jump suits they all wear, and that hair, even redder then and rivaling the crimson blood in her veins, that hair whipping about her neck and shoulders in the slipstream she creates. Ping! Her toes, agile and strong then, grip the stand as her body swings upward in a majestic, sensual arc.

Cheers.

She calls out as she lifts her beer mug, one of the many we wash in dirty, lukewarm water, being half-drunk ourselves and a little more than lazy.

Once, this guy comes in: young, bitten with craziness, but not bad-looking, understand. Dart-eyed and drunk. That kind. He comes in and sits next to her, miscuing on her red hair maybe, I don't know. A few beers later and his hands run her calf, squeeze her knee, tumble under her dress. *Not here,* she glances, *not in here. Wait.*

Wait, at her age. At his age. But he sure does. The old gal hasn't lost her touch. She's going to do her drinking, and the hot colt will just have to steam.

Damn! I bet she could really get up there in the air.

The one she calls Mom and the other "girls" giggle and watch. His hand will be back for more, they know. His lips will kiss the French.

I walk by her table.

"Falls City." The young stud eases a finger into the air like he's ordering Lobster Thermidor and Pouilly-Fuisse '64 at the Peppercorn Hunt and Spice Club. She laughs. "For her," he explains, proudly patting her thigh, though careful to keep his hands outside her dress as she'd directed.

Damn!

Then was then and now is now. Now, I turn to watch her push the cart over each crack of the sidewalk with a pop and a rattle. She's being so meticulous that I think of the child's rhyme, "Step on a crack and break your momma's back." But her shoulders are held straight, and son-of-a-gun if she doesn't put a little sway to her walk. I hold my finger in the air, wanting to say *Hello there, tell me about life, would you?* Instead, I quietly watch that little sway slipping farther, farther away.

It was, as they say, the armpit of the night, the time when stray cats yowl and fools walk. It was two o'clock, to be more scientific, less precise. I'd just gotten off work and had a pocketful of tips and a place to spend them. It was an unlikely place—the Holiday Inn—but it offered a good jazz band, decent snacks, and ever-steady booze. Two potted palm trees outside assured passing pilgrims of its inner swank. And oh yeah, in that swank worked a nice gal bartender I always pretended I knew. Bosom buddies, to hear me say.

The hotel bordered the intra-coastal waterway, a bridge, and a strip joint. The area was prime roving for wineheads. I usually managed to hopscotch out of their way, but this one night I wasn't so agile: my being tight from a few after-work shooters generated the mistake.

"Say, sir, excuse me, sir, I've never done anything like this before and I'm ashamed as hell. I just sailed in from New Haven and I don't have a cent. You don't suppose that you could see a man—"

"Beat it!"

It was the whiskey in me talking; I can't reckon for the panhandler. He had a white windbreaker, wore a normal face, and God above, for all I knew, could have been telling the truth. The whiskey, like I said. He stared at me for an instant, long enough for me to realize one severe miscalculation: he outweighed me by an easy forty pounds. But it was a good bluff I pulled, and he walked away.

I went inside and proceeded to spend my tip money on drinks after complaining (jokingly) to the lovely bartender about the neighborhood riff-raff. She smiled and I quivered. Bosom buddies, as I said.

A few weeks of the same ritual passed, minus the winehead, though everything else chugged in an orderly chain-of-being. I came, I drank, I was conquered. Then one night the winehead rejoined the chorus. He wore the same white windbreaker; it was, as before, straight out of Hemingway, and he had the same New Haven line as before. He bumped the palm tree to the door's right, I bumped the one to its left.

I was sober this time, so I didn't press my luck but mumbled I didn't have any change or some such rubbish. He stared again, holding onto a palm frond for balance. He'd really rolled downhill since last time. Dark, nightlife circles under his eyes threatened to turn him into Bela Lugosi or one of Dracula's brides (one could never be certain of a stranger's sex in West Palm). Those eyes focused as he staggered, considering my answer. Then he left, dragging the tree a foot before it snapped his shoulder back and he had to let go.

I touched the bar's copper door, congratulating my vague reflection on such perceptive judgment, assuring myself I'd known the guy was a bum all along and that four bits of charity wouldn't have made a shred of difference, either one month ago or now. *No walnuts bouncing off my noggin. Moi, I've balletted well beyond the Darker Middle Ages.* Giving a whistle, a bow, and a swallowtail strut, I slid forward to battle and open the heavy door.

LET ME TELL YOU something. Sometimes. Sometimes in night's dark lurch I spy a window or mirror and I shout, *Declare yourself! Friend or foe?* When the inevitable silent answer arrives, I stagger and close my eyes. Then I count angels, dancing on a pinhead.

Faithful Companion

On the party train and all but dropping out of college, popping a beer and tooling my restored Austin-Healey Sprite down Lexington's Main Street, I was driving toward a blind date, a promised beauty. My pal Art, who fixed me up with the date, was sitting at my side. Ha! Let UK's atomic clock click its loudest: what care I, with such a faithful companion close by?

Then a traffic light turned red and a scowling cop eased alongside. My friend Art, fresh out of the navy, lit what he swore was a Cuban cigar and I cradled my unsipped American beer. While we three obeyed the red light, I managed to open my door and ease that virgin beer onto the road's dividing stripe—antique Sprites being unbelievably low to the ground. Sans incriminating beer, I pursued my civic duty and nodded at the cop, the cop pursued his civic duty and frowned at a soon-to-be-ex-college punk—Art, who'd evidently completed his civic duties with his stint of naval service, puffed and polluted.

Then we all pulled away. In my side mirror was reflected the can—blameless, full of itself, and alone. Art gave a puff and said, "Slick move with the beer." He paused, studying maybe a bat skittering through the dusk. "She's hot, Josey. I've met this woman, and She-Is-Hot. What else can I say?"

You could say, 'Even a once and future dropout like you, Josey, can sweet-talk her.' You could say, 'Let me handle anything involving social graces, you just guzzle beer until she's lathered like a racehorse.' But I kept quiet, not from political correctness, but because I was the only one lathering, too young and too stupid to know what I was lathering about.

As we drove on, Art wouldn't let up: "Are you going to try this time, Josey? I mean, I've set you up with three women. No excuses this time. If you can't make it with this one, even clam juice won't help." True to his four years in the navy, Art's favorite aphrodisiac was clam juice, though hardly his only. I, on the other hand, spent four years cooking pizzas and restoring this car, passing the GED and weaseling into college to major in physics or something stellar and smart. So far, women had resided in another nebula altogether.

"Well?" Art insisted.

"No excuses," I replied, imagining colliding nebulas glowing pink and purple, like silky undergarments.

"You promise?"

Hadn't my physics professor recently asked for just such a promise about my studies? The guy had adopted me for some reason. Did I resemble his lost son? He sure didn't remind me of my father. He'd have to be an anti-neutrino to do that. Non-existent, as far as this flowing world was concerned.

"You just come on as slick with her as you did with that beer can...."

Art's girl, Karen, shared her friend's apartment, though there was only one bedroom. Art confided that when we arrived I should quickly motivate to the adjoining dentist's office with the roommate since he and Karen were going to motivate to said single bedroom and do what every twenty-five-year-old male and female do immediately upon convening. That was all right for the old folks, but at twenty I needed prep time. How would a dentist's office help?

"She'll figure something out for you. Maybe laughing gas is an aphrodisiac."

"Maybe that squirting flavored water is."

"That's the spirit."

Art indicated a driveway. We parked then lugged two fat jugs of wine and two six packs of beer up a rickety fire escape. As I glanced down I thunked one of the jugs against the metal railing.

"Careful! That's our key to a good evening."

Art had pronounced Sneaky Petes an aphrodisiac comparable to clam juice, Sneaky Petes being a mixture of cheap sparkly Rhine wine and even cheaper bubbly beer. His concoction tasted like you'd imagine, horse piss, a taste that working part-time on a horse farm gave me ample opportunity to imagine.

A woman stepped out onto the landing. She was twenty-five or -six, an ageist conspiracy forming against me. Though old, she had the coalest black hair I'd ever seen—better than that, her breasts were slag mountains, her eyes eastern Kentucky blue skies, her lips western Kentucky wet lakes, her voice ("Hello down there.") a cardinal's chirp, her legs a thoroughbred's canter. *My God, my God, why hast thou forsaken me?* I quickened my climb, unsure why that New Testament verse resonated, maybe delusions of grandeur, which is what got me booted from high school in the first place. So what could I blame flunking college on?

"Sarah, this is Josey, my friend I told you about."

"Hi Josey. Let me help." Taking a jug, Sarah was duly impressed with our drink selection, and upon stepping inside her apartment she offered containers that resembled spittle cups dentists give patients.

"That's what they are," she said, swaying her hips against her kitchen sink in a way that spurred me, a stud stallion roaming bluegrass, to heave into a sweat. And her sputtering window air unit prompted further sweat.

"Sarah, why don't you show Josey Dr. Grey's office? We'll be over in a while. Take a jug and some beer with you."

Good ol' Art. Certainly not one to wimp around when anything close to shore leave heaved-ho. I hadn't even said hi to his girl, a sultry redhead with the largest Paris lips imaginable outside a *Cosmopolitan* cover, because she was still in the bathroom performing nebula-like chores or making spirals. When she did emerge, he shoved us into the hall—even before she nodded. He closed and locked the door to drive the point home.

Click.

Sarah tossed her black mane: "Kicked out of my own apartment."

She took charge to hug the six-pack of beer and tote the wine jug while I carried our drinks, careful not to squeeze the spittle cups too hard. We walked along a hall overlooking another set of stairs, this inside set cavernous—cracked plaster must have given that illusion. The hall itself smelled of dust, mold, and termite juice. The floors screeked, and a single bare light bulb dangled from cloth wiring to glare wantonly at a yellow-and-black moth dancing around it.

"What kind of moth is that?"

"Dead, if it keeps that up." Sarah set down the jug and beer, then gave a life-saving jump and swat, but the moth ignored her warning. I, meanwhile, gave her Appalachian hips a glance, planning my seduction.

Seduction? Who was I kidding? It was clear even from the way Sarah heaved the jug over her shoulder who'd be this night's seduce-er and who the seduce-ee. *Pop! Pop!* My soulmate the moth was already back at it, drawn to scalding electrical love.

Sarah produced a key to the dentist's office from tight black jeans. Keeping pace with my thoughts, the opening door did a squeak thing. When we entered, an obligatory black dentist's chair dominated pink linoleum, which spun outward from that dental throne like gum disease. The chair's black leather was cracked, revealing yellowing foam rubber. Backed along two walls, chipped white ceramic countertops hung off-angle. Fluoridated water had evidently set this dentist back. I imagined his only customers being victims of chewing tobacco, and even they would lower his profits by stuffing stacks of spittle cups into their pockets when he wasn't watching.

We talked for about an hour, Sarah showing me denture molds, trays of scissors, and enough pries, picks, and knives to resurrect the Inquisition. She kept the office door open, and occasional moans slid across the dank hallway, oozing from under her apartment's locked door. They gave us both a laugh, and in frolic I picked up a set of dentures and inserted my thumb to have them clamp down. Boldly phallic, I realized, amazed at my audacity. Was radiation from the physics lab skewing me?

Sarah giggled and led me into a cramped office with one filing cabinet, one desk, and one bright orange shag rug. Orange shag struck me as emblematic of contemporary love, so I tried my arm about Sarah's waist, pretending to reach for a paperweight. She eased aside, tingling my fingertips and electrically tugging me back into the larger room with the dental chair's cracked leather. Upon hearing the moth pop! pop! against the hallway light, I also observed emerald and yellow love plasma cascading from Sarah to me. Sneaky Petes, working their magic. I reached again, but Sarah deftly shifted to open a closet. My love-reach boomeranged to slosh my drink, for in the closet hung a skeleton, like a winter coat.

"What's he doing with that?"

"Come on, touch it."

"Is it real?"

"Of course it's real. He's a dentist, he can get things like this. He tells me he used to study chiropractic, but I think the skeleton's just his sickhead idea of a joke. Scare some poor kid into flossing. There's a tooth missing. Come on, touch it."

"No thanks." Hanging from its hook, the skeleton was taller than I was.

Sarah shrugged and edged her plenteous hips into the closet. "Excuse me, Francine." She reached for a box, sliding the skeleton aside with a frail rattle.

"It's so tall—are you sure it's a she?"

"A woman can't be tall?" Sarah pulled out a pair of thin, translucent ivory rubber gloves. "Go sit on the chair and I'll show you a glad surprise." She popped a glove by stretching it. The sharp noise reminded me of something, but I couldn't place what.

A button to her blouse had opened itself during her short stay in the closet and revealed to my glaucomic eyes was a heavenly arc of the palest, milkiest bosom I could ever hope to see. By midnight would that bosom and I intertwine? I envisioned its relative, Nina Nipple, a raspberry atop a creamy mound, awaiting my lips. . . . Ahem. You can see that Kentucky pasturage had given way to Vermont dairies, Maine backwoods, and my puerile *Penthouse* imagination.

Sarah closed the office door. Clack-clack went her steps, even though she was wearing red sneakers. I mean, this was a woman's woman, maybe even a man's man.

"Go on," she said. "Sit. And keep your drink. There's a tray."

I did as I was told and set my drink on the tray, my body on the chair. A crack in the leather pinched my thigh, since I was wearing shorts. Sarah slipped the second rubber glove onto her hand, then bent to kiss me fully. Resting her right leg between my two, she began running a Latex finger along my lips, my teeth, my gums as she kissed—pressing until I could feel two luscious raspberries, firm, ripe and erect, imprinting my chest.

Another moan—from Karen, Art's girlfriend. Unable to hear the moth's sharp pops anymore, I laughed nervously for fear that the creature had died. Sarah eased aside the tray holding my drink and climbed over the chair's arm. The Latex glove was replaced by her swollen tongue, which had somehow acquired the wildest cinnamon flavoring. What? Was my mouth becoming numb? Panting, I wrapped my arms about her, hearing the rubber gloves snap. She reached for a lever and we were eased back, though the leather cushioning got in one more pinch.

"Get this." She grabbed what looked like a drill and flicked a switch. The drill started rotating, but it wasn't a drill, just one of those tiny rubber cups hygienists use to pick up gritty cleaner and polish grimy teeth. After rotating the cup in some paste and her Sneaky Pete, she told me to turn the thing off. I brushed past her breasts to hit a button—which incited an ominous whirring to my right— "No, the one next to that one," she said. I flicked the first one off then pushed the correct button. She went back to insinuating a deep, thrusting dollop of cinnamon and Sneaky Pete into my mouth. The chair moved us upwards as she purred and ground her hips against my pelvis.

"Umm, it's like a dental drill down there," she commented, feeling my erection.

I didn't laugh, so she said, "Oh, this boy needs loosening."

She continued grinding, then moved her blouse toward my mouth. One more button undone, and no bra! I searched for that elusive raspberry. Meanwhile, farther south where the banana trees grow,

Sarah was unzipping me. Feeling her fingernails nip, I squirmed, but she only laughed. "Maybe not a dental drill but a big, gushy Texas oil derrick."

The chair hit top, shivered, then started down. "Automatic pilot," she giggled, pulling her breast from my mouth to drive her tongue deep, implanting more cinnamon and Sneaky Pete. I felt her wrapping something around my sac and stiffened, but she whispered, "It's only dental floss; that's the surprise; just wait, you'll like it."

She kept pressing her tongue like a probe. As the chair descended, I could hear Karen and Art let out mutual moans, which Sarah echoed softly, comically. Or was she imitating the chair's electrical surge? She'd wrapped strands and strands of floss around the base of my sac and was now wrapping more around my penis. The chair hit bottom and started up. She squirmed and the lights overhead went out; a dull greenish examination light over the chair came on.

"That better?"

I didn't have time to answer, for she arched until her hair was silhouetted green, like an emerald angel guarding paradise. I began tugging her jeans; she kept wrapping my penis. My hand made a miraculous discovery: no panties! I felt her fur and she obligingly spread her legs.

Then the door downstairs squeaked. "Sarah?" a voice called.

"Shit." Sarah spit this out like a too-hot cinnamon ball, pulled me off the dental chair, and led me to the closet with the skeleton, shushing me with her fingers and giving me a rub where I needed it most.

"Sarah?"

"Up here!" She shouted then turned to me. "Be quiet. It's Dr. Grey." She ran to the chair and tossed me my clothes. Catching them, I squeezed next to the skeleton. Sarah licked her lips, smiled, and closed the door on me. Before she did, I heard the moth's *Pop! Pop!* in the hall.

Came a last squeaking step. He must be underneath the moth battering itself on that bare bulb. Would he shoo it off and save it? On instinct, I sniffed the skeleton, but all I could smell was the cinnamon dope Sarah'd rubbed on my tongue. I wondered if Francine really was a she skeleton. *Some svelte babe you must have been, Babe.* I swear I heard an answering clack of her mandible, but the overhead lights went on just then and I could hear Sarah toss something into a cabinet with a clunk. My shoes. Damn.

"Sarah?" the dentist called.

I scooted down to the sizeable crack between the door and the floor. I could see Sarah's bare feet walk toward the office door. She opened it.

"Sar—"

"Sh!" She giggled, standing there addressing a pair of shiny black shoes. My brow furrowed. Art's and Karen's moans reached another plateau, near the Himalayas.

"What the hell's that?"

"Sh. I loaned a girlfriend my apartment so she and her fiancé could be alone together. That's why I'm in here."

Good. Great lie. Now go home, Doc.

"That explains the lights. That's why I stopped."

A cataclysmic moan from Art's girlfriend, followed by one from Art himself.

"Fiancé? The two of them sound like they're on their honeymoon."

There was a pop, pop—oh yeah, the moth. Then a hiss, then a motor whirred. She'd forgotten to turn off the chair! But what was the hiss? Had the moth been fried?

"I was sitting in the chair listening. It's sort of kinky. Want a drink?"

After one galactic spiral came a boorish, slo-mo sip.

"God. What is it?"

"Sneaky Peter."

Sneaky Pete, damn it!

"Goes right along with what's going on over there, doesn't it?"

No answer. What the hell's she mean by offering him my booze? Get him lost.

Quiet.

"You're barefoot. I've never seen you barefoot. You have ballerina feet, strong and defined."

"I should run around barefoot more."

"You should."

Sneaky Peter is right. Get him moving!

"My divorce is final next week."

"I know it's been hard for you."

Quiet.

I was getting cramped and I was getting tired of watching feet—ballerina or not—so I shifted to peep through an old skeleton key hole. *Sneaky Peter! Sneaky Peter!* Sarah was bent backwards over the counter under Dr. Grey, who wasn't gray but darkly around thirty. The old folks, crucifying me again. Her hand was rubbing his back, her legs were spread at an angle that allowed him to squeeze into her, her mouth was open wide enough that her cheeks hollowed. All that cinnamon going to waste. The old fart was probably diabetic. The passengerless chair hit bottom, but they didn't mind in the least.

My nose had pressed so hard against the door that I'd forgotten to breathe. Inhaling, I felt something tingle my head and thought it was a spider and turned, almost blowing my quiet, for bony fingertips brushed my nose. . . . Cinnamon, even the skeleton was using it. I could hear the dentist and Sarah writhing, their mouths emitting sucking sounds as vacuums suddenly created were just as suddenly filled. It was the fabled neutrino and anti-neutrino seeking one another for cataclysm. Then Francine's fingertips touched my lips.

"Nice," the dentist said. Was he already discovering the same lack of panties I had?

"Nice," I echoed, gritting my teeth enough to give a dentist some work. Not this one, though, damn it. I think I may have whispered that. At any rate, Francine seemed to appreciate my conversation, for her fingers caressed my cheek. "Nice," I told my sole companion again. But my voice squeaked, while the dentist's damned voice floated suave and mature, like maybe he smoked imported cigars. *Nice.* Why hadn't I said that? Or even *ballerina feet?* Something dangled on my thigh, and my eyes widened in fear. But of course it wasn't a rat or even Francine being forward; it was the spool of the dental floss still wrapped around my drooping derrick. I tugged angrily and almost went through the closet door in pain. *You're going to enjoy this!?* Hadn't she said that? As I unwrapped inside, those two wrapped outside. I heard something drop . . . a damned belt buckle. I jammed my eye to the keyhole. Francine leaned with me, her thumb caught in my hair. I could see them moving to the chair, which was still going at it. Sarah took bottom this time. "Oh, ohhhhhhhhhh!"—Coming from neither Sarah nor the dentist nor the moth, but Art. Evidently he'd brought a gallon of clam juice to accompany his Sneaky Pete. Francine kneed me, wanting a peep. Or was she offering caressing companionship? Was it possible? Three lonely couples, passing like ships in the night. . . . Tilting, I rubbed my hair in her fingers—she surely wouldn't mind post-teenage dandruff in all this dark. Oh Francine. . . . Will we rent a raft and float the Ohio River to the Gulf of Mexico? Will we discover Einstein's secret universe?

The overhead lights once more went out, and once more the examination light over the chair went on. The trick had lost its shazzaam, at least from my vantage. The chair's motor hummed. More clothes dropped, and some change, one coin rolling to hit the closet door. All I could see through the keyhole was an ivory rump bumping like an ocean wave. Francine's fingertips nuzzled my cheek.

If you can't make it with this chick, even clam juice won't help. I leaned against Francine's hips to rub a finger over her lowest rib, wondering if she were ticklish. You certainly are a slender lady. Would it be proper to kiss you here? The lowest rib—derived from Adam?— felt cool against my lips. "Ooh" drifted from outside. I stared at the keyhole, its pinpoint light shining like some ghostly light-wave experiment. Is it a wave? Is it corpuscular? Screw you, Art. Screw your nubile Karen with her Paris lips, screw your damned navy stories about whores in Spain and screw your sure-fire aphrodisiacs too. Sink on a battleship—or better, a hospital ship, stuck in the dental hold beside an X-ray machine, why don't all three—four—of you? Francine's wrist rested against my left earlobe. My right, she knocked quietly with her wholesome hipbone. *Your origin and your resting place, lover. For eternity and a midnight more.* As she whispered this, dark warmth seared my packed brain meat. Meanwhile, outside my and Francine's noir boudoir, the two in the office began a tropical storm, now that Art and Karen had finished their gale. Ah! Whir. Click. Oh! Um. Ah! Yes, yes. Whir. No more "ballerina feet"—the vocabulary had dropped substantially to ur syllables, maybe even pre-Big Bang.

Francine, ever mindful, tapped me again. *Lover*, she whispered, *I'll always be here for you.* My freshman comp teacher, a blonde whose husband raised thoroughbred mares, had taught me about seizing the day. Inspired, I kissed Francine's fingertips like a true gentleman caller, then dressed as quietly as I could, though I needn't have bothered, what with the Force Two hurricane building outside. I opened the door then lifted Francine off her hook—she was heavier than I expected, a real woman, Rosie Riveter, Carrie Nation. *No, just Frankly Francine*, I heard her whisper as her teeth gave my ear a sweet nibble.

For a moment we danced cheek to cheek, our coming-out party to the world. Feeling her thin, thin breasts, her sturdy clavicle, I led lovely Francine toward the green examination light and the humping ivory that proved to be the dentist's rear end. *Slip-slide, back one, forward two, then spin.* Francine and I coasted the pink linoleum, which looked turd brown in the green light. *Your feet*, I whispered, *so articulated, like a ballerina's; your cranium, so capacious, like Madame Curie's.* She pressed against me in response.

This dentist in the chair, he was some grey grinder. No wonder business was slow. As Francine and I completed a last spin and dip, either the dentist or Sarah accidentally kicked me. Francine and I held our breaths. Needlessly, for we were beyond the pale.

I want, Francine sighed into my ear, her teeth cool and smooth in the heat, *I need, I want. . . .*

Looking into her lovely, sympathetic eye sockets as she glowed green in the examination light, I nodded and rubbed my hand down her ribs, to where her belly button would have been. I gave it a tickle all the way through to her spine. She smiled. Then I hung her, by that rude hook drilled into her skull, onto the swivel-arm for the dentist's drill. She tilted her head and watched the wallowing. It must have brought back memories, for she grinned fully, gat-toothed. I wedged her fingertips into the drill's pulleys and moved the tray so she could comfortably lean. Ignoring the dentist's two huge, flopping anal molars, I used surplus dental floss to tie Francine's willing hand to the drill—not the polishing tool—aimed at his butt. Francine blinked flirtatiously. *Keep your promise. Go home and study physics*, she advised. *I'll attend the rest.* She was tired of being kept in a closet, miffed at the hook in her skull. *I want . . . I need . . .* she whispered as her lovely eye sockets absorbed the ongoing scene. Her grin reflected greenish, just as her ballerina toe bones reflected the pink linoleum. I brushed her mouth with cinnamon-Sneaky Pete mix, fitting my little finger into a gap, a tooth missing. *Surely, Francine, no lover hit you there? / No, dear heart, it was too many sweets and chocolates, not enough kisses*, she sighed. As the chair hit bottom, I blew her a smooch to let her know that a missing tooth offered no impediment to eternal love. *Goodnight Francine, I'll kiss you in my dreams.*

The chair had started its ascent and fetching my shoes would take too long, so I retrieved my beer and wine then hopped into the hall. The moth was still popping the bare bulb; taking pity I flicked out the light. I paused by Sarah's apartment to place my ear against the door and hear revived osculation from within. Behind, in the dentist's office, a hurricane was building: Force Three . . . Force Four . . . Force . . .

"AAAAGHHH!"

Yes! Skittering armloads of metal instruments and a heavy crash! Had the entire chair capsized? A scream, then the unmistakable vengeful clatter of Francine's lovely bones, at last getting what they needed. Out of the closet! Freedom!

Leaving the wine jug where Art would trip over it in the dark, I hopped the fire escape three steps at a time, raising my beer in a thermonuclear toast, "Farewell, faithful companion, farewell!"

In Whose Palms We Trust

Go, Child of God, upon the shining desert,
Where, with eyes of flame,
The roaming lion keeps thy road from harm.
—Thomas Merton

WHEN I WAS TWELVE and Oedipally trying to fill a fatherless household, Bardstown cupped me in history: nearby Hodgenville where Abe Lincoln was born, My Old Kentucky Home where Stephen Foster composed lilting songs, Talbot Tavern where Jesse James drilled three bullet holes, and Our Lady of Gethsemane Abbey where the monk Thomas Merton wrote.

But Lincoln left for Illinois and Foster drank bourbon to a stupor. They say Jesse never rode east of the Mississippi, and anyway, Talbot Tavern was a restaurant serving staid Kiwanis luncheons. Thomas Merton? Some hermit crackpot writing poetry no one in town liked or understood. Still, as morning corn mash lifted from local distilleries, all of Nelson County and Bardstown seemed to cup its palms and urge: "Slumber on; the rooster has yet to crow."

After school I worked for Howlett Hardware, often running errands and marching through town, virile as a Knight Templar commissioned by the See of Rome. On just such a march I met The Infidel: to my incredible plantation ignorance he seemed to invade My Old Kentucky Home like Martin Luther King stirring the darkies, like

Elvis the Pelvis twitching away the tuneful Sewanee. But even New South Insight wouldn't have altered my final judgment of the Infidel: a slick city lawyer fouling pasture outside Holy Gethsemane. But the story isn't about him, or myself.

For when a person's lungs wanted respite from corn mash, they'd naturally guide the legs into Howlett Hardware to breathe Mrs. Howlett. Her gray eyes, large and shiny as a tractor's harrowing disc, made people do that, made them inhale sharply and turn to study splintering floors. Her gray eyes were as sad as the gilded Greek Madonna in our cathedral's vestibule. Her gray eyes were as soulful as a deer's. Her gray eyes were . . .

"Josey, would you go to the back and dolly a roll of black mulching plastic out to Mr. Guerney's truck?"

"Yes ma'am." I looked to where my right shoe was poking at a crack in the floor.

"Josey?"

"Yes ma'am?"

"Did you hear me?"

"Yes ma'am. Right away."

And off I'd stumble, wondering why the girls in Bethlehem Junior didn't have eyes like that.

Mr. Howlett loved her eyes too. He loved her whole body, her whole self with the uncontrollable blazing of a hayloft fire. I saw his eyes roam to hers from counting axe handles, from cutting a length of chain. I saw his quick fingers drum his thin stomach. During the second winter I worked there, he could hardly bear to be beyond arm's reach.

"Mr. Howlett, you should give your wife a rest from all your attention. It'll go to her young head."

"Mrs. Walsh, God made women for attention. There's nothing wrong with a husband proving he's aware of the fact."

As this second winter began, Mrs. Howlett spent her time near the window arranging, rearranging the toy display. At her insistence, the store sold this small selection of toys, goods it hadn't carried for six previous years. All day long a small train chugged her wishes around satin-dressed dolls and pyramid-stacked cans of Pla-Doh.

"Do you like the train, Josey?"

"It's okay for kids."

"Don't be in such a hurry to grow up and leave your mom and me all alone." She tousled my hair, something she'd done even before I began working for her and Mr. Howlett. She must have followed my eyes, for she then said, "You like rifles and shotguns, now—is that it?"

That was it, and I didn't even have to nod.

Mr. Howlett walked up: "Coincidence, coincidence—the tall fellow in here yesterday looking for a chain saw, that new lawyer, told me I could go squirrel and rabbit hunting on his farm anytime."

I looked from Mr. to Mrs. Howlett.

Mrs. Howlett's gray eyes darkened to slate. "Bill, don't be getting his hopes up; you know Louise has to give her okay on something like that."

"You and his mother both need to give the boy a little breathing room, Anne. Sunday'd be a great day to hunt, wouldn't it, Son?" Mr. Howlett raised his hand to forestall objection from his wife. "I'll talk with Louise," he said, making a tiny cross on his forehead to seal his promise. So the two of us walked to the gun case and looked at the shotguns.

"Check to see it's unloaded first. Always check that first. An unloaded gun won't do you any good, but it sure as hell won't do you any harm either. And point the barrel at the floor, Josey. Not my leg."

I could see Mrs. Howlett watching after I broke down the barrel like he showed me. Her fingertips rested on a doll's forehead as if checking its temperature. Outside, snowflakes barely drifted.

Thursday of that week Mrs. Walsh purchased two rolls of chicken wire. She said a fox killed her rooster and was stealing her chickens. Even as I helped load the wire I knew a fox hadn't killed that rooster. There's no foxes in town, just mangy dogs. The year before, a nun had told us that roosters were a medieval symbol for Christ. "Why do you think that is, Josey?" / "Because Christ flew to heaven?" I guessed. The nun had scowled. "No, but that's close. It's because Christ represents a new day, just like the rooster." When it was alive, Mrs. Walsh's rooster made for the sickest new day I'd ever heard; it crowed halfway then stopped like a broken record. No wonder some dog killed it.

On Friday Mr. Howlett sent me on an errand. I was to take a chain saw to the lawyer so he wouldn't have to trouble about coming by. When I stopped at the drugstore to warm my hands, Mrs. Wilson, who used to be the town librarian, bought me hot cocoa, then asked about my mother. "She's fine," I told her. Mrs. Wilson rattled her cup until the waitress came.

"And Mrs. Howlett? Is she still as thin as ever?"

The waitress poured hot water for tea while I tried to figure out an answer.

"I suppose so, ma'am," was as bright as I could muster.

"Well, cold winter nights and Mr. Howlett should put a coat of fur on her soon enough, don't you suppose?"

The waitress clinked the cup and laughed with Mrs. Wilson like they were sharing a whisper. I swiveled the stool and bumped Mrs. Wilson with my knee as she dipped her tea bag. Feeling bone instead of skin, I hurried my cocoa and left.

His office was on the second floor of the Todd Building. The lobby was a post office and the floor made loud sounds because it was marble, sounds that followed you like the finger of Uncle Sam or the bloody wound of Jesus hanging on our cathedral's main crucifix. The Todd Building, which rented its space to the post office, lawyers, insurance agents and accountants, was one of the few places in town where you couldn't smell corn mash from the breweries. Instead you smelled cigars. Mom said the deals made there smelled as bad as the tobacco. I walked upstairs, looking back at the finger of Uncle Sam, which followed me step by step. I'd be a sergeant in the next war, I decided well before reaching the top.

The cigar smell was strongest on the second floor. His office was to the right and had a line of frosted windows. A man I recognized from when my father was alive stood painting a sign on the windows. He smelled enough like corn mash to cover the cigar stink: it was the first time mash ever smelled good to me.

"Hello, Josey. You up here to sue Mr. Howlett for back wages or are you after that pretty, big-eyed wife of his?" He opened the door with a chuckle and gripped the wood until it shivered.

"I'm just delivering this chain saw." I shifted the box, struggling to port arms like the marine in the poster downstairs. Over the box I could see him finish the bottom of the R in LAWYER, sweeping it into an effortless, perfect curl.

"I remember your father." The man turned to squint at me. "You come to me when you finish school and I'll teach you to do this and billboards too if you want, if you don't move to some big city like my kid and every other kid around."

I nodded and walked into the office. *I'll move all right*, I thought. *I'll be a sergeant.*

The secretary looked up with her long red hair and lips to match. When I told her why I was there, she snapped, "Stay," and slapped down a paperback book. Too stupid to shed the chain saw and its box still smelling of cold cardboard, I leaned it on her desk after she left. Her book was called *Love Knocks but Once*. It pictured a blonde woman pressing a pencil to her lip while turning from a dark-haired man whose three fingers rested on her neck. My fingers tingled, imagining a girl named Becky who sat in front of me in class.

"He'll see you now." The secretary grabbed her book like I'd lost her place, then pointed angrily in the direction I was supposed to go.

He was standing by the door to his office and I nearly bumped into him because of the box. My Adam's apple retracted as he reached with big, talcum-powder palms and took the box like he was weighing it, then set it on the floor.

"You have a receipt for me, don't you?"

I reached into my pocket.

"That's the most important thing to remember about retailing: always give the customer his receipt." He took the receipt and walked to a life-sized bronze rooster on his desk. He tapped its tail feathers and its beak dropped, emitting a crow that sounded even sicker than Mrs. Walsh's rooster when it was alive. He placed the receipt in the bronze beak and it snapped closed.

"Cool," I said, intoning my daily attempt at rushing puberty.

He looked up. "You the boy who's going hunting with Howlett?"

"Yes sir."

"Does your father know you're going?"

"My father's dead."

"Well, don't take potshots out there anyway. I've got twenty head of cattle on that land and it's no place for smart-aleck antics." He waved and nodded toward the door. "You can go now."

Sunday morning came, even colder. I heard my mother coughing and banging cabinets in the kitchen and stuck my head under the blanket. When she called me, it was still dark out, so I sat at the kitchen table drinking hot chocolate and making craters in my oatmeal while glancing backwards through the door to the black-faced living room window.

Both the clutch and the brake pedal in Mr. Howlett's truck popped like rifle shots, so through the winter air I heard him pull in our drive. I ran to the front door, my mother close behind with my coat and hat. She told me to be careful at least ten times before I got them on and left. The truck's passenger window had a draft, so I moved to the center of the cab where the heater worked. Mr. Howlett passed me his mug.

"Don't tell your mother."

"I'm old enough to drink coffee."

"Then wipe the hot chocolate from your lips." He laughed, not mean, but I was hurt anyway.

Grown-ups, it occurred to me, spent a lot of time laughing at their own jokes. It was like every grown-up kept a make-believe grown-up beside him and the two of them were sharing a big joke on the world.

When we criss-crossed over the winding Elkhorn Creek for the third time, we turned down the lawyer's private road. We were supposed to watch for dead squirrels as markers.

"There's one!" I spilled coffee as I pointed at a squirrel slung over a strand of barbed wire, its head and paws pointing downwards. As we passed, its tail lifted in the wind and I remembered school stories about Christians hung outside Rome. We counted three more before reaching his gate.

"The lawyer must think he's Daniel Boone." I laughed at my joke. Mr. Howlett just lit a cigarette, his lighter making a click then a snap. I gave up laughing to look out the window.

His house wasn't the white one with a front porch spread out like a welcoming grin. That one was too old for a city lawyer just out of law school, Mr. Howlett explained. We drove a hundred yards farther and passed a low brick house with a concrete stoop and a four-foot walk.

"What's he going to do with the other house?"

"Sling it over a fence, most likely." Mr. Howlett mashed out the cigarette he'd just lit.

We got out and began to hunt, crunching frozen dirt, breathing frozen air, drinking steaming black coffee. Mr. Howlett had me shoot into a high squirrel's nest, but nothing happened. Then we spotted and shot a rabbit. I ran to pick it up and saw it had one brown foot and one white. Mr. Howlett said that was because it had mixed signals in molting. He said it was good luck and he thought my shot had hit it. I didn't mind the coffee and the cold so much after that.

A little before eight we shot another. At nine a stiff wind crossed the field, kicked snow in our eyes, and howled through winter-bare trees like a moaning angel. So we left, passing the four dead squirrels and the three bends of Elkhorn Creek, rubbing our hands and stomping our feet.

"My granddad warned me I'd be useless this far north, as sluggish as an alligator out of season, that I should stay in Florida with the rest of the family." Mr. Howlett stared at the road, then turned on the radio. It was a Baptist preacher, not a Catholic priest, but Mr. Howlett kept it loud anyway. I tried not to listen since it was a sin to hear a preacher, especially one who shouted like he was angry with every puff of air: "What do we MEAN when we say *worldly*, friends? The Thirteenth Apostle tells us the world was 'not WORTHY' of the prophets who roamed its deserts. Now, WHY would he say that?" The preacher exploded: "Because WORLD MEANS CITY and CITY MEANS CORRUPTION! City means Sodom! City means Gomorrah! . . ."

Mr. Howlett clicked off the radio. "I can't imagine listening to that trash every Sunday. We'll drop by for your mother and go to Mass after we skin these rabbits."

"It'll be Father Simmons at noon." Father Simmons was old and sang the slowest Masses and gave the longest sermons. Everybody said the Monsignor put him on noon Mass to punish late-risers.

"At least he won't be raving," Mr. Howlett said.

We cleaned the rabbits in Mrs. Howlett's washroom. Her gray eyes hooded while we did. I held up a rabbit's foot and she made a sound that was half laugh, half cough.

"Might as well get used to things like that before we have one of our own ch—"

She ran from the washroom before he finished. He asked me to start my rabbit alone, like he'd shown me. In the tiny paneled room I cut off the rabbit's rear feet: the brown one for my mother, the white one for Mrs. Howlett, to bring good luck. Bones crunched against porcelain as I stared the rabbit in the eye.

THERE'S A CERTAIN DAY in spring, a certain warm day which ambushes your skin to draw it from your bones. That day came, mixing the smell of tar from the roofers a block away with moisture from the earth. It was a Tuesday, the second one of March; and it seemed that overnight, because of some off-season electrical storm, every blade of grass had lustily unfolded from its straw-brown genuflection.

On the second Tuesday of every month Mr. Howlett drove to Louisville to pick up special orders, so Mrs. Howlett was alone talking on the phone when I arrived after school. She waved me on to the stockroom, covering the receiver like whoever was on the other end might hear her wave. There were three metal seed racks in the stockroom. I knew Mr. and Mrs. Howlett would be anxious to get them out for planting days, so I sorted the first box of unpacked seed.

"These should have already been out."

I jumped at Mrs. Howlett's jittery voice.

"I'm sorry, Josey honey. I didn't mean to yell. Here, you can help now that you're here."

Together, we sorted the last box, and as we placed the third stand outside against the storefront, I saw Becky with her long brown hair coming down the sidewalk, and I nearly knocked over a stand.

"I'm going to the drugstore for a Coke," she called out. When she got near, she fingered seed packets and smiled from me to Mrs. Howlett. I could smell what always smelled so good about her—not perfume like you'd think, but something with a bit of a tang—her hair, I guess.

"I'd like to let Josey go, but I'm depending on him this afternoon. There's a man coming on important business. I'm sorry, you two."

Mrs. Howlett placed her hand on my shoulder instead of rubbing my head like usual. She apologized again and asked if Becky couldn't come back another time for Cokes, promising she'd buy for us. He— the Infidel—walked up then, and the two of them went inside.

"I don't like her," Becky said, shaking radish seeds and pouting.

"Mrs. Howlett? Why?"

"My mom says she flirts."

"No she doesn't."

"Then how come she's with him when Mr. Howlett isn't here? My mom says he's the biggest masher in town because he's a new bigshot lawyer."

"You heard her. They have business. He's a customer. He bought a chain saw that I took him and plenty of things."

Becky snapped a seed packet. "I bet she's divorcing Mr. Howlett. Mom says Mrs. Howlett can't have babies because of him."

"You're crazy, Becky. And your mom is too."

Becky dropped the radish seeds on the sidewalk and spun about, clutching her dark blue purse and some books as she walked off. I picked up the seeds and sorted through vegetable and flower packets. All the while I tried to see the stockroom from the window. I could make out Mrs. Howlett fingering papers on the worktable. I looked up the street: Becky was turning the corner for the drugstore. I waved timidly, but she only slung her books to carry her around and out of sight.

Closing time came, so I went to ask for the key and saw Mrs. Howlett sobbing against his shoulder, tissue in her hand. His stupid head jerked at me just like when I brought him the chain saw, but I stayed. He jerked his head again and waved his talcum powder hands. Mrs. Howlett turned.

"Josey." She walked awkwardly over and squeezed me. I remember a button from her blouse catching my ear while she cried. I remember wanting to cry too, but not knowing why. I remember her telling him in a cough that she'd be in his office tomorrow at ten. I remember his briefcase clacking shut, his stupid talcum-powder hands touching her shoulder. I remember her kiss after he left, her assurance that she loved me and Mom no matter what.

Four days later my mother ladled out oatmeal. I stared.

"Did you hear me, Josey? You'll probably have to quit. Anne's going through with her divorce and it will be better for you not to be there."

"Why?"

"Because I said so!"

"No, why is she getting divorced? Doesn't she love Mr. Howlett anymore?"

"Yes, she still loves him."

"Well, he loves her."

"Yes."

"Well?"

My mother poured herself more coffee and walked to the window.

"Mom, she doesn't flirt, does she?"

"Honey, I told you that she was upset when she was with the lawyer."

"I know."

"Well?" She turned and frowned until I ate a spoonful of oatmeal.

"Well, why then?" I asked after a swallow.

I didn't have to quit: Mom said I might as well learn about the world and that with spring and summer coming, work would keep me busy. Mrs. Howlett stayed with me and Mom awhile, though her door was always closed. The lawyer called one day and she left for dinner in Louisville after a kiss from Mom. Next night I heard them talking.

Mrs. Howlett said Louisville had really gone down, that paper bag winos and whores were everywhere. "Louisville's getting to be a big city," Mom offered.

"What bothered me was I felt like one of them," Mrs. Howlett replied.

A month later, Becky took me to her 4-H cornfield, and between the fourth and fifth rows I ran silt along her neck and down her blouse. That Saturday, guilt-ridden from the sin of petting, we were at the county fair when a taxidermist scared us with a stuffed rooster that could crow. When it did, I could see the inside of its beak, which was caked black as a soul. One day Mrs. Howlett told Mom that she was going to marry him. She and Mom spent the night out. Alone, I watched for a moon that was supposed to be full, but clouds came. Two months after the marriage, Mrs. Howlett said she was pregnant.

In August, Mrs. Walsh came in to buy a .22, saying the chicken wire didn't work, she needed a rifle to shoot that fox. Mrs. Wilson, the retired librarian, died that same month. Mom, Mr. Howlett and I went to the funeral. On the way back, Mom thanked him for driving and said he was a blessing to her and me both. Perfume filled the truck. I grinned, seeing Mom hold my rabbit's foot inside her purse as she invited him to dinner. He came but announced that he was moving to Florida to operate a Western Auto store, saying we wouldn't believe it, even hardware stores were air-conditioned down there. Next morning my rabbit's foot was in the garbage, half-hidden under Kleenex. Mr. Howlett was gone before Halloween, since the new owner was anxious for holiday sales. By Christmas, Becky loved Bill Cox and I didn't like the new storeowner. By next summer the lawyer divorced Mrs. Howlett and returned to Louisville, calling us a bunch of red-faced rubes. In school I wrote an essay about a Thomas Merton poem and the nun claimed I misunderstood: the poem wasn't about the evil of cities, but atomic bombs. I didn't know: I'd never seen an atomic bomb.

The Trappist monk Thomas Merton died years ago while visiting the Dali Lama, electrocuted in Bangkok's city heat upon adjusting an electric fan. I try to imagine his ascetic, bony hands reaching—I saw him once when our school went on retreat—but can envision only a bronzed rooster clamping talcumy fingers instead. Though it's become a modish bedroom community for Louisville, there's no doubt that Bardstown's corn mash haze still rises each morning—not like God *Pater Noster's* comforting palms, but like blighting urban smog. Mrs. Howlett? The perfect ending would be that I grew up and married her, or at least her gray-eyed little girl. But no, in the city—and *city* means *corruption*—God's palms simply swelter, rabbit's feet bring mismatched luck, and hollow mechanical roosters crow, they crow, they crow.

Learning To Fall

At that time, Su Lin had immigrated to Lexington and commandeered a monopoly in teaching karate. No peaceful lotus position, no meditative kata, no gentle art of tea, though—paranoia was his commodity, sold in incremental, aery packets. For instance, a once placid friend, while strolling UK's campus, feared that an approaching couple's giggles indicated a conspiracy to pounce, to waylay—to force a Stand and Deliver! So, spin-kicking the male—whump!—then shoving a palm into the coed's jaw—whap!—(reasoning that her shrill scream presaged the deadly Black Mantis eye-jab) this friend fended epically. But to my friend's dismay the couple so soundly defeated now sprawled on UK's ivied walkway amid a single, piteous poetry book. Assessing those poems and the couple's fearful glances, she had the sense to transform her nunchuks into wind chimes that very hour. Yes, my friend was female. What wearisome paranoia was Su Lin selling the testosteroned half of campus?

My little nose kept clean, though, for it stayed in books at UK's bookstore where I worked. Well almost clean, for I was taking judo lessons from the campus barber. And Tim was no slouch: he'd won or placed second in state tournaments eight years running. Rumor had it that the first time Su Lin stepped on campus Tim bounced him off the mats right onto the gym's scoreboard. If the match had been a basketball game, the score would have been Judo-137, Karate-24.

"Heh-heh," Tim commented after I mentioned my friend. Always, Tim laughed just like we literally spell it: "Heh-heh." And when he did, the thick eyebrows abutting his square head always bunched as if retracing a life lesson from a deep-jungle, Shao-lin temple where a bevy of blind monks taught self-defense and irony underneath watchful, cackling monkeys.

"Heh-heh. Su Lin, he was a black belt when he first came to Lexington. One summer vacation he left for one of them Pay-cific isle-lands and waltzed back with a ninth degree red belt." Tim sang his words in up-and-down intonation, so his heh-hehs sizzled counterpoint. "Got belted by some miss-ti-cal master no one's ever heard of, heh-heh, or seen." Tim's eyebrows hooded, Buddha-fashion.

Twisting in the barber's chair to see the mirror, I edged tentative fingers toward my precious golden locks, the envy of every woman I knew, though you shouldn't get any idea about my being a Casanova. They just wanted to scalp those locks. A coed was staring through the open door even then, figuring she could sweep the floor when I left, no doubt.

"Where's Don today?" I asked, worrying that Tim would block my hair into a square like his own.

"Oh, taking his Cad-il-lac to the body shop, I suppose." Snip, snip.

"He wreck it?"

"No-o, someone ka-raa-tay kicked a dent in it."

"He run over whoever it was?"

"Heh-heh. Not yet. Not yet." Snip, snip.

I touched my hair and Tim popped my knuckle with his scissors. "Ree-lax, Josey. You're as upp-tight as Don."

Don worked for Tim and was a Kentuckian's Kentuckian. Straight from Pineville's hills, Don believed the best items a man could procure in life were a white convertible Cadillac and a hefty woman to ride shotgun, preferably cradling home-fried chicken and a firearm instead of a baby. Since Don was on the rebound from his first wife—a terribly sad affair as she'd lost weight, stopped cooking with Crisco, gotten college, a job, then a divorce—since he was on that rebound, he lavished all his love on his Cadillac. And now someone had dented it. Conflagration. Lexington's streets would be an open battle zone until he wreaked vengeance.

"He'll be along to play jujitsu with us tonight," Tim said as a mop-haired student walked in. The boy needed professional help—maybe some of my clipped curls, if that coed didn't beat him to 'em.

"Judo? Serious?"

"Heh-heh. See-ree-ous." Snipping his scissors, Tim motioned for the student to sit. The kid looked as if he'd arrived for a calculus final. Maybe Dad or Mom had threatened to clip his money unless he clip his hair. Tim spritzed me with aftershave. "Wild Boar musk," he said, twitching his nose under his bifocals.

"Serious?"

"Heh-heh." Tim squirted my nose and I coughed. "Don swore he's going to get whoever smashed his Caddy, by the way."

After my haircut I went back to the bookstore and stared at the mess I'd made trying to alphabetize our stock of Prentice-Hall. My own love rebound had lost its bounce a year before. God knows I needed control over something, and the alphabet offered a harmless choice. Suddenly, I felt fingers drawing through my hair.

"Sandy, loooook. Josey got a haircut."

Sandy, a freshman, was punching in on the time clock. She shelved her card to join Mildred, our administrative secretary, and both ran their fingers through my hair.

"Ooooh, and what's that perfume you're wearing? Mmmmm."

They giggled and left the stockroom. Was a good thing for them I was learning judo and not karate, it was.

We played, as Tim always called it, jujitsu in the basement of the local Y, in a room hung with water pipes whose yellow and red arrows pointed this way and that. They confused my twenty-two year old mind, especially when I was on my back, underneath someone's ghi, staring up at those conflicting arrows. *Whither, Josey?* They seemed to ask. Or was that a command? *Wither, Josey.* We played in a small group, usually four to six people. Don was already there when I arrived, grudgingly nodding at what Tim was telling him.

"Jujitsu just doesn't work that way. You're going to spend all evening learning how to fall."

"How's that going to help with the sonofagun who dented my Cadillac?—Hi Josey. You hear what happened to my Cadillac?"

I waved and told Don I'd already heard, but he decided to demonstrate in his bare feet, giving a twist and shouting "Boom!" at the end of his side-kick toward the wall.

Tim walked to the concrete wall, bent, and held his palms an inch apart. "Don, you're going to break all five of your litt-le toe-sies if you don't calm down.—He wants to learn how to punch, Josey." Tim tossed me a Zen grin, because that's exactly what I'd wanted to learn when I first started, too.

"I just wanna dent that skinny, out-dated hippie like he did my Cadillac, is what I wanna do." Don had a smoker's voice that would have added weight to his threat except for his eyes, which bulged like a frog's. All this made him look like an eight-year-old. I suppose that's what he was, emotion-wise. The stance . . . oh it was familiar.

"Don, ka-raa-tay boys don't know how to fall. They nev-ver get taught."

This was a masterstroke on Tim's part. Knowing anything the karate boys didn't know was just fine with Don. So he spent the next hour and a half bouncing off the blue mat—with Tim, two other guys, and me playing the heavy's part of slinging him over our hips, then higher up on our shoulders when he got used to falling.

Don was one green frog hair under six feet, and a lily pad over two hundred and ten pounds, so I'd undergone quite a workout by the time we hit the showers. There, he told me that the Cadillac dealer couldn't see him for a week. And Don refused to let anyone besides a Cadillac dealer work on his baby. He confessed, as we stood amid steam, that he thought of driving either to Cincinnati or Louisville. But Tim had ixnayed that, saying he couldn't afford to let Don off in the middle of fall semester when the students, all hot to find their Mr. or Ms. Wonderful, needed coifs at least once a week. Ah, so that's what the mop-head was doing in Tim's shop earlier: a squirming crush on some girl six rows down in socio-bio-statisticology. Well, he was out eight bucks for a haircut and the girl'd have to dislocate both her upper and lower cervix to turn around and see him.

After our showers, Don coaxed me out to his car, croaking a secret whisper on the way. "You know how to cut hair, Josey? If you do, you can fill in for me next week."

"No, Don. I just know how to alphabetize books."

He grunted *huh*, twice. Less than a year with Tim and he was picking up that Buddha laugh, bit by bit. If only his questions could keep pace, he'd undergo a mind-miracle to do Kentucky hillbillies proud.

"Huh. Huh," he laughed again. Practicing. Then he pointed. His car was parked at the bottom of a hill. I'd never ridden in it and wondered if this would be the meltdown point. Tim had ridden twice and swore that both times they went to Jerry's, our local chain drive-in that refused to die, where Don drove around in circles until Tim became so dizzy he had to order a vanilla milkshake to coat his stomach. "Josey," Tim confided afterwards, "pretty little high school girls gathered like bunn-ches of roses, all of them staring at us in that crea-my con-verr-tible Cadillac. I don't think my wife would appreciate me riding with Don too very often." Tim was one of those men with a mystery wife—does she really exist? No one could confirm the fact except Tim—and his wife, of course. But that was the point: no one would ever see her to ask if she were real. Love, it was taking a beating in Lexington.

We stopped fifty feet from the car and Don shook his head. "See it?" he said, pointing at his Cadillac.

"Well, no, I can't see anything from here." But I was trying, honest.

"That's 'cause the dealer sold me some touch-up paint. But wait till we get close; it looks terrible."

As we closed in I could see the dent, sure enough: a ten-inch crease that made me glad I hadn't run into this killer karate chump on a foolish drunk at the Paddock Club. Don knelt—both knees!—by his car to rub its sore. Then he picked an offending pebble from a tire tread and angrily tossed it into the grass; then he gave the Caddy a sniff, then an on-the-spot spit-shine to its left taillight. God knows what perversions he'd've enacted if I hadn't stood there watching.

He looked up at me, keeping a cheek against the back panel, as if listening for a heart murmur or mis-fired bowel movement. "I'm going to describe this guy to you, Josey. He ever comes in the bookstore, I want you to promise to call me and keep him there. Jam the register, show him a new *Playboy*."

"Don, I—"

"You got to! You've just got to!"

"All right! All right!"

Tim came out the front door of the Y and I waved him down the hill. *Help. He's your employee.*

Meanwhile, Don continued his description: "He's about my height, but skinny. I don't know how the pencil-neck SOB could do this much to my Cadillac, especially in the rain. He must be one of these bookworm students, 'cause he didn't have any complexion to speak of. And no beard. A skinny nose."

"That's not much to go on, Don."

"The black ponytail. Just hold that black ponytail in mind. Halfway down his butt. How many guys have ponytails these days? Hippies have been gone forever."

Tim walked up and sang, "Is he giving his mug shot, dee-tailed, eye witt-ness account?"

I nodded, then asked Don: "You gonna take us for a spin?"

"Like THIS?" He pointed to the dent with horror, eyes bulging as if he'd been gigged beside a moonlit pond. "No way. I'll take you next week when she's out of the shop. I can't have people seeing her in public now. It'd hurt her feelings." Don knee-walked forward, checking for further damage, or maybe lung obstructions.

"And just what are you going to eat for supp-per if you don't drive to Jerry's?" Tim asked.

Don's froggy eyes croaked. This was evidently something he hadn't thought of. His mouth worked like it was catching flies. "Guess I'll walk over to Candy's."

"Heh-heh. For lunch and sup-per both? For a full week?"

For once I understood Tim's laugh: the Buddha chuckle of world-weariness, the yangless yearn of yin, the yinless yarn of yang. In brief, Candy's was an institution whose greasy, yellow walls rendered eggs, hamburgers, waffles, apple pies, and iceberg lettuce not only visual, but gustatory, even moral equivalents. Food to dilapidate dharma. Not *Om*, but *Ug*. Could any sentient being survive Candy's menu for a full week? I appraised Don as he nuzzled his Cadillac's chrome door handle. Not only his eyes, but his lips bulged amphibian. Maybe his taste buds ran Pleistocene too.

"Huh. Guess I'll walk on over to Candy's. Anybody joining me?"

Tim and I quickly searched out our cars.

A WEEK LATER and Don was definitely off his feed. He'd taken to spending his lunches by the Cadillac, eyeing pedestrians for leg twitches, since he was a firm believer that the criminal always returned to the scene of the crime. Sometimes I carried him a hamburger or popcorn. After work, Tim taught him how to fall.

Then came a second trauma: the Cadillac dealer told Don that the crease folded so much that it'd be better to order a new panel. That would take two weeks. For those two weeks, jujitsu was no longer play, no matter how Tim tried to make it so. Don described the side-kick that the guy'd used, and insisted that Tim teach him how to counter it. That's all he wanted. So now it was my turn to take falls as Don practiced leg sweeps whenever I side-kicked. And Tim taught Don a chokehold that he was getting the hang of—well enough that I'd have to remind Don it wasn't me who'd dented his damned Cadillac. We collectively tired of it, and the group threatened to dwindle to one frog and a lily pad. Finally, I became impatient, and when Don swept me for the hundredth time one day, I took him over my head as he grabbed my ghi for the chokehold. To his credit, he'd learned to fall, and he hit the mat nicely, though his eyes bulged when I twisted his own ghi in a chokehold.

"Want to ride in the Caddy tonight?" he croaked when we were in the showers.

A peace offering.

"I thought the panel hadn't come yet."

"It hasn't, but I'm tired of waiting. I suppose the dent don't matter all that much. She's a tough gal, she can take it."

So I rode to Jerry's with Don, Tim having shook his head no-no, emphatically no-no. "Heh-heh, you two baach-el-ors go."

"What's bachelor got to do with hamburger?"

"Heh-heh," was the only answer I got.

BY THE BLESSED BEARD of Abraham Lincoln! Holy Mint Julep! I saw all after half a circle around the lot. Twenty teenage hands waving, twenty charm bracelets jangling. "Don! Hey Donnie! Don-Don!"

"Open my glove compartment, would you, Josey?"

I hesitated, even as Don pulled into a slot. What would flop out? Lolita lollipops? Barbie bubble gum? Perfume samplers? Trojan-Enz? I hit the button. A pint of cherry vodka.

"Two cheeseburgers, two fries, and four Cokes?" This was the drive-in's speaker repeating our order. Don looked over to me, and I nodded, though raising my brow at the number of Cokes.

"Thass it, darlin'."

"Don, is that you? You have someone with you?"

"Sure do, darlin'."

"Male or female?" The speaker scraped with a tinny edge, as if it might spit electricity.

"Male."

"Oh honey, this I want to see. I'll just carry your order out myself, Sweets." Now the voice crooned, mature and sensual.

We sat a few minutes, talking about judo, haircuts, and the latest gossip on campus—a sociology professor had run away with a hooker—and, of course, Cadillacs. Maybe he got a grant to do research on the social underbelly, I mused, still stuck on the professor, not sharing America's obsession with cars.

"There she is!" Don nodded toward the service entrance. At Jerry's there were five steps the waitresses had to descend while carrying a full tray on their shoulders—I'm sure this worked wonders for their spines—but this woman's descent made Miss America's stroll look like amateur night on a duck pond. She weighed over 200 and her swaying hips vibrated the iron banister—who knows what damage they were doing to Jerry's stone facing.

"Ain't she somethin'?"

"She sure is, Don."

The waitress's name was Eve. "I only got ten minutes tonight," she said. "We got a new manager and she's a P in the A." Eve was rubbing her silky brown carhop slacks all over Don's Cadillac and buffing the driver's side mirror with a sleeve at the same time. Don reached for the cherry vodka and gave all four Cokes a dollop.

"Who's that other one for?" Eve asked, that same tin creeping into her voice.

"Josey. He's a lush. This is Josey, Eve. He works at the bookstore across from me in the Student Union."

"Glad to meet you, Josey. Haven't I seen you somewheres before?"

"Could be. I've lived here all my life."

"I'm from Paintsville myself. Just twelve miles from where Don lived when he was a little boy."

Don gave an obligatory blush then drank his Coke and cherry vodka. Eve gave him a good slug in the arm.

"Didja hear that Henry Johnson and Mary Lou Lyons are getting married?"

"Naw."

"They sure are and . . ."

And teenage tires squealed as I looked around the drive-in I swore I'd never return to once I got out of high school. *I truly thought we were going to eat in the dining room,* I told myself. *Drive-ins are like dinosaurs,* I told myself.

"Eve, break's over. Miss Walker's asking where you are," the speaker crackled.

Don reached for the button. "Tell Miz Walker to—" Eve grabbed his hand and shushed him.

"Tell Miss Walker I'm in the Ladies' Room and will be right in. Thanks, Jean." Eve slurped the last of her spiked Coke then shook her head with a flirtatious laugh at Don. "You gonna give me a call this weekend?"

"No calls until I get this Cadillac fixed. But you're top on my list."

The instant—the very instant Eve walked up those steps and into the restaurant, I heard giggles and turned to see two teenage girls skipping around the Cadillac's rear fins.

"Where've you been, Don? We've been looking for you nearly every night."

"Who's your friend, Don? Aren't you going to introduce us? His hair's so pretty."

Their names were Tina and Lena. No, that's not true, but it may as well have been. Two bleached blondies who thought make-up meant clown dots. Well, I guess a forty-year-old woman would say the same about two twenty-two-year-old guys: Toby and Joby: a duet of punks who can't grow their beards past Brill-o. At any rate, the night coasted downhill as we passed the fourth Coke back to the girls and ate bomb-burgers and fries and took Tina and Lena for a ride . . . to their car, which was parked three rows over.

"This is the life, ain't it, Josey?"

I was sucking my third cherry vodka and Coke, approaching sugar overdose. "You think?" I croaked.

"No." Don finished his drink and put it on the tray. "I think I need to get married again. I think I miss going to Roger's and watching Thelma Sue—she was my wife—eat fried chicken." He took my cup and placed it on the tray. "Want to go to the Office Lounge? It's ladies' night."

"Sure. Why not?"

But once we reached the bar Don fell into a blue funk and began ranting about the SOB who kicked his Caddy. Female lips grimaced; female legs chose barstools or booths time warps away.

Don was counting down. It was Tuesday and the dealer double-dog promised the panel would be in on Thursday. I was having coffee with Tim, who'd let Don off early for lunch.

"Lunch? It's only . . ."

Tim smiled. "That's right. Someone told him she saw somebody walk by his car yesterday and stop to look at the dent. At about this time." Tim gave a glance to the clock. We watched the second hand.

"Do you think he'll wind up in jail or the emergency room?"

"Heh-heh."

A coffee-and-a-half later, Don walked in with a gashed lip, but he was all smiles as he nodded to Tim and me.

"Did you find your ka-raa-tay boy?" Tim asked.

Another grin, though this one caused Don to reach for his lip with a jerk. He was holding the door, waiting for someone. Seeing blood, Tim tsked and walked over with a Kleenex. As Don dabbed, in limped a lanky graduate student from the math department who'd worked at the bookstore last summer. I waved, but she homed in on Don.

"Did it start bleeding again? I'm sorry." Her voice matched Don's bullfrog croak. I remembered how surprised I was when I heard her speak in the stockroom the first time.

Don leaned against the door as she took the Kleenex and did some personalized dabbing of her own. I could smell her perfume and blinked: talk about wild boar musk. Funny, she hadn't worn perfume in the summer; she hadn't even run her fingers through my hair like every other woman. Life on the number axis must have gotten lonely over Labor Day.

She gave Don's lip another dab; then Don looked at us. "Diane, this is my boss Tim. And this is—"

"Josey. I remember you from the bookstore."

I nodded.

"Diane's the one who kicked my Cadillac."

"But I didn't mean to. It was raining and Don accidentally splashed me and I lost my temper. I've been taking all this karate from Su Lin."

"Su Lin. Heh-heh. And did you give my mass-ter barr-ber that nasty lip as well as denting his car?"

"I didn't mean to. He jumped and yelled at me, and when I side-kicked he swept me to the ground. . . ."

Don started to apologize again, but Diane assured him she was okay.

"I saw that she was a girl—woman—just as I was about to choke her. . . ."

"And I thought he was a madman going to kill me so I elbowed his jaw. . . ."

"I told her I'd give her a free trim." Don's chest inflated and his double chin worked with bullfrog absorption. "You can take it out of my pay, Tim."

"And I'm going to fix his Cadillac. My sister's husband owns a body shop." Diane was rubbing her haunch, playing the cherry-red clip in her ponytail about the barber shop like a fisherman's bobber on a farm pond. Don gulped and hunkered to watch, while Tim strolled to study Diane's hip as she rubbed it. He tsked as she grimaced.

"Su Lin—he ever teach you to fall?"

"No. Just kicks and punches."

"Maybe Don here will inn-vite you to play jujitsu."

"Not tonight, Tim," Don croaked. "We're going out to Rogers to eat fried chicken."

"It's been over a year since I've tasted fried chicken. Cholesterol be damned. Being a graduate student has kept me on beans and rice." Diane added, "That's why I was working at the bookstore." She looked from Tim and Don to me. "All the women in the store love your hair," she said, giving a non-numerical smile.

"It's these danged Student Union Building fluorescent lights," Don said, his eyes bulging sudden and possessive. "Thought it looked peculiar and skagly myself, out in the open air, in my Cadillac the other night, I mean. No offense." That was the last he had to spare for me. He blinked at Diane, Diane blinked at him. Both of them swayed.

"Heh-heh."

"Heh-heh."

Surprised by the echo, I realized that Tim and I had both laughed, sharing the same cosmic thought: *Lexington's streets are safe, 'cause Don's truly learning to fall.*

My Life as an Imaginary Number

Looking down at myself as a tannish speck on a brilliantly green meadow. So it must be a planet we're talking about. The grass, it's that coarse St. Augustine strain that springs like a coil, so it must be Florida. There are other specks, active on the trampoline grass, and there's a stage that the specks face. A woman sits docilely next to me, the tannish speck with the luststick bulging his shorts. The woman, she's talking about Thomas Edison. The woman knew Thomas Edison, who lived on Florida's other coast. At least I believe that's what she said at lunch yesterday when I waited on her table. No, it was Thomas Edison's wife she said she knew. Right after ordering Caesar salad and a dry gin martini.

She—the woman, not Edison's wife—has blonde hair mummified from the late sixties, resembling that modishly nebular swirl with which *Star Trek* coifed all Kirk's would-be amours. In fact she could very well be cast in a bit part for the same. Then who would I be? Charming Kirk almost in love? Spock, Bones, offering calming reason, or a molecular antivirus? I have it: The Mad Computer.

We just came from meeting her parents. Approval for their thirty-two year old daughter's date, I suppose. Or is she older? Lines crevasse her make-up and she did say she knew Thomas Edison's—forget it. Myself, I have been grasping the number line for twenty-seven years, sometimes as a fraction, sometimes as a mixed number, sometimes as a negative. Today I'm an imaginary number. Never-Never-Never have I been a positive, whole integer.

Her parents. One hour ago she and I'd shuffled into a shotgun shack shelved in Lake Worth where immediately I spotted a white form pegged to a bed in the bedroom one shotgun blast back. Listening, I could almost hear the form's milky sinews straining for release from the heavy sheets and pillows. *Halloo back there. Are you real?*

"This is my mother," she'd said, pinioning my elbow with her pale, puffy, sweaty, intriguing hand and pulling my attention from that back room. Her grip was strong; one of my tendons popped. She pointed to a bundle piled against the wall that I'd mistaken for a GoodWill donation. "And that's my father." She then pointed to the aforementioned form in the bed, one room back, as the shotgun shack pellet flies.

"Hello. Hello," I squoaked.

"Hello," the recumbent bundle said, shifting blue house slippers from under migratory dust.

"{ }" The null set announced from the bed. Then its hand jerked as if attached to wire. I smiled and bent, searching for a pulley on the next room's ceiling. It was possible, I realized while searching, that she said her *parents* knew Thomas Edison. That would make things okay. I mean, that would shift things back onto the real number line because Edison and Henry Ford were neighbors, so Edison could have died in the twenties, thirties, even early forties, I suppose(d). And these parents of hers, well . . . they could have died about anytime.

"Hello." Her mother repeated again. Or was that the scooting of her blue slippers?

Like sand in an hourglass, the timegraph slipped along, and after twenty-five intriguing minutes we were leaving the house. The visit, you might say, had been splendid. The hand rose again and I nodded, forcing myself not to reinstate my search for a pulley or cable. The GoodWill pile scurried, shifting bric-a-brac amid a flurry of two blue mice—I mean two be-slippered feet. A small Hummel was moved from the TV to a bookshelf; a red book was moved from the bookshelf to a windowsill. "Shush, shush," the blue mice went as each item was moved. Or was that sound really someone saying, "You schildren have a schfun time"? Whatever, outside the house, Florida sunlight and its showering accoutrements of heat, vitamin D, and ozone-gap ultraviolet had reassured me.

So now, let's return to point x(i), y(i); OR, back to the present and the green field and the special Gulf Stream breeze that always blows about Lake Worth:

But no, that's not what she said. That her parents knew Thomas Edison's wife, I mean. Because now she's telling me a tale in a rich voice that wells from beneath her breasts, themselves reassuring potential repositories of antibody rich milk, and I suppose, vitamin D: "Men! You *know* that Mrs. Edison poisoned Thomas, don't you? She was tired of him puttering all the time. He had a whole workshop across the road, you know, and she had to constantly stare at all these workers scurrying over there, playing with all these chemicals in what was really her own front yard. The whole block could blow up anytime! Besides, he was mean to their son and he was mean to her. Don't tell this to anyone because I promised Mrs. E. that I wouldn't."

The secret's safe, I swear.

"Hey, Paul! Hey! Wait up! —Will you excuse me for a minute?" She waves vigorously at some passing Florida Adonis and blinks her widemost and roundmost until sapphires tumble from her eyes.

I lean to catch one, simultaneously trying to grip my tiny plot on the timegraph, but my hands slip completely through the thin number line, while both of hers flit through the air to attract Paul. *Paul? Who's Paul?* She's standing and waving now. My God, I'm to be abandoned on our first date. I look from her waving, happy hands to the bright red purse she's leaving at my feet. So I was reassured that she'd come back . . . *unless she's placed an explosive device—stop it*! It was just a quirky little story, what she said about Edison being murdered by his wife.

She's in the crowd now, trying to hop high enough off the ground to attract Paul. The number line quavers as she lands, for she is a bit plump as I've mentioned, but delicate in a cotton-bole way that intrigues my feeble mind. And by all the Holy Number Line Axes, talk about minds! Friends, there hops a woman of whom no one will ever utter, "She's got a really nice personality," in trying to arrange a blind date. As she hops for Paul, I watch her green dress change coordinates—well, in truth I watch her hips, feminine but akimbo. None of this seems strange, considering the number line we live on.

Oh no. Oh no, no, no. My shoulders vector in downward empathy, for the SOB Paul has purposefully asymptoted off before she can reach him. Ashamed of my fellow male, I look down at the coordinates I'm sitting on, and am amazed to find grass instead of line squiggles and fractions. I keep staring, feigning obsession with a small decimal point I've discovered. I toss it upwards and watch it tumble: she needs to have the privacy either to chase after the guy or pretend she's said what she wanted to him, conveyed an interesting and fully balanced quadratic equation, say.

Five minutes later she returns. The decimal point drops and disappears as her white-white sandaled feet approach. I could worship that cotton candy. Her toes, I mean. And the accompanying toenails are painted with a violet nail polish that kindly complements her green dress and the large red handbag. Myself, I'm dirt on dirt—no color coordinate problem for this sector of the graph.

Her sapphire eyes loom hugely, nearly filling her face as she sits: "An old high school friend whom I haven't seen . . . in a long time." Lots of teeth grin at me—so even, so perfect.

Her lie, too, is so perfect that I think maybe she caught up with Paul and maybe he turned away only because of a pressing engagement: an errant square root attack or some other polynomial aberration. She blinks, though, and I know the truth as liquid sapphire logarithms exude.

"Good," I say. "Me, I never heard from *anyone* in my high school after graduation. All parties concerned seem happy with the arrangement."

She smiles. "You shouldn't be so negative, you know. Negative vibrations can keep house plants and even grass from growing."

I look to where I'm sitting: I pet the grass, cooing, "Really a gorgeous day for stretching the old blades, isn't it, guys and gals? Say, how can I tell you guys from you gals? Ticklish in different spots?" I pretend to tickle the grass.

She laughs. Good.

"Did you know that Thomas Edison was working on perfecting a rubber plant that could be grown in America?"

"For Henry Ford?"

"No, for cars—oh I see. Yes, for Henry Ford. And for their friend Firestone."

Thomas Edison again. Well as long as his wife stays out of the way.

Despite Thomas Edison, we have many things in common, I think, still pretending not to see her sapphire tears. Sapphire? How about sap for hire? Well, of course you have things in common. You're deeply in love with female toes, lips and eyes, and she owns a quantum of all three.

"But he died before he could perfect it."

"He?"

"Edison. Poisoned."

AT ANY RATE, my plan was this: After the concert (Who played? A band. What'd they play? Why, music, of course.), after the concert we would zip to the mall for a slam-bang fancy dinner and some wine, zip-zip-ZIP past Mom and Dad's housepital, forget about electricity and Mr. and Mrs. Edison, and roam my West Palm Beach batchartment which claimed a jalousied window's back view onto Big Daddy's Liquor and Lounge that could not be beat in seven Southern states, including Lookout Mountain, Tennessee.

The plan starts. Car ignition. Pull off main number line into a number depository, more commonly known as a mall.

"I love pizza."

"There's a seafood restaurant down there, it says." The mall's map glows on my face like a console charting the entire Milky Way. "I thought we could have a nice relaxing dinner with some red wine."

"I'd rather not. Remember: I'm buying my own."

"But . . ."

"I'd rather have pizza. Pizza costs less."

"But . . ."

It wasn't even a real restaurant but a grab-and-gulp stuck in the mall with fifteen dirty tables surrounded by chrome banisters, pizzeria lights, and two screaming pimply kids shoveling tomato catastrophes in and out of three ovens, one of whose hinges squeaked immeasurably. I looked, I looked: yes, they had beer. Axle grease for the axle!

"Let's get a couple of beers first; then we can decide."

"I know what I want." She turns from me to the walking Clearasil ad who's been kindly awaiting our equations to form. "Could I have two slices of pepperoni pizza, thick crust, please? And a large iced tea. Unsweetened. I always use my own sweetener." Her eyes and lips deliver fillips to the high school kid taking our order, just as they did to me yesterday when she ordered a Caesar salad and gin martini.

But don't you want a beer? —Even though I speak in my imaginary number voice, she shakes her head emphatically while the kid waits politely for the two of us to get our act together.

Speaking of Edison, did I ever tell you about the time I met René Descartes? Yes, right before he learned that he existed! What a mind that man had: I think; therefore I am. *Me, I told him it didn't always work that way*: I think; therefore I amn't *better suits me.*

"You sir?"

I look over my shoulder. I, sir? My chest puffs a fraction on realizing the kid is addressing me: "I'll have plus-two slices of bacon pizza and plus-one large beer."

"Uh, what kind of beer would you like, sir?"

Pernod on the rocks with wormwood and heroin.

"Sir?"

"Sir?"

Tracking back to the zero point, I focus on the youngster. "Schlitz."

"Schlitz. Fine. I'll bring it right to you."

We sit with a commanding, if not impending, view of the mall. The floor is scuffed with intersecting graph marks, quadratic equations gone completely out of hand, nearing the chaos phase. I'm thinking of something stupendous to say, when through the chromium turnstile walks a motorcycle would-be and his would-be chick. He's nervous— God, he's going to pull a gun and rob the place. No, he orders pizza.

With a damn sight less indecision than I did, I notice. So I vaguely form plans to buy a Harley-Davidson and some chain oil.

She's stopped mid-tear on a packet of Sucrose. She's staring at the Harley kid too, but her sapphire has taken on the iced mortuary glaze that occasionally haunts one corner of the walk-in cooler in the restaurant where I work. She turns quickly to me. "Have you ever studied what's inside these?" She finishes tearing with a slow relish, her fingernails enjoying their task so much that they shimmer, like a myriad of subtraction signs scootering down Highway A-1-A on a Memorial Day Parade. Then she cascades out a fine white powder from the torn packet.

"It looks *exactly* like nine different poisons. Do you realize how easy it would be to slit one of these with a razor and slip a poison in, then carry it in your purse and when someone isn't looking—or even when they are—tap it into their drink?" She dribbles the grisly white remainder of the packet . . . into *her* tea, I'm happy to say.

"Tell me," she says in all cheerfulness. "Do you ever use sweetener in your coffee or tea?"

She gives me a look that echoes the one she gave the Harley-Davidson would-be. That ice patch vaporizes, however, as she props her feet in a most neighborly manner onto a nearby chair and wiggles her purpletop toes. As I wave back at them—*kitchy-kitchy, kiddies*—she grins alluringly with her female lips, her female eyes, her female love-dimples while she taps a new pink packet of Sweet N Low lightly—tap-tip, tap-tap . . .

Stop! Did Thomas Edison invent Morse code? Why not, he invented everything else.

I listen to the freshly ripped Sweet N Low packet: tap-tip, tip-tap . . . *I've come for your bones, I've come for your bones. . . .*

TINY IMAGINARY NUMBERS OF THE WORLD, UNITE! O brethren O sistren, keep your imaginary antennae extended late into the night. Sip your beer slowly; carefully peek into all red handbags, billfolds and knapsacks. Never ever wear your club colors in public; always be polite to your ex-high school chums. Travel alone. Keep an eagle's eye on Nutra-Sweet and Sweet N Low. Keep a cat's ear for tapped Morse code. And if you *ever* meet a woman who claims friendship with Thomas Edison's wife—ahh, hook your imaginary toes hard into the number line; don't drink a sip; glance neither left, nor right.

Alpha and Omega

"Stop! Stop!"

It had started a week before, when the man, who was a priest, said he needed someone to help him retrieve shelves for the parochial school from his mother's house outside Covington. That day after school, the boy had asked his own mother if he could go and she said yes because this young priest was energetic, because he worked about the parish and the church, unlike the older priest whose dandruff snowed his eyebrows and who randomly tottered into classes to drill students on the ancient Greek alphabet, *alpha* through *omega*. "Stop! Stop!" the boy always wanted to shout when this old priest's hands fumbled at the blackboard to scrape chalk.

So the next week with the young priest had come about, as if ordained. On the drive to Covington from Lexington, about sixty northward miles, the young priest must have noticed the boy leaning forward and squinting.

"Read that license plate ahead," he ordered.

Even as the boy's mouth spewed numbers and letters that landed nowhere near reality, the man asked him to read a road sign. The boy couldn't.

"Mary, mother of God," the priest half-whistled through wet lips. "Have you ever had your eyes examined?"

The boy said no, and the priest told him he should, that he needed glasses. To drive the point home, the priest pointed out a closer second license plate then asked the boy if he could read it.

No.

"Mary, mother of God," the priest repeated.

All the altar boys liked this young priest, because he let them sip the sacramental wine—not on purpose or blatantly, of course, but he always poured more in the decanter than the old priest did, so there was always a taste left after Mass. He also told them little jokes in the middle of Mass, which was confusing on such a serious occasion before such intent parishioners kneeling in such a hugely somber church. But the jokes were fun compared to classes with the so-serious nuns. "Jesus, Mary and Joseph, the flood of the Nile," he once exclaimed to the boy, who'd poured too much water for the preparatory rite of cleansing the priest's fingers. During that same Mass, when the boy tried to be stingy with the wine, the priest had nudged the small glass decanter twice with his knuckle, until the boy had been forced to empty the contents.

"That'll teach you to keep your mind on the Mass," the priest leaned to whisper, with a wet admixture of logic and illogic oddly comprehensible to the boy, who straightened his starchy cassock, clinked the crystal salver on the marble topped stand, then turned and tiptoed to his place, studying the granite floor to avoid the taw eyes of parishioners in the church—parishioners who had witnessed the exchange and no doubt recognized the boy was well on his way to becoming a wine drunkard or worse.

So. So it was a week after asking his mother when the boy and the priest drove to the priest's mother's house, which was in the country, on the outskirts of Covington. Outside her yellow frame home a willow permanently and grandly wept while an old gray dog shambled to sniff the boy's hand, then lumbered back into shade. Just beyond the house, a sunny field plotted out a welcoming handshake, despite grass dried from that spring's lack of rain. Altogether, the day smelled of coming summer vacation and happiness, for the boy was too young to care about drought or rain.

The priest's mother let a screen door slam behind her. She looked at the boy quizzically then smiled, then wrung her red, swollen hands on her apron and thrust her chin at her son.

"I came to pick up some of that old shelving in the garage to take back for the school."

"It's good to see you, Son. Are you going to spend the night?"

"No, I'm going into town to see Ben."

Ben was the priest's brother. The mother, whose brown and gray hair strayed just like the dog's who had trotted out of the shade, looked at the boy.

"What's his name? Has he eaten?"

"Didn't I tell you, Josey? Hah? Didn't I tell you that mothers exist for the sole purpose of fattening sons?" The priest, whose wet lips grinned loosely, pinched the boy's shoulder. The priest had a voice that, although deep, could peak in piercing sharpness. The boy had heard it do that very thing during one Mother's Day sermon when the priest castigated America for lavishing affection on the mother while forsaking the father. The church's gothic revival architecture enthroned a huge artificial Mary-blue seashell over the lectern. This shell focused the priest's voice and undulated it over pews and around pillars in crashing waves. "MOTH-ER'S Day?" The priest had jerked his pink palms upwards like a puppet. "And what do we do for FATH-ER'S Day? It's time for the FATHER to get a little respect in the household. It's time for the MAN who goes out and WORKS forty and fifty hours a week to hear an 'I LOVE YOU!'" He harangued until the boy was nervous, until adults squirmed in the pews, grinning uncomfortably or cracking knuckles and crinkling their brows, remembering awaiting rose bouquets and ham dinners at home.

"Josey. For Saint Joseph?" This was the mother, who gave the boy a second glance.

"Geeza, Mom. Of course. Did you think he was named for Stalin?"

The woman tsked and shook her head at her son. "You know where the garage is, Frank. I'll go on in and fry some chicken. You like drumsticks, Josey?"

The boy nodded and the woman smiled faintly.

Out in the wood garage they were attacked by yellow jackets and had to retreat with only one piece of the shelving.

"You can throw gas on them and it kills them right away," the boy suggested.

"Jesus, Mary and Joseph. You'll have me burning the whole county down."

But gasoline was what they wound up using, since the priest's mother said she was out of any kind of bug spray.

"Women don't know how to run a house," the priest rumbled as he poured the gas into a Mason jar. He leaned away from the rising fumes. "You sure this will work?"

The boy nodded. "It kills them right away, they don't even have time to fly."

In the golden glow of the garage's lumber, they watched the yellow jackets, twenty or more, tumble crookedly from the nest onto the dirt floor. There, their bottoms briefly curled as if to sting their own bodies in self-flagellation. Then they stiffened and died.

"Some trick. Looks like the parishioners when I'm delivering a sermon."

They loaded the wood into the car's trunk, a huge trunk in a new blue Ford Fairlane that the parish had bought for the priest.

"Frank, you and Josey about ready to eat?"

The priest mumbled something the boy couldn't make out, then told him to wait. The boy was glad to do this, for the dog had come out again while they were loading the car, and was sniffing the boy's legs, wagging its tail slowly like old dogs do. The boy squatted to pet it as the priest opened the screen door and walked inside the house. The door once more banged shut.

"Stop! Stop!"

The dog was licking his face and the boy was laughing and staring into the distant field, wondering what it would look like when he got his first pair of glasses. It looked dry and yellow-green now, though with the breeze that had just picked up and with the dog tickling his cheek, that off-color didn't matter. The boy wondered if someone in the field was waving at him, but decided it was just a small tree or maybe a scarecrow.

"Geeza. Of course it's a tree. You really do need glasses. Come on in, she's not going to let us get out of here without filling us with chicken and gravy."

That was a disappointment to the boy, for they'd passed a hamburger shack where the priest promised they would stop on the way out. For some reason, ordering hamburger-all-the-way seemed a magically adult thing for the boy.

Though the woman tried to be friendly, she mostly talked about Ben, the priest's brother, who lived in Covington and whom she was worried about. The boy ignored her frets and the priest's quick comments; instead, while chewing the gristle off a drumstick he studied the kitchen. Its walls were yellow like the outside of the house, but brighter. A picture of Jesus with an atomically glowing Sacred Heart hung in one corner; above it, a picture of Mary with her halo. No picture of Joseph was to be seen.

"I just don't think your father would be very happy about things if he was alive, that's all I'm saying."

"He was never very happy about things period."

"That's no way to talk about your dead father."

The priest let out a tiny burp and lifted the napkin to his lips. His mother pushed the gravy boat toward the boy.

"You get enough, Child? Why is he gnawing the bones, Frank? Did you tell him he could only eat one piece?"

"Mom, he's had three."

"Well, when you see Ben, you remember what I told you about your father and see if you don't agree. He'll listen to you."

They left after peach pie, swirling up so much dust on the long driveway that when the boy looked back he couldn't see the house or garage. They passed the hamburger stand and the boy stuck his nose out the window to smell.

"Sorry about that, Kid. We'll make up for it tonight, though."

"*Nyx*. That's Greek for *night*. Father Wilson taught us that."

"Ancient Greek—it keeps him off me, anyhow." The priest lit a cigarette and turned to laugh and tousle the boy's hair.

"He said he memorized a long poem by reading it aloud to himself every day and that now it will always be with him."

"It will, huh?" the priest replied.

To someone young from Lexington and horse-farm country, Covington's reputation as a sin-city of gamblers, hookers and Mafia murderers loomed, so the boy pulled his arm inside the window once they entered the city proper. It was barely after midday, but dust motes and noise thickened into a yellow paste that coated the streets, the brick buildings, even the trees, whose leaves and trunks shunted to olive drab. People teetered near gutters and stared dull-eyed. They too seemed olive and drab.

"Stop! Stop!" the boy shouted to all those olive-drab people. No he didn't, but he thought he might.

"Geeza," the priest commented as they hurried past a corner grocery with chalky, peeling, red paint and a dozen black and white people slouching in tee shirts. Evidently the priest had lived in Horse Country long enough to be uncomfortable with Covington too.

Ben, the priest's brother, rented an apartment under a brick house. He stood outside when they drove up, and soon the two brothers leaned against an ironwork fence sporting spearlike points. They talked while the boy ran his hand along the same fence some fifteen yards away. A girl pedaled by on a bicycle, her silly frilled blue-and-white dress seeming more suited for Easter parading than riding the pasty streets of Covington. A sparrow chirped in agreement, mockingly jumping from limb to limb of a tree obstinately rooted beneath the brick sidewalk.

The boy let go the fence and walked to the tree. The brother was shorter and heavier than the priest and the boy didn't like him from the way his eyebrows thickened and the way his sleeveless undershirt showed through his sweaty yellowed shirt. The priest had mentioned that his brother sold used cars. The boy could believe it. He looked from the bird in the tree and the receding girl on the bike to see the brother's fat stomach lean into the iron fence, as if trying to section itself like a boiled egg in a wire slicer.

A few minutes later, the girl came back, her head rigidly forward. The boy wondered if she'd read his mind about her dress. She was riding in the opposite direction but on the same side of the street as before. Sirens sounded and he searched, but spotted nothing other than the yellow haze. Sin City.

The priest walked over and pinched his shoulder. "HE-Y Kid, you're great. Most kids would have been nosing around listening and getting in the way instead of standing off by themselves. You're really great, you know?"

2.

They went to dinner that night at a Howard Johnson's, at the same motel where they were staying. They sat in a huge circular booth in a corner and the boy noticed a woman picking at an odd orange-pink thing on a nearby table.

"What's that?"

"Shrimp cocktail," the waitress answered.

"Fella! You've never had shrimp cocktail?" The priest's voice was shrill and he ordered the boy a shrimp cocktail.

When it came, the priest took one in his big fingers, peeled it and dipped it in the sauce, showing the boy what to do.

"How were they?" the waitress asked when she returned.

The boy nodded, and the priest commented that the boy liked them so much he'd searched the sauce for more, which was true. The waitress gave the boy's blonde hair a tousle and took their order. When she came back again, she set down three more shrimp she'd sneaked from the kitchen.

They ate the rest of their meal, the boy finally getting his hamburger-all-the-way, while the priest talked about his brother, about the nuns at school, about his mother, about the boy's mother, and about where they would put the shelving.

The boy told the priest how one of the girls had dropped a bloody Kotex in the middle of the hall the other day when they were leaving school and how their nun had straddled it with her long black skirt, held up her hand like a traffic cop and yelled "Stop! Stop!" to reroute all the class outside and around the building.

"TH-AT'S great!" the priest said, his voice momentarily booming. He picked up a napkin to stifle his laughter when a nearby couple looked. The boy was proud of himself for telling the story; it was like it was his own now. He could barely hold in his smile. When the waitress returned, the priest ordered coffee, the boy dessert. Afterwards, they went to their room.

The room was very cold, as the priest had left the air conditioning on high. Earlier, they had sat by the pool, the priest reading a magazine, the boy jumping off a low board, afraid to really spring and dive because in the summer of third grade he had to pass a swimming test at a local park by jumping from a high dive. Even now, in the seventh grade, the smell of chlorine made him nervous. So he hadn't really dove from this board, but more or less fallen into the water.

The room had been cold when they had come back in then too, and the priest had seen the boy shivering and held him next to him in the bed under the covers for half an hour.

But now the room was even colder. There was only one light on, by the bed, and the boy took off his pants, wondering if the man was looking. He kept his underwear on but almost tripped getting out of his trousers. When he turned around he saw that the priest was already in bed patting the covers next to him, so he got in and the priest's warm arm reached. Things mixed in the boy's head then. The priest's chest smelled very good, not of chlorine, but of heavy cologne. The man began to caress the boy, to kiss his forehead. After a while, he took the boy's hand, his right hand even though the boy was left-handed, and placed it on his penis, which in the dull light was red and bald and reminded the boy of an animal, even one of the shrimps in the cocktail. And so the night began.

Nyx, to slantly rhyme with *pixie* and *jinx.*

Night, to truly rhyme with *fright.*

3.

Where can any story stop but with death, the *alpha* and *omega,* our final epiphany? It was thirty years later when the boy's mother died. With his wife, he returned to Lexington to see her cancer-worn body spread like a sheet in a hospital bed, the hospital where she had worked, the Catholic hospital where she had worked faithfully, refusing work in any other, for she was a stolid convert to Roman Catholicism. Seeing her silted eyes, her parched hole-of-a-mouth, one need not ask a doctor's prognostication. He called the hospital's chaplain, asking if he would perform the last rites for his mother, who was Catholic.

"And what about you, friend?" the priest queried on the phone. "Aren't you Catholic?"

The son was listening to the voice.

"HE-Y, that's all right, Fella. We all go through it," the priest said on hearing that pause.

It was the same priest, the son knew.

Upon seeing the son the next day, the priest too knew, for after a whispered "Oh Geeza," he rushed through the rites with the mother, who was barely able to perceive that there was indeed a priest in the room, indeed a son and daughter-in-law in the room.

The priest still retained his booming voice, his wet laugh, though his hair had thinned and he now of course appeared much smaller to the son. The priest too now wore glasses, the granny frame popular in hippie days. Had some friend, riding with him in a car, asked him to read an approaching road sign?

The son watched the purple stole used in the last rites, he watched the priest's hands rubbing on sacramental oil, watched them giving a blessing, and he watched his mother, now vaguely aware and able to cross herself in response.

After finishing the prescribed rites, the priest rushed from the room, keeping a nurse and the son's wife between himself and the son. He had a secretary call the next day to inform the son that the priest would not be able to perform the funeral service as he had to travel to a meeting in another state.

How odd to have so many things tumble together at once, the son had first thought on hearing the priest's voice on the phone and glancing down at his mother's matted hair and emaciated face. He had envisioned, like Saint Teresa of Spain, flaming walls with mourners wailing before them, the Holy Ghost decked in seashell wings hovering *illuminatio* above. Life and its Scattering would merge into the Sensible as the flames etched glyphs into the walls, as the polyglot voice of that nebular member of the Trinity crackled. Closure, happy

happy closure, he had thought while standing by his mother's bedside, not knowing what to do with the phone until she coughed dryly. He'd hung it up and dabbed her lips. But then the priest with his wet mouth fled without a direct word, then the mother passed away with not even a throat-rattle.

Death, of course, does offer closure to the deceased. "Stop! Stop!" it shouts. But amazing and mysterious are what rhizomes tangle on, gripping dirt that should have gully-washed away. So. Is *alpha* and *omega* a deception? Do Hindus call it right when they describe this world as a gossamer, entangling veil of Maya?

4.

So the priest had been guilty of depriving the son of closure, among other items. But he'd gotten the boy to go to an eye doctor, something no one else had been perceptive enough to do.

Should the son have lifted a finger in that hospital deathroom; lifted a trembling, accusing, wasplike finger and pointed: *This man took me as a child and. . . .* No, that wouldn't have played well in front of the dying mother. Should he have waited in a corridor then, and ambushed the man with thrashing fists or brought criminal suit against him at an appropriate date?

Appropriate?

After getting fit for his first pair of glasses, the boy had noticed that trees bear leaves. That is, he could feel, imbibe, what he had always known. Their discrete, emerald green blossomed a magnificent revelation that caught his breath; at last he felt his welcome as one of the world's true wriggling creatures. O Brave New World!

Appropriate?

How so, when the seed thrown off by a troubled young priest thirty years before grew like a wild, variegated rose—replete with piercing thorns and evanescent blooms. For the priest, it reportedly caused severe mental episodes that took him from duty and left him, in prime age, not an active monsignor directing a wealthy urban parish, but tucked quietly from schoolchildren in a Catholic hospital. For the boy it meant his first pair of glasses, with which he could see the world in emerald clarity. Of course, of course, it meant something else, for long after both hamburger-all-the-way and shrimp cocktail passed through his bowels to feed bacteria lurking some Covington sewer, his eyes clung to a sin-city smog that would taint green leaves and fields even through an adulthood switch to contact lens, even through . . .

Closure, then.

This was all the mother ever knew: "Mom, Father Putnam thinks I need to see an eye doctor."

Closure. What if the boy had screamed "Stop! Stop!" in the hotel room? What if he had run out the door and yelled over the balcony to adults lounging by the sunset pool? What if he'd fallen from the booth to tug the waitress's tan uniform dress the moment she brought out the three extra shrimp? *Help me. Please call my mother. I have the number. Please take me from this man.*

Or what if the priest's own mother had said: "Frank, I want to talk with you. Alone. Leave the boy named after Saint Joseph out playing with the dog and climbing in the tree where boys belong. . . . Frank, I'm worried about you. Ben can make it, despite his used car lots and his loose women. But you, what are you doing with this youngster? . . ."

Closure. What if the boy had been the only left-handed pitcher in little league, and the coach, a kind but firm man, insisted he begin workouts early? What if he'd had a father who lived with him and the father'd said, "The priest needs help moving shelving? Fine, no reason for Josey to miss school. I'll drive up instead." What if the boy's own mother had said, leaning close to study her son's myopic eyes: "Covington's only an hour away, why does the priest keep you overnight in a roadside motel? Why? Why?"

But those closures offer only more beginnings, more *alphas* with their own entangling rhizomes. Who but the most myopic would prescribe *appropriate*, who but the most myopic would desire *closure*, when the in-between of *alpha* and *omega* is what binds us all.

Who? Who? Who?

The Evening Star Is Not a Star

1.

I'm sure he's dead now, so I can use his name. But here's some so-sad right off: I only remember his first name—could it be I never learned his last? His first name, though, was Jeff, and Jeff had the pearliest teeth I'd ever seen outside a TV commercial. In a party mood he could flash a grin that would puff his cheeks and buoy his blue peepers into an elfish squint, even though he weighed two hundred-sixty pounds. And most of those pounds were muscle since he worked day labor, which lent him a piecrust-brown face—a very important beach/party attribute in Florida, despite the disappearing ozone.

Before you get carried away picturing him as Don Juan, I'll warn you that his blue peepers were usually ninety-percent glazed with alcohol and marijuana, so that you could daily predict a sea fog banking ashore in them. And too, he floated from job to job because he had a temper and was a bit of a reformed thief—he once confessed to breaking into his mom's house—this was when he was hard on heroin—and busting her antique mirror for meanness then stealing her purse for money. So no Don Juan; other concerns demanded his time, other concerns dropped him into the sand.

He was one of the few people I'd ever met who was born in Florida, from a real Florida cracker family. He had two brothers, the younger a giant who could have made it in big-time wrestling with the right breaks. As life twisted though, this brother wielded a socket wrench for minimum wage at a local Texaco station. I once saw him cold-cock some guy for smarting off to a waitress. As his ogreish fist thudded the back of the guy's head—I swear, no theatrics here—it lifted the guy off the floor to deposit him through the door and outside in a pile. I always wondered why Jeff's brother felt obliged to sucker punch like that. Maybe he figured it wouldn't make any difference how he fought and a sucker punch would at least return him to his beer sooner. Or maybe it was just a good, honest reaction, because to tell the truth the guy *had* been an asshole to the waitress. Well, that was Jeff's younger brother. His older brother was as thin as his graying moustache, and he too worked construction—concrete—but held jobs for years at a time, just as he held onto the concrete from them, for it was constantly flaking from him onto the bar. Every time a flake flaked, this older brother lost a goodly portion of his weight. How these three ever became related was a question only God might answer, for I doubt even their mother could.

Once I saw Jeff charge his pick-up down the centerline of Highway 1 at midnight for over five blocks. Oncoming cars zigged and zagged. Once I saw him pull a knife on a guy whose bragging was wearing heavy, then jab the point ever so lightly into the guy's leg. I saw because I had the misfortune to be sitting between them. But the knife wasn't aimed at me and I knew damned well the skinny kid on my left wasn't going to start anything. So I sat tight. Spectator sport, right? Once Jeff saw a rookie cop, scared out of his West Palm blues, shoot a kid trying to break into a drug store's back door. "He's dead, man. You killed him," Jeff told the cop. Seeing how scared and young the cop was, Jeff tried to coax him out of his gun, figuring what a fine prize that would be to take home. But the cop wasn't buying, so Jeff opted to leave before the gun got turned on him. In his spare time, Jeff raced demolition derby, complaining about the stupid safety rule regarding the small amount of gasoline his car could carry. So he rigged an illegal spare tank with a hand valve. . . . Well, you do understand why I'm certain that even if I could remember Jeff's entire name it'd be safe to use now, twenty years later.

But I can't remember it, and I want to sing about a night when

Jeff wasn't just some aborigine Florida cracker, but a winner. Because everybody should be a winner for—well, Warhol's fifteen minutes are compressing tighter and tighter with reality TV and all—so let's say for eight minutes anyway. And Jeff especially should be a winner because he was a male counterpart to the proverbial Whore with a Heart of Gold. So . . . Punk with a Penis of Platinum? I'm not sure how that would go. Anyway, I'm going to bestow Jeff with a name to suit his night as a winner. The Crimson Tide's a winner, or at least it used to be—see the above comment about Warhol and fifteen minutes—but since Crimson would too harshly resemble Jeff's likely eventual fate, here's the story of one special night when Jeff Tide rolled in:

Though no Don Juan, Jeff Tide had been training his eyes on Diane Thomas for some time, and his eyes momentarily lost their glaze when he learned that I worked with her at Mama Sorrento's. Diane was a prep cook during the day, I was a pizza cook at night. Our shifts overlapped enough that we became friends, especially since the two of us were new to Florida, Diane from Pennsylvania while I was from Kentucky.

Diane carried some sad and mysteriously festering hurt—a common enough story for Florida. Her hurt manifested itself in two things: her size, which rivaled Jeff's and echoed the endless vats of pizza dough she concocted; and her roommate, who was a hard-line lesbian doing her best to convert Diane. But you could see neither was going to stick. Diane was still a kid, and given a chance would snap back from one louse of a boyfriend, shake off the pizza-dough weight, shake off her anger at men, and get her act in gear.

"So you know her pretty well, huh?" Jeff flashed his teeth at me.

"Yeah. She's fun. We've been out for drinks together. I've been down to her duplex in Lake Worth."

Jeff bit his lip and rounded his shoulders at that.

"Her roommate's some dyke who's always hanging around, though, so— "

"So you haven't gotten anywhere." His white teeth flashed happily at my revelation.

"We're just friends and I haven't really tried, but . . ." Though bar conversations often mist away like beer foam, Jeff wasn't going to let this one drift off with a simple set of ellipses.

"So if you're just friends you won't mind if I meet you guys over to The Black Forest tomorrow night, say about seven?"

"Sure, that'll be swell."

At work the next day, my only day shift out of the week, Diane half-wiped a patch of flour from her nose, leaving a white racing-stripe in its place. I'd recently borrowed from someone, somewhere, a laugh like a pickle barrel, never having much originality about me. I gave this borrowed laugh, then wiped her racing-stripe clean with my index finger—clean because I was just coming in for the lunch crowd while she'd been at it since sun-up preparing pizza dough, ravioli, and garlic bread for the starving minions of West Palm Beach. Her green eyes laughed as she looked at the flour on my finger.

"Some guy I know, who knows you too, invited himself along tonight."

"Who's that?" By the sharpness of her question, I could tell she wasn't trustful at the mention of a strange guy, though bless her, she did keep a smile and her cheeks did remain as red as ever under their pale sift of flour.

"Jeff Tide. He said he met you at The Black Forest. A big guy with pearl white teeth."

"Oh yeah. He's sweet when he's sober, and he has a real cute smile. Where'd you meet him?"

"At the Red Lion."

"Seems like everybody in Florida meets everybody they know at a bar."

I raised my eyebrows. What else to do when wisdom has been invoked? For the next four hours I tossed and baked pizzas. What else to do when you need to make a living in order to stuff food in your mouth in order to make a living?

Then at last, hurrah! My time on the Italian crucifix expired for the day. Diane wanted to take a shower before going out, and though I always suspected soap to be a good policy, I rarely had the patience to wait so long for my first beer. Um, speaking of Don Juan, could that be why my own streak with women twittered so thinly? Diane suggested this very thing as we stood on the back porch watching a garbage truck swallow Mama Sorrento's Dumpster. As tomato-stained paper products, rotted spaghetti, and flies spewed, I told Diane about the new dishwasher who was eating food off the plates before he scraped them. I described the kid eating a handful of ravioli while his Neanderthal brow, his shovel-mouth, the splotches of tomato paste—

"On second thought, Josey, it may not be just your showering habits that need improvement before your dating life picks up. Maybe you could use some conversation material. Why don't you subscribe to *Time*? Think about it." Diane grinned and walked to her car as coquettishly as a two hundred pound woman can, which is pretty coquettish if the woman is young enough, her cheeks rosy enough, her eyes bright enough, and her grin sincere enough.

But on driving home, instead of following Diane's advice, I stopped at The Red Lion for a beer. For some reason I sat there and imagined Diane in an earth-mother sack dress with pale yellow and green flower patterns. A puff of wind came up in the hollows of my mind and her dress flapped. Behind her on a mountain loomed the smokestacks of Pittsburgh. It was sort of an every man's *Mona Lisa*, and I wondered if I should be a painter. They were starting lessons at the local junior college.

The bartender laughed when I told him my vision and my plan.

"You got tomato sauce on your chin," he added. More advice to add to the *Time Magazine* subscription.

So with a wipe I drank up and drove to Diane's. She'd showered and was looking good for a Pennsylvania Mona Lisa, wearing one of those Mexican dresses that can cover a world of past pasta. I noticed her chest was a Dairy Queen size for a real beef man, and naturally, Cattleman Josey's horns emerged. But then her lesbian roommate walked out to snort like a Brahma bull and his branding iron withered. . . . Maybe instead of being an artist, I could be a poet?

We drove to the bar in Diane's car, which was spotless enough to confirm my suspicion that she'd snap out of this Florida phase. My car, you ask? Well, Momma Sorrento's Dumpster had nothing on it.

At that time The Black Forest Bar was a delight for connoisseurs of tawdry. The owner was a greenish-blonde darling who'd saved money from robbing convenience stores or knocking off a husband so she could do what she loved most: drink in the privacy of her own bar. And she clearly relished that privacy, because she treated customers— not Chamber of Commerce style, but Chamber of Horrors fashion. Jeff's brother swore she once hit him with a pool stick when he was in the middle of a fight with some punk who'd poured beer on his head. Needless to add, this wasn't Jeff's giant brother, for the owner was still alive, the Black Forest still standing.

Jeff was waiting inside, beer in hand, smiling at something in the upper right hand corner of the bar mirror. His eyelids had begun a declining sea fog droop until they noticed Diane in her *senorita* outfit; they then squeezed in boa constrictor focus.

"Right on time," he said. Though we were really twenty minutes late, I'm sure he meant this kindly, dealing in time as he did, on a carefree plain that took up where Einstein left off.

We drank beer for two hours until a nine o'clock summer glow drifted through the door. I was standing at one of four pool tables, and Diane and Jeff were at the bar fetching beer when in walks this skinny, pony-tailed blonde kid. He grabs a pool cue from somewhere and the next thing I know he's beating a table and screaming, "You've all been sons of bitches to me. There's not a damned one of you's my friend!" Balls were bouncing, low-slung fluorescent lights were rattling, beer mugs were breaking, and everyone was moving pronto fast out of this poor waif's way. He smashed a cigarette machine then stood screaming at the entire bar who'd scattered onto a patio out back. From my pool table I could see moths hover in the artificial light over their heads—how dark, how quickly dark, things can turn in our time-warped universe.

"Not a goddamned one of you! You've all laughed and treated me like shit!" He ineffectually hit a pool table, breaking the stick at last, leaving a nasty-looking splinter in his hand.

"I've called the police and you better get out of here!"

"Fuck you, Jean. You've treated me like shit too. And fuck the police too! They know where to find me!" He heaved the broken stick along the floor and walked out the side door.

It turned out that darling Jean the owner hadn't called the police; one more disturbance and they'd promised to shut her down. I suppose word of this eventually got out and quite a few people having scores to settle with her took advantage. I hope Jeff's older brother made his way back to even matters up. At any rate, the storm was over as quickly as it had appeared—typical Florida weather.

"I can't believe you just stood there while he was banging all around with that pool cue," Diane said, her eyes wide.

"Hell, he was just too afraid to move." Jeff's pearly teeth pushed his lips apart for stage presence.

But I'd already scored points on Diane's invisible macho scale. Truth was, I was caught off guard. Truth was, I thought the kid was sloppy drunk and I was Speedy-Toe-Josey eyeing his opponent's every move in slow-mo, ready to deftly parry, kick, and thrust. Truth was, I was blockaded by his swinging pool stick. Ah truth, jested Pilate, who as we all know is one dead and sand-blown corpus delicti by now.

Diane sipped her beer and gazed at me.

"Fug this place," Jeff said. "Let's go to the pier in case that jerk comes back with a gun."

2.

Unlike Jeff, Lake Worth Pier is still alive, so I'll say only good things about it. First, it's famous for an annual shark-fishing tournament—this is not to suggest that a person should feel jittery about swimming around the pier the remainder of the annum. No, not at all. And secondly, part of its attraction is its length and age— long enough to swirl an occasional mean current, old enough to have impressive barnacles scaling each of its eighty pilings.

The Pier is where we went that night. Even though I sat in the back seat of the car on the way over, Diane's eyes kept finding mine in the rearview. *Hell, I'm not on the make; look at Jeff, the guy next to you, who most definitely is.* But she wouldn't, so I smiled my crabby pizza-maker smile and popped a beer.

At the pier we got out and stood by the car, listening to the surf, looking for a moon and spotting it timidly peeking around a cloud, as if it too had just encountered a maniac swinging a Herculean cue stick and intent upon bashing innocent stars. The surf eased our paranoiac thoughts.

Khtshooo.

Khtshooo.

The sand was still warm, though the air was cool. Ghost crabs skittered under the parking lot's lights and we joined them. At the period I'm talking about, the pier was open only for fishing and necking at night, though surely someone by now has installed a lounge so people can plaster their minds with a CD player, booze, and pink stucco to escape all that ugly Nature pressing in.

Khtshooo.

Khtshooo.

The waves turned less rhythmic as we climbed the steps. A lone fisherman at pier's end eyed us, then saw Diane and relaxed. We stopped a third the length of a football field from him.

"It's high tide," Jeff said.

When I looked at the water below, its black motion stirred primal brain cells. As far as I could see, Jeff's statement was valid, though it could have been low- or mid-tide, and I wouldn't have known the difference. My home state of Kentucky is landlocked, don't you see.

"Up there's the evening star! Know why it's not twinkling?"

"Because we've had too much beer?" I answered.

"A Las Vegas comic. No, it don't twinkle because it's not a star, it's a planet. It's Venus, as in love. Venus is a planet, dummy."

Diane was standing on my right side. I felt her hip against mine, warm in its honey-milk way.

Oof!

That sharp poke came to my left side, where a rib ached like a thoroughbred had kicked it.

"High tide. We could dive off right now. Wanna bet?"

I looked down, catching a hint of foam flecking about a piling.

"Hell no," I answered.

"I've done this spot right here six times." Jeff pounded his fist on a loose bolt in the rail. "This'll make the seventh. I'll show you where to dive. As long as you land right and are a strong swimmer you don't have to worry."

In the light I could see Jeff was talking out the side of his mouth in the same smug way he had when he'd pulled the knife on that kid. "I'm not a strong swimmer. I'm barely any kind of swimmer," I countered.

"Too bad. See you on the other side."

"Jeff, that looks dangerous." This was Diane. She'd grabbed my arm to lean toward Jeff, who'd kicked off his shoes and tilted his beer. He tossed the empty can toward a wastebasket and made it, of course. It's one of those weird laws of confidence that when you're on a roll you're on a roll, like stockholders and Republicans. Thank god for Heraclitus: everything changes, so all rolls eventually stop.

"Jeff!" Diane's voice or mine? We were at the same pitch of frantic because with even our mousy modicums of reasoning, the water below gleamed with jaws of death.

But Jeff rolled on. Off went his shirt. Out went his barreled chest. Up on the rail, then in went Jeff.

"Hey, you crazy son of a bitch!" This was the fisherman at the end, who stuffed his rod in a holder and ran to the side to look down just as Jeff hit the water in a perfect shallow dive that carried him ten feet out before he came up.

"Motherfuck!" The fisherman said, running down to us.

"Are there sharks down there?" Diane asked as Jeff turned and began to swim below us.

"Hey you!" The man stopped to yell over the side. "Don't swim toward this pier! It's high tide! The current's too damned strong! You hear? You hear?" The man turned to us. He was a healthy sixty, with lean muscles looking like dried beef jerky. "That fool'll be lucky to come out dead. I'm gonna call an ambulance. Sharks? Honey, the damned rip current's too strong even for them tonight."

He gave one last look and beat on the rail as if Jeff could hear. "Stop! Stop!"

Jeff was underneath us now; we could see his white skin merging with the foam. He was nearly dead center between the two pilings below. Three, four seconds passed. I thought I saw kicking feet, then foam again.

"Just cause your friend's a suicide don't mean you two need to be. You better both go down right away and see if you can drag him in. Don't get heroic and dive in yourselves though. This damned water drops from a foot to five quicker than a ghost crab can scoot. Here's my belt. Maybe you can figure something to do with it, I don't know." He stripped off his belt and ran for a phone at the pier's beginning. I grabbed the belt and we followed, clomping down wooden planks that resounded like a cattle call.

Under the pier my pupils dilated to golf ball size. Still, I couldn't see a thing. Water splashed my ankles like warm blood, and something stung me, probably part of a dead jellyfish. I kicked it off in a nervous reaction and held onto wood jutting from a piling.

"There he is!" Diane said.

But there wasn't anything. The jumbled roar of surf bouncing and echoing was so overpowering that it seemed more visible than anything.

"Hey you down there! The ambulance is coming. I told them someone fell in drunk. You see him?"

"No!" I shouted up into dark timbers resembling the arches of some forgotten Episcopal Church.

"I'm throwing down a life preserver I found. If you see him, toss it near him, not at him. And don't try to go out yourself!"

I nodded to the angel scurrying in the choir loft. The preserver flopped dully in wet sand. My breath smelled of sour beer.

"There! There! Jeff!"

Diane had spotted him, stumbling up the beach. Whoops! Down once in the surf, up again, holding his side. How many minutes had passed? Four or five, I guess. Diane, the old man and I all ran toward him, toward those pearly teeth, like phosphor on a flying fish. Smiling. Smiling.

Khtshooo.

Khtshooo.

"You all right, young man?"

"I'm all right. Who are you?"

"Je-eff!" Diane sang this out, halfway as a reprimand and halfway in astonishment at his right side, which had several long gashes and accompanying streams of blood.

"I'm fine. I've had worse than this happen from racing demolition derby."

He was shaking and his lips were purple—I don't know whether that color came from the fluorescent parking lights, the gashes, or the chill. Or all of the above.

"I called an ambulance, son. You better let them take you to a hospital."

"I don't need no damned doctor. I need a damned beer. Alcohol and sea water'll clean this right out."

"Sea water'll infect the hell out of it, is what it'll do."

"Go on and fish, old man, and leave me alone!"

"You're one lucky son-of-a-gun," the old guy said, shaking his head and walking off.

"Luck didn't have a damned thing to do with it," Jeff yelled at his back. "Skill!" He turned to us. "We gonna hold a tent revival or we gonna get some beer?"

Diane grabbed Jeff's arm and we walked to the car. He poured half a beer over his side, inhaling enough air to inflate a truck tire as bubbles foamed in his cuts.

"Jeff, maybe you should go to the hospital."

"You two sound like that old man."

"At least let the ambulance drivers look at you."

"What ambulance?"

"The old guy called an ambulance. He just said that."

"Let's blow this place. Ambulance comes, cops won't be far behind."

So I drove while Diane sat in the back with Jeff, who laid his head in her lap as she dabbed his side with a towel and fussed over him in general.

"Right when I jumped I saw all the stars twinkle, even Venus." Jeff's loud voice and laughter were undercut by the chattering of his teeth.

Venus is a planet, dummy. But I just gripped the steering wheel. I heard movement in the back, like they were positioning themselves. Jeff let out a small yelp, which Diane echoed empathetically.

"Could you open me a beer?"

She did.

"I'm going to take Jeff in and bandage him up. You okay to drive yourself on home, Josey?" Diane asked as I made a turn near her house.

"Sure." I looked in the rear view mirror, thinking I caught Jeff's big pearly grin.

We never saw an ambulance. With Diane around, Jeff didn't need one.

3.

From the look on Diane's face two days later I could see that not only had the cock crowed, but the kitty had mewed. Which isn't to say they got engaged, married and settled to produce the national average of children, salary, and happiness. Neither was anywhere near that stage, though Jeff had shone like a nova.

According to astronomers a nova explodes only once every 120 years—I figure the odds infinitely higher that any two humans will concurrently change their lives for the better. But I do say this: Jeff Ti—well, whatever his last name—saw starshine's twinkle that night instead of the inside of a body bag at Lake Worth's city morgue, and Diane immaculately cleaned flour off her nose for nine weeks running before wising up and moving back to Pennsylvania.

And now? What about now—as if that's the only star time that matters. By now Jeff has achieved his murky wish and is dead. Diane? My painterly premonition in the bar surely solves that: through the layered veil of time and space I envision her wearing an earth-mother dress in an upper Pennsylvania town, where she owns a pastry shop that caters to tourists seeking Amish buggies on parade. Me? Go ahead, you can answer for me. After all, this isn't just about Jeff, Diane, and some sap named Josey. All of earth's children want their eight, ten, or fifteen minutes. So go ahead; answer for me. . . .

Well, since you're shy, I'll speak:

Me? In my incarnation as Josey I'm still finding myself blockaded into corners, imaginary or real; I'm still dodging pool cues of that same ilk; I'm still ignoring each evening's twinkles like a prime time fool. And yet on certain nights I peer intently for an auspicious supernova on Venus, though I know damned well that particular evening star's never yet, nor never will be a star.

Meanwhile on Limestone Street: Time, Mass, and Energy Masquerade as Free Will

1. Id

Josey's hometown of Lexington had a street named Limestone, a generic street most cities claim, one that threads richest glitter to raunchiest gutter. It was just blocks from Main where the gutter started in earnest. In these days of crime and crack cocaine, despite the new millennium, I'm sure no child of twelve—no middle-class child—walks that part of Limestone alone. Even in those days when Josey did, the pavement tended toward barren. And for quite some while that pavement's geography enmeshed his life like a tyrannical parent or drug-dependent spouse. Or say like the inevitable plot of a tragedy, or like the quirky crossroads where Clotho, Lachesis, and Atropos spin, measure, then snip life's thread.

There was a skinny, yellow, three-story hotel on Limestone—you'll have to believe this, though even Josey found it stunning—a hotel called LonelyHearts. Unless an errant breeze should parade by, its chalky blue sign with a chalky red heart kept noiseless vigil over its mildewing stairwell; and with any breeze the sign would sway in a haunting, "*Lonely*, screek, *Hearts*, screek." But be it breezy, gusty, or calm, Josey remained certain that only the darkest of dark lurked atop that stair.—Here now, let's watch him one brave day as he peeks inside the ajar door: there, see his baggy tan shorts, see his tenuous forefinger touching the doorframe's peeling yellow paint? Instantly if not sooner he recoils from falling morgue-blue plaster and the rising bone dust of the stairwell proper. And when a wet hack shambles down the wooden steps in a ghostly *coup de grâce*, his leg muscles knot and his back tingles for a full block of nearly sprinting.

Interestingly enough, this pale yellow hotel still operated when mid-twenties came to Josey, when his friends who lived in nearby refurbished apartments laughingly told of gunshots, fistfights, broken wine bottles, derelicts, and ambulances. "*Lonely*, screek, *Hearts*, screek."

In the next block of North Limestone, farther distancing itself from Main Street and what civilization Lexington could offer, a bar rolled the world's juiciest hot dogs on a window grill. Not even LonelyHearts could make Josey shun that circulating vision and aroma, so on the day we're talking about he slowed. But a clever sign adorning the bar's screen door read, "Ladies invited. B 21 or B Gone." No hot dogs for a growing boy of twelve. Unlike LonelyHearts, this bar itself was gone by Josey's coming of age. You'd think the owner, presciently realizing he was failing in business or maybe even dying of drink and cigarettes, could have tossed out a compassionate hot dog.

"Here, kid, take a breather and a dog. You look like a spastic in the county fair, one that's just heard a ghost hacking sputum."

Clearly from this politically incorrect statement—had the owner only thought to make it—we're discussing a pseudo-occurrence from decades behind. For in this new millennium (Oh will we ever tire of ladling out that phrase?) we no longer charge sideshow admission to gawk at nature's mistakes. In this new millennium we burrow under layers of euphemism and blithely lisp "differently abled." Nonetheless, that bar owner, had he only been humane enough to speak those words, would have judged correctly: Josey was and still is a capital M spastic Mess. There's something clean in the honesty of admitting it, just as something clean clung to the jerk of the owner's bald head whenever he caught Josey staring open-mouthed at those hot franks.

"Flies, kid, flies. You're attracting 'em. Business is bad enough already. Shut your trap and jump along."

Now here comes a decision to be made: Was the day when Josey huffed after peeking into LonelyHearts the same day these two approaching girls pass him? If so, then it must be the day when even juicy rolling hot dogs can't draw drool from his mouth, for though the owner hasn't spoken, someone inside has coughed and Josey's young boy heart again drops at so sudden a reminder of the stairwell. His legs shove him away to a grocery store (one heartbeat!), a junk shop (two!), and a nondescript venetian blind shop (three!). Just as he feels safe from the evil cough and the withered pale hand cupping phlegm, two girls pass, heading toward sin city's very center. He's heading toward what he's always heading for on Limestone: Dennis Book Store, which lured him past LonelyHearts in the first place. So you see, it wasn't a puerile, idlike, gustatory infatuation with hot dogs that pulled him so far from Main—oh no, Josey was forming character and excellence already. Honest.

"You could take that home with you, couldn't you, Darlene?"

Holy Virgin Mary, Pray for Me. (200 days indulgence toward Purgatory's Early Release Program if prayed fervently, and this was at least thought fervently, for Darlene's companion was indicating our character-forming, conscience-forming Josey.) While he stumbled and gawked, Darlene bobbed and leered. Afterward, he dreamed of her for a year, but at that moment he feared for his masculinity, his virginity, his soul, and worse. For Darlene was a dishwater blonde in a tiger brown skirt who gave an arched glance and grin no schoolgirl had ever before given Josey. She and her friend were a year or so older, a generation or so shrewder. Northernmost Limestone was no doubt where they hailed from. Josey envisioned a single shotgun shack, three green and peeling shutters, and a dank, dark living room with Darlene sitting open-legged on a . . . daybed?

Well here now. Just why Darlene and friend's interest in the first place? It must have been a joke, and it worked. But let's defend Josey's emerging soul, manhood, and pride, shall we? Let's argue that this was before he wore eyeglasses and that it was also summertime, so he was sporting those tan shorts. And so? And so one of Josey's attributes of excellence that you should know about is his Arnold Schwarzenegger legs. Everything else of Schwarzenegger's—the toothy smile, biceps, triceps, deadpan humor, outspokenness in political affairs—Josey lacks. But legs, the two must share. God—or Mary or Clotho—knows that's little enough equipment for someone who's trying to emerge beyond pantomime and stimulus/response. So let's theorize that the outburst came as both a joke and boy lust on Darlene and her friend's part.

Vanity, vanity.

Josey and his id-ridden hormones, still pondering that daybed with its single dirty sheet scantily covering Darlene's bare left thigh, wobbled on toward Dennis Book Store, feeling heat skim his shoulder blades, worrying that at any moment Darlene might swoop and pinch his arm to tug him into the shotgun geography of northernmost Limestone. What would they enact in there? Would a daybed and stained sheets play a leading role? Josey had no idea, though Darlene surely would have supplied ample stage directions.

2. Ego

THERE, AHEAD! LOOK! LOOK! A black sign with silver lettering momentarily eclipses Darlene:

DENNIS used BOOKS

Now, the geography of Mr. Dennis's store was divided into three parts—not clearly divided like Caesar's Gaul, understand, just as Limestone Street itself never clearly jumped from antebellum homes to run-down shotgun shacks. But divided nonetheless, maybe akin to Freud's ego, id, and superego. Logically enough, the front part of Mr. Dennis's store housed his best sellers: left wall hardbound, right wall paperbound. Then came a bargain table of comics, then a cash register where the great man himself presided with a shock of silver hair, pulling paternally at a cigar and looking bemused in his gaunt, six-foot bespectacled frame. After stately Mr. Dennis came a cubbyhole on the left that encapsulated history and travel, plus a tawdry bathroom on the right to accommodate roaches of any ilk. Think of it, my friend: roaches have toyed on this planet longer than either streets or free will, and so deserve their portion of any geography too.

This middle division faded into children's books, which Josey had about outgrown, though fond memories always surfaced of Dr. Doolittle talking with animals, and Tom Something-Or-Other and the RAF blasting those nasty Germans. Tom. Well, Tom was present at the evacuation of Dunkirk, it seems. He was also with the ambulance service in Belgium and with the French Resistance outside Paris. Tom got around for a British lad of sixteen. Likely, he could have handled even Darlene. Dr. Doolittle, on the other hand, would have sent that nymph packing across the ocean floor, restrained in a giant purple Nautilus Snail with only an Anabuse prescription for company.

This particular day, which you shouldn't judge to be that particular day, I mean the day that Dar . . . well on this particular day Josey paused and smelled the air in the bookshop. So much paper, so many words, so many free-thinker ideas! The ideas themselves smelled as austere as Gaul, even if they never divided themselves so cleanly, and he churned in their possibilities. Did you know that Freud, since we're thinking in triads, added a fourth urge in his later work? The thanatos or death urge. Had the man lived to pal around with Tom at Dunkirk, he might have added seven, eight, or nine urges. Darlene, I fear, would have confirmed only the primal and primary one.

Opposite from the children's books languished stacks and stacks of *National Geographic* and *Scientific American,* which is where Josey has presently turned. Let's watch him bend and pretend to read a triad (of course) of the latter magazines, a habit that he's retained as faithfully as breathing. The ones with deep space pictures of stars still remain his favorites, in fact. After that, come artistic renditions of prehistoric men. These cave men, they'd be comfortable with Darlene, wouldn't they? Just like the British boy Tom. And Darlene herself, wouldn't her teeth gleam like a saber-toothed tiger's, wouldn't her big eyes glow like a supernova? But then, I've already forgotten my own admonition: today isn't necessarily Darlene's day.

After these magazine stacks came the dustbowl. In this final section, books reeked of amazing age and indifference; nonetheless, Josey occasionally sorted through them to prolong his stay if it were hot or rainy or snowy outside. Yes, I have it now! Look, look! See!

See! This is a slush day, and Josey has had to stomp his feet at the entranceway under the watchful eyes of Mr. Dennis. And now Josey nestles in the back, in the cold, cold back where no space heaters are lit. His presence there seems to unnerve poor Mr. Dennis even worse than stomping galoshes.

"Listen, Son, I don't mind you going back there, but be sure to pull the light chains off when you're finished." A chomped cigar not only emphasized the situation's high economic seriousness but it delimited matters, much as punishing amperage would delimit a laboratory rat's choices.

So there you have Dennis's, on Limestone. Can it possibly serve as a breeding ground for a transcendent mind? Perhaps. Buy a book, Josey, even a set of Edgar Allen Poe, walk it home and read some, forget more. Didn't you once buy a complete set of Bulwer-Lytton from the dust bowl? Josey! For a pre-teen that was a ridiculous purchase of a ridiculous nineteenth century obscurity. But the bookworms—actual, pale, and writhing!—did intrigue you, didn't they? Look! Look! See, see how they etch through paper, cocooning on their own. But your mother wasn't as intrigued: she threw the whole caboodle out.

But this time, this day, it is Poe, and it is to be wrapped carefully in brown paper by Mr. Dennis, and tied with twine, and no bookworm will show except Josey. Lenore, Lenore, how she beckons. And those clanging alarum bells—just Josey and Darlene's style. But wait, is this before Darlene? After? During? Will she be walking back soon, searching out Josey, who even now counts change for his intended purchase? To quoth the raven: "*Nevermore.*"

So out from DENNIS used BOOKS. There was also a somewhat misplaced school for rich kids on that block of Limestone. It was called Sayre and still operates, let's say. After all, rich folks' kids gotta go somewhere to escape the Darlenes and Joseys of the world. Give 'em a break. Sayre School was set back on a quiet lawn full of aged oaks, and its halls no doubt resonated with *ciao's* and *merdre's* that Josey pretended to hear even in the heat of summer vacation. Josey himself went to a Catholic school and was oddly curious, even jealous, of Sayre. So he would walk by, but never cross to its side of the street. Once he saw a drunk pushed against its iron fence. The man was frisked then shoved into a police car. Bad, bad; Josey knew he was bad. He knew that he himself would never choose to grow up so moldy, so damp, so worm-ridden, so bad.

But let's forget Poe, the drunk, Sayre, and Darlene. Let's shoot past Main Street and the bronze plaque honoring "Smiley, beloved by all" and travel south down Limestone. Hurry, Josey, get those thick Schwarzenegger calves of yours moving! We're free spirits, and blithe!

No, on second thought pause, for Smiley was a mongrel, part Border Collie by the look of his bronze memorial muzzle, and he deserves some notice, even if he didn't attend finishing school. Bend down and look at the plaque, Josey, would you? Of course it's embedded in the sidewalk; that's why you saw it, you dope! With your head constantly dumped toward the ground as if a road map to life were etched there, I mean. Well, perhaps one is. But don't go philosophical. And don't worry about those adults shoving by.

Yes, evidently Smiley the mongrel camped outside this corner restaurant for six years, to be beloved by all. Of course neither the pound nor the health department would now allow such ridiculous goings-on. In this new millennium, Smiley would be availed of a "temporary home site" and once his "residency period" expired he would undergo the "humane alternative" of carbon monoxide from a Briggs & Stratton lawnmower. Clean, cleaner, cleanest. Why . . . we of this millennium must be the cleanest humans ever to trod limestone!

Here now. Has a whine crept in? The good ol' days? Is that the refrain? Character ethics? A man's a man for a' that and a' that? Even Dickie the dim newsboy can deposit his dimes and . . . well, let's just bounce back to Mr. Dennis's Antiquarian Book Shoppe, wherein Mr. Dennis proudly displays a photo of Lexington's last public hanging—a nigger, of course. To Josey, the black man in that photo looks as straight up and down dead as those times were. And notice there's no bronze plaque for the nig anywhere in sight. Only the word "me," an arrow, and an inked circle inscribed on that photo indicate Mr. Dennis's ineffable presence. Josey, would you go up there and look? I'll keep an eye out for Mr. Dennis. He's gabbing in the travel section with some blue-haired horsy dame about art books on the Louvre. Yes, the one in France, you've got it. Now hurry. . . .

Yeah? I'll be damned. Listen, Josey says that Mr. Dennis is smoking a cigar even in that picture. Was it all those white spectators who gave Mr. Dennis the idea of opening a business? Did he strike a match just before the trapdoor snapped and think, "This burg's really packing in some class, I bet a used bookstore would go just great here."

But Smiley, Smiley, we should concentrate on Smiley, so let's hop back. Smiley must have been a wonderfully tolerant pooch, always responding to the petting hand with a lick, regardless of that hand's race, creed, or sex.

As long as we've whisked Josey back in time to sniff the restaurant's luncheon air—doesn't this child ever eat?—let's look caddy-corner from Smiley's plaque. There looms a Woolworth's Five-and-Dime, in front of which Josey once got lost as a three-year-old. Consequently, all throughout childhood he dreamed of bright lights and faces spiraling upon him. When he finally recounted this nightmare to his mother she said: "You must be dreaming of the time you got lost in front of Woolworth's as a three-year-old." Poof! Shazaam! The dream disappeared forever, just like Darlene, just like Smiley, just like the lynched black man. Time. It's easily as fragile as a street's geography. Wasn't there a *Scientific American* cover indicating as much? And if time flip-flops with such disregard, what are we to think of ever-fasting Josey, masquerading as an emergent soul? Here now, Josey! You've lollygagged enough over that pooch's bronze plaque and your troubles in front of Wal-Mart. I mean Woolworth.

But not lost this day—at least not Woolworth's lost. For this day, in all honesty, is not the Poe-and-slush-Day, nor the Darlene-LonelyHearts Day, for those have become ragged and torn like a month-old newspaper. No, on this day Josey—fool that he is—is not even remembering that he's ever been lost, nor imagining he ever could be. This is the day when Josey encountered "Just Paul" having a seizure on Limestone. Just Paul dropped right before Josey's eyes, right as Josey was readying a social nod, a low-level skill he'd recently acquired in his effort at character building. But Just Paul just slid against the bricks of Woolworth's, his own eyes focusing far beyond Josey's vision—maybe to espy a sprig of interstellar gas while his mouth chewed itself. Josey pulled out his wallet, for he'd heard this was the thing to do—stick a wallet in their mouth, money and all. But a man strolled up and admonished,

"That's just Paul. Don't bother. He'll be okay."

So walk on, do whatever adults say. On until you don't hear Just Paul gargling, on past a shoe repair shop that always smells more of illegal betting and cigars than shoe polish, on to a clearing for the train tracks that once carried you—I mean Josey—to Corbin and Irvine, click-clack, click-clack, then up a slight hill toward another used book store, though Josey really went to this one for the used post cards and their stamps, which he collected in a most anal-retentive way.

Now here is an interesting fact: Evidently most people collect used post cards for A.) their pictures and, B.) some mild voyeurism in reading private messages: *Dear Sarah: Things haven't turned out as they should. He's doing it again. Your loving friend, Anne.* I say A.) because these postcards were placed picture-out and the proprietor was always surprised when Josey turned them stamp-out. I say B.) for the obvious example given. *Anne, Anne, do have faith. Please come back to Limestone where it will all work out.*

There was a record shop across the way from the faux bookstore, but it only sold Hank Williams and Ernest Tubb. Josey wasn't no damned hillbilly. He'd gotten at least that much straight.

Hold up, Josey. Could you trot back a few steps? Pretty please? Because there's something familiar about that stairwell and its beckoning emptiness. But this is blocks away from LonelyHearts Hotel, you say? I know, but look up, Josey, look up. Josey does, and he envisions his own rear end ascending.

Time, you see, flows many ways given the proper geography, and Josey was seeing his future self walk up bare wood steps with a male friend who would shock pretentious world-weary Josey onto Jupiter's smallest moon. *Bad, so bad, I'll never grow up that way*, Josey thinks, watching his rear end ascend.

"You could live here, and I could support you. I make enough money," his friend would say, with obvious sexual overtones.

This friend had convinced Lexington's draft board that he was a conscientious objector—no small feat, I assure you, for Lexington's horse people wanted the city's Joseys, not the fine graduates of Sayre, to serve as Gelignite and Agent Orange fodder. And if they could, they would have even sent all the Darlenes. So to convince that draft board of the validity, even the possibility, of middle-class conscientious objections was Socratic in depth. And for a moment, this friend's other argument almost convinced Josey. But then Josey looked past those tinted hippie granny glasses and saw a smile lift sidewise like a jackknife's blade. For once in Josey's stupid life he knew that not a damned thing is free. It was a discovery akin . . . not to learning one's own ignorance, but at least to learning that you can't breaststroke through limestone.

"No thanks," Josey managed to whisper. Or will manage to whisper, since it's only the street we can presently be sure of, not the time.

A banshee grin. "I'll be here, if you ever change your mind."

Later on, Josey will actually live on Limestone, not with Mike of the jackknife grin, but in a top floor apartment with five very straight guys, one a Viet-vet bordering on wooly after serving as a helicopter gunner. He'll awake one night screaming because a rat has dropped on him. "A rat? You're kidding," Josey and the three others will chorus. Their roommate will assure them that after Vietnam he knows exactly what rats feel like. This rat, I should mention, will allay his dreams, for in them he awakes from machine-gunning a pregnant woman, having thought she was an armed man. So Josey will move toward another discovery: As a species, rodents are geometrically more discernible and kinder than either political causes or humans.

Well, we've taken a leap—not of faith, but of time—so let's remain in that future a moment more: One Saturday, the window in Josey's turret bedroom will get rammed up against its flat black sill: "You goddamned hippies!" Another of his roommates will lean to shout this at two longhairs passing below on Limestone. Josey will squat on his mattress, cuddle a beer and howl in laughter. God bless America and Limestone Street, where public opinions might abound!

Now, back up . . . far back to DENNIS used BOOKS. Josey, you're still idling in there, aren't you?

Actually, it was Josey's neighbor who introduced him to Mr. Dennis's store. Josey was friends with Timmy, who was a year older than he was, while Joe, Timmy's brother, was two years older. Josey should have stuck with his namesake, for Timmy never meant him much good.

Now this neighbor Joe was a confirmed Anglophile for reasons Josey couldn't fathom—maybe due to Episcopalian leanings, or maybe due to a dark Freudian secret. Anyway, Joe once convinced Josey to write to the Queen of England. You shouldn't worry, for America and Lexington's horse people—who may be one and the same—saved face since the letter came back marked "insufficient postage." Something else you should know about Josey besides his legs: he's a cheap son of a gun.

Joe was also a bibliophile. And the three of them—Timmy, Joe, and Josey—were at Dennis's when . . . oh my, it's that day. A metallic thunk resounds into the store. Looking through large plate-glass windows, they see people running in the direction of the traffic light, so they run out too, dropping books back onto shelves.

Brains, in case you ever have occasion to wonder, are pinkish white and seem to foam or suds with soap bubbles. Under the traffic light, two cars have collided. But the real problem is the child caught between their steel. No one is there to react with a scream—no mother, father, sister, or brother. Alone, alone, alone on Limestone. Timmy, Joe, and Josey stand queasily, watching others standing the same. Then they turn, not to re-enter Mr. Dennis's, but to desert Limestone and walk Main, entering a record shop to listen to rock 'n' roll, which assures them that an infinite number of broken hearts and new loves await, assures them that they're partaking in the launch pad's countdown to fling their souls into cool outer space.

Years later—this is perhaps too bold, for it slips far ahead of Darlene, Just Paul, the accident, or the postcards—years later Timmy owned a Head Shop on Limestone. In fact, it may have been exactly where the hillbilly record store once stood, the one that Josey refused to enter. *Plus ça change, plus les memes choses*, no? Josey did walk into this store, and he recognized Timmy, who laughed and said, "Yeah, yeah, I remember you." Then Timmy continued putting the moves on some hippie girl in a floundering paisley dress. If I had to guess, since Josey is shifting his big legs in a muted, crestfallen manner, I'd say Timmy could tell he'd spotted a hillbilly who wouldn't purchase a solitary scrap of drug paraphernalia.

About this time, Josey landed a job. So he must be eating, yes? Why else would anyone work—unless maybe to earn money to buy books at DENNIS used BOOKS? But just how many books . . . ah well. So, mobile and eating—he's well on his way toward free will, we can assume. Anyway, Josey landed a job just ten blocks from all this, farther south on Limestone Street, and surprise of surprises, it wasn't at Dennis's but at the University of Kentucky's bookstore. He worked as a trade book buyer there for five years, encompassing the time Timmy's hippie head shop went in and out of business. One day Josey displayed a big counter-culture book called *Steal This Book*. Sure enough, someone broke the glass and stole it. The general manager said whoever did it was lucky the heavy glass didn't slice through his arm, bone and all. Josey—didn't Timmy and I warn you he was at heart a hillbilly?—was becoming sorely disappointed in the emergent counter-culture and half-wished the glass *had* severed the idiot's hand. People—so this isn't just Timmy and me—were always telling Josey that he wasn't much at being a hippie. Josey always answered that hippies weren't much at it either.

Now, a great deal of the University of Kentucky abides on Limestone, though the obligatory protest that burned down the obligatory ROTC building took place a block away. But that's okay, for rumor had it that ROTC itself did this for insurance since the building was decrepit. In other words, the faux-Limestone scene that has crept in may have been a faux-protest, too. Still, Josey got pepper gas in his eyes despite the bookstore's air conditioning. And five months later, as if to vindicate Josey's opinion, some hippie SOB strolled to the bookstore's buyback register and passed Josey a note: *Give me all your money*. Josey laughed and walked away, being used to students threatening to firebomb the place whenever he didn't repurchase a text at their exaggerated counter-culture concept of its worth. This hippie, Josey figured, saw himself as an eighth member of the Chicago Seven, out to liberate money for whatever worthwhile cause he could find: Patty Hearst and the SLA; LSD and wine.

"I can't believe it. The man just laughed and walked away. I can't believe it." The hippie threw up his arms and stomped out the door after yelling this to other cashiers. It dawned on dull Josey that underneath the hippie's heavy tan coat some shiny blued metal had been deadly serious. Oh well.

While living on Limestone Street Josey asked his first wife to marry him. Or did she ask him? Oh well.

They lived in a hillbilly trailer court in hillbilly Nicholasville. Oddly enough, Nicholasville Road was a twenty-mile extension of Limestone Street with a different name. Oh well.

Dennis's Book Store sold comics for a while. Josey's favorites were *Donald Duck* and *Uncle Scrooge*, though Joe, the older neighbor, tried to convince Josey that *Little Lulu* was more mature. Josey liked Lulu fine: She and Tubby were mean squirrels of a kind—but squawking Donald and cheap Scrooge: how could Josey deny his genetic heritage? Indeed, isn't that our whole question to be considered, Dr. Watson?

But if we must needs talk of Josey's favorite books: Despite Bulwer-Lytton and *Scientific Americans*, they were those great adventures with Tom at Dunkirk and in the ambulance corps. Wasn't young Tom standing up to show the nasty Nazis what a free individual could do? Isn't that what this lumbering, circumnaviating earth's all about? Say . . . perhaps we should pose that question to the real Dr. Watson and his friend Holmes. Here, let's give them a ring-up: "'Ello? 221 B Baker Street. 'Ello?" / "Uh . . ." / "'Ello? Can't 'ear you. Sorry. Ring again." Oh well.

Limestone Street did have its oddities that often enough struck Josey. For one, the owner of a red brick boarding house kept monkeys in the back. Lots of monkeys. Josey sneaked there once and was amazed to see a hundred swinging about a cage stretching over sixty feet. They screed if he approached; otherwise they happily groomed one another. He tried this five or so times, as a type of controlled experiment.

Walk forward: "Scree!" Walk back, they comb one another.

Walk forward: "Scree!" Walk back, they comb one another.

Now, I've been deputed to tell you the monkeys' side of the tale:

That small, two-legged, featherless biped: if we pick our fleas, it approaches; if we screech, it recedes.

Pick fleas, it approaches; screech, it recedes.

While conducting his experiment, Josey was waiting on his mother, who was getting her hair done. On his last approach to the cage, he spotted a relatively empty space, large enough for a young boy to squat in forever. *If only Mom had come to this hairdresser three years ago when I was really small*, he thought, peering wistfully.

"Boy! Boy! Go find some friends! Leave the monkeys alone!"

3. Super-ego

THERE WAS A LOVELY girl Josey met on Limestone. Her name was Robby. They fucked like thoroughbreds intent on the Derby, but Josey thought he wanted a mind, and hers wasn't fine enough. It was plenty damned fine, I'm sorry to tell you—maybe Josey should have read the self-help section in Dennis's instead of gawking at *Scientific American's* galaxies and stars.

Robby and Josey went into a restaurant on Limestone, near where the lady used to keep the monkeys. Josey watched the waitress trundle a beer around to a male customer sitting at the bar. You see, in Kentucky it once was law that women couldn't hand drinks over a bar, so she would always have to do this. The law had been repealed a few years before, but the owner, he was some type of guy. As I say, Josey watched the waitress, in her sixties, heft the beer while he listened to Robby talk about her trouble with an insurance claim. On she talked and on.

"Stop it," Josey said. "Stop it, stop it. I hate insurance."

His hands twitched like angry duck feathers, or say like prehensile monkey tails in summer heat. The waitress carried the mug of beer around to the customer. Josey wanted a mind. Josey took the beer, for he was the customer. Josey wanted to discuss Plato. Josey sipped the beer. Josey wanted to discuss Nietzsche. Nietzsche hadn't sold insurance. So Josey broke up with Robby, but kept going to the bar, sitting at the counter and ordering cold beer after beer, making the waitress trudge around while he told her how dumb and out of it the owner was. And yes, Josey did use his prehensile thumb to clasp the mug.

Go around comes around, especially on Limestone. There was a fine Italian restaurant across from the huge granite central post office. Sarah, the would-be archaeologist and unrequited love of Josey's life—if you except Darlene—Sarah and Josey would eat at this restaurant nearly every weekend, drinking a pitcher of beer, waiting for their spaghetti diavolo or Toni's hand-stretched pizza. Aha! So . . . eating, moving, and a prehensile thumb. We nearly have him there, I swear. This bobbling mass will attain personhood any moment now.

But this night we're talking about, this night everything unearthed Sarah as if she were one of her own archaeological shards exposed to ozone and modernity. Time again, you see. Energy and matter again. The jukebox was too loud, she complained. Too many country songs. "I hate hillbilly." The two winos tottering outside the window, befuddled by a street sign written in English, were frightening, not amusing as usual. The spaghetti was too spicy, too hot; the beer too warm, too flat; the salad too wilted, too busy. Plates and forks clacked; like Donald Duck, people quacked.

"What's wrong, Sarah? What's wrong?"

"I'm moving to West Palm Beach with a girlfriend."

Oh well.

In the central post office on Limestone Josey once spotted sheets of an 80-cent airmail issued in 1952, still tucked in the postmaster's green drawer decades later. The violet stamp depicted a placid bay with a mountain in the background and two leaning palm trees bordering either side. Over this flew a calm transport plane—not the type that crashes into a World Trade Center, just the type that carries goods to the good. One plate block of the stamp is now worth two hundred hard bucks. Josey's cost three-twenty. The postmaster smiled as he handed it over, his eyes shaded from the fluorescent lighting by a card shark's green visor. His hands were so puffed, cracked, and yellowed that Josey feared they wouldn't let the stamps go, but they did. Clop-clop, clop-clop—Josey's proud and miserly shoes carried him along the PO's halls, past the hunchback who sold magazines and imported cigars. The hunchback—he didn't know better—smiled as if he'd bought the same bargain stamps. When Josey descended the PO's granite steps, a wonderful spring air promised to be crisp, blue, and free—forever. It promised to fly him toward romantic palm trees—forever. Oh well.

4. Thanatos

ONE DAY MR. DENNIS died. They say even Sol, our own sun, will up and implode/explode some day. Josey's seen enough pictures of novas and supernovas to know that's true. You can't browse *Scientific American* for decades without increasing the suds factor in your brain by some percentage.

The man who bought Mr. Dennis's store cleared out the dustbowl in back to find scads of first edition primers worth thousands. They always looked like worm-rid school texts to Josey. The man took down Mr. Dennis's picture of Lexington's last hanging, along with Mr. Dennis's favorite sign: "You'll find the proprietor where the cigar smoke is thickest."

So Dennis's had changed. A friend of Josey's had known the place was for sale and offered to front capital if Josey would move back and run things. *Have Faith. Come back to Limestone, where it will all work out.* But Josey was attending a university in Florida—oh don't ask how he was lured there!—a university that boasted offering America's only undergraduate major in circus performance. What a bald-faced lie: they all do.

Well? Did Josey major in circus performance and minor in, say, the transcendent freedom of interpretative dance? You're asking this, remembering his prehensile thumb, his eating abilities, his amazing motility. You're asking this, realizing that he must no longer drag his knuckles along Limestone Street. I'm afraid he did neither. He still wanted a mind, a mind. Besides, who's to say he ever truly left North Lime?

A Jungian Postscriptum

Limestone: CaCO3. An omnipresent, sedimentary rock originating when oceans covered the globe in a great, archetypal web, when shellfish entertained little choice concerning their place of death. Typically, limestone deposits are peppered with cavernous aquatic abscesses whose walls foam—merrily if not pinkly—during abundant rains. And during drought? During drought, my friend, they collapse all too soon.

The Phantom Tipper

1.

Flashback: When I worked as a waiter in West Palm Beach, rumors persisted about the Phantom Tipper. This gentlemen, hailing from the glitzy-ritzy, toilless-roilless isle of Palm Beach, was reputed to unfailingly leave a discreet five hundred dollar bill under the plates of any servers who waited on him. A very democratic gesture, don't you agree?

Consequently, I spent much of my productive time eyeing customers and wondering if THIS were the one. Jeans or suede sports coat, it didn't matter, for the gentleman might be slumming, you see. Three-piece suit or evening gown, it didn't matter, for we lived in the funky Palm Beaches, and maybe the gentleman in question enjoyed dining in drag. Or maybe the rumor sexistly assumed the situation, and *he* was truly *she*. The Phantom Tipperess? It didn't matter, as long as I got my five hundred. A very democratic gesture, don't you agree?

Even now I don't know what a five-hundred dollar bill looks like—frankly, I don't know if the government really issues them, nor am I likely to find out. No store *I'll* enter could ever change such a large bill, so tendering one would be as useless as pulling pressed green toilet paper from my wallet. No matter. What I really want to linger over is the exuberance of being on the *qui vive* for the Phantom Tipper. . . .

We waiters and waitresses—we humble serving people—would occasionally broach the subject and giggle stupidly, drunkenly, cynically, each according to his or her God-given genetics/potty-training. It wasn't like any one of us had personally received such a $500 boon. No, the receptor was always a friend of a friend of a friend who was working in X-Y Ristorante that, don't you remember, went out of business last year. But despite our doubting giggles and guffaws, our fingertips would trace wanton, late-night restaurant air: *Me, it could have been me. It could **still** be me, maybe with this last couple tonight, or maybe tomorrow night.*

"Would you care for a dessert or an after-dinner drink, sir?"

"Drink? Ah yes. Martell Five Star—and, does your establishment employ a cigar humidor? No? Ah, things haven't been the same since the demise of the Vanderbilts and rails, have they? Well, no matter. Bring on the Martell."

Oh where, oh where will he slip it? Under the dinner plate, while reminiscing over the decor of the Vanderbilt, Post, and Kennedy estates? But we had to remove the dinner plate with its offensive scampi shrimp tails. Well, under the bread plate then? Yes, that could remain unobtrusively enough.

So we would leave the bread plate and furtively watch so-soft and so-white and so-refined fingers swirl a cognac, while our sweaty thin fingers polished silverware or clasped a drink slipped to us by our friendly bartender. All *por nada*, for of course the gentleman in question would leave the standard Palm Beach nine-percent. Hey, the sonofabitches didn't get rich to give their money away to West Palm *hoi polloi,* after all. . . .

2.

Flashtinyback: But hope springs eternal, as does Phantom Tipper *qui viveness*: Why, just a week ago I spotted the Phantom Tipper again, even though Palm Beach lies years and miles away and I'm no longer a waiter in any sense other than crudest earthen metaphor, and even though this Tipper was a Tipperess, not a Tipper. . . .

Yes, just one week ago, on a Sunday with a male friend in Mobile, I immediately saw through her skillful disguise. She stood beside the same Confederate monument as my friend and I did, wearing a slinky autumnal one-piece dress embroidered with golden leaves that gave her identity away. And of course it wasn't a five-hundred dollar bill this autumnal Tipperess would leave me, but the chance of a lifetime when she would turn and say, "Josey . . . did your friend call you that? Jo-sey?" Yes, she would ice my name in the air like a medallion-laden French chef finishing royal blackberry pastry. "Well, Jo-sey, I'm just a Northern tourist type heiress gallivanting Mobile," she would then whisper, "and you, Jo-sey, seem sensitive, seem knowledgeable, seem . . . could you just spare your precious time to guide me through this city's sights?"

Could I? *Ahem. This particular sight we stand before is a replica of the first submarine ever to sink a ship. A replica because the real Confederate submarine, the H. L. Hunley, became entangled after piercing its Union prey, and said entangling ignited its own gunpowder canister. Hence, dear Tipperess, all the Confederate seamen in the Hunley were blown to atomic bits or drowned, and all the Confederate iron was scrapped and sunk, while all the Union sailors were rescued by a sister ship. This, my dear Tipperess, occurred in Charleston Harbor. . . .*

My friend, accustomed to my rambling fantasies, jabbed my fourth rib and urged, "Hey Josey, wake up. You think they actually took this thing under water, like Jacques Cousteau?"

I was about to impress both my friend and the svelte, autumnal heiress by saying, *Sure, see the two portholes on top?*

But the Phantom Tipperess upped and explained: "No, look. There's only a horizontal rudder on the stern. No vertical rudder for descent or ascent. This ship was designed to skim under the surface with only those two portholes showing. It really wasn't a submarine, in other words." And then she waved to someone in a long, gray Lincoln towncar that had just pulled up. And then she left.

It was like I was once more waiting tables in West Palm Beach and she was some high-powered lawyer who'd dropped me change in an ashtray for serving her and the mayor spinach salad, shrimp diavolo, and two extra-dry luncheon martinis.

3.

FLASHFORWARD: SO I'M AT a carwash in mid-Alabama now, and my brain cells are reeling. Damned if they don't almost tingle with insight from all these flashbacks. . . . Almost, but my skull evidently isn't prehensile in the very least and it can't keep up with my thumbs as they index past memory pages.

So, at a carwash, I say, about to drop in a final quarter to spray-wax my '85 Ford, when the *real* Phantom Tipper drives up in a maroon Jaguar sedan. I've been pontificating to yet another friend (where this vanishing species springs from, god knows). "Nietzsche's concept of the Overman fascinated Jack London, who was a socialist, blah-blather, blah." Anyway, I think I just told that to this friend (where this vanishing—oh gee, I've already mentioned *that* concern). My voice breaks as the Jaguar's windows ease electrically down and the driver, who's puffing a large black imported cigar, stares at me or past me. "Uh, Nietzsche thought that most humans should willingly serve Overmen who have the ability to make global decisions." I murmur this, musing that perhaps the fellow in the Jag comes from the MacArthur or Guggenheim Foundation and is roving America's backstreets in search of thwarted philosophical genius. A Phantom Tipper on the *qui vive* for phantom trippers?

"You two fellas work here?" he asks, emitting a blue cloud of imported Caribbean smoke. "Because I need to get this car cleaned real well before I drive to Atlanta. It's worth an extra buck to each of you."

My face falls and my prehensile thumb drops the damned quarter, which rolls through a filthy iron grate. I'm instantly on my knees, grunting: the guy in the Jag gets the picture and roars to the Texaco across the street where sorority girls are spraying one another in a fund-raiser.

4.

FLASHFLASHFLASH: CONCENTRATE, I TELL myself as I scrape my forearm reaching for the quarter. *No, really concentrate,* I tell myself as I ignore the smell and the furry dead thing protruding from a large pipe just under the grate. The quarter, it's between my thumb and forefinger when I hear a thud. It's my foot kicking my Ford, it's my face hitting the grate. And the quarter's gone because soapy water from the pipe is flushing it and the furry thing away.

I sit up and wipe rust and soap off my cheek. Hell, never mind Nietzsche, never mind the quarter. Stay on the *qui vive* for the Phantom Tipper. Where will you spot him/her next? In a public library by the *National Geographics*? In a grocery aisle by spaghetti sauce? Nuzzling the snout of a Greyhound Bus? Whereever, whenever, you'd better be wearing a hunter's-orange hair shirt, a velveteen tam-o'-shanter, or maybe polka-dotted pantyhose to render yourself conspicuous. And you probably should move to Atlanta and take lessons in Manhattan elocution.

Another quarter drops from my fingers into the grate, and as I once more shove my arm through the rusty iron a wet furry voice squeaks, *Would any of it help?*

The World's Thinnest Fat Man

Now this story comes sort of *apres summo dummo facto*, I mean it comes in the fresh, Pampers rear-end of our new millennium, when America's children are raised placidly in two-parent homes, taught racial tolerance and non-belligerent sexual mores—when, in short, they are educated into the arts of self-awareness and epiphany by the globe's leading public school system and its concomitant TV networks. But in those antique twentieth century days, Josey—a child without a father—whirled in a bollix.

Because of his situation, mysteries enough for ten TV detective shows filled Josey's life, and Old Man Garner presented the most puzzling. As did all adults, the old man towered, and Josey would strain to search his godly white moustache for some wise word congealing there. "Old Man" Garner's nickname originated from Josey's grandmother, and as it indicated, he couldn't have been Josey's father—even at nine Josey recognized a problem in that area insofar as hoary age. Yet the old guy visited, come every spring, with paternal regularity. His ostensible motive was to attend Keeneland horse sales and The Lexington Trots, but Josey always suspected . . . well no he didn't, he did what all kids back then did: he took whatever adults tossed him at face value, so this weeklong houseguest was just that: a weeklong houseguest from the hillbilly hills of Kentucky.

The one spring Josey really remembers, for whatever rumbling biological reason, the old guy stayed two weeks. Whirls of shared walks to the liquor store, rattlesnake rattles, pocketknives, snapping suspenders, chewing tobacco, and good luck buckeyes assailed the lad. The only down side was that Grandma was staying too. Like magnets flopped wrong-end, she and Old Man Garner repelled.

At dinner the first night the old man taught Josey the proper way to eat peas. Josey watched in amazement as little soldiers, one by greenish one, were forked onto the old man's pocketknife in a neat parade line of eight. Was that Grandma snorting? Never mind, for the old man lifted that knife and slid that green squadron past his snowy moustache, gave three satisfied chomps, forced the mush past his Adam's apple, delivered a gray-eyed wink, and braced his liver-spotted hands by the plate.

"Well shit." Josey's mother, as always, gave those words a musicality one wouldn't expect. And she sang this again on seeing Josey attempt the same operation with a pocketknife Old Man Garner'd bought him that day, positioning three peas on the blade, knocking the trio off with a fourth brethren.

"Joe-seephus, you'll wind up sticking that knife down your throat like you was a toad," Grandma warned.

Mr. Garner had already lined up another squadron, readying them for a march to oblivion. Josey watched as he slipped them down. No sliced throat, and the women kept quiet.

There was school for the next two days, but Friday was a holiday, so Mr. Garner and Josey took a cab to Lexington Trots. It was early morning, late spring, and trees hung in emeraldcy, their buds having blasted into jeweled canopies overnight. Wind whipped to bulge Josey's eyes as he and Mr. Garner headed through dewy grass toward horse stalls painted virginal white. When a pair of men waved, Mr. Garner veered toward them while a black mare trotted a buggy by, its driver holding a whip to his goggles in a smart salute. Patches of hosed-down dirt peeled and spattered from the buggy's thin, receding wheels. Years later Josey would learn that the actor who played Tonto on *The Lone Ranger* was a favorite driver at Lexington Trots.—Who knows, *Kemo Sabe*? Maybe it was Tonto saluting Josey that very day.

While the three men talked, Josey sniffed the air, which, of course, smelled like horse manure. But the smell didn't bother him; in fact, he liked its difference, for it wasn't school and it wasn't diesel from a dirty bus taking him to school. And though Lexington Trots lay well inside Lexington's city limits, upon whiffing that air Josey became a country boy who bent for a grass blade to chew. Did he envision fields of corn slinging golden tassels? Herds of free-born horses wilding over hillsides? Well, that's his business. You just need to know that he was never a kid to hang around adults when they didn't want him, and even though Mr. Garner introduced him to Eddie and the other man, both of them noted Josey about as much as they did the upside-down water bucket the one named Eddie rested a foot on. So . . .

So glancing back from a distance, Josey saw Mr. Garner hand Eddie some bills from a money clip. Eddie was short and wore one of those silly horse-people caps that wasn't quite a beret. He eased the money into his tight tan vest and the three men walked toward a stall where a horse's gray rear end stuck out, brooming a magnificent black tail to shake off flies. Old Man Garner patted the horse's rear, sending a quiver through its flank. The horse moved deep into the stall, but another horse in another stall stuck out a chestnut head and chewed a mouthful of hay while observing the men as if it had been deputized from the animal kingdom.

Josey chewed his grass blade in time with that horse's bulging jaw, then sauntered near the track's rail to watch the black mare in its workout. The section he went to had a tunnel built under its turn, which cars used before and after a meet, and the trotters themselves used the rest of the time. A breeze swam through the tunnel as the black trotter stopped at the catty-corner turn. The driver got out and appeared to take a leak, then climbed back in to pass slowly around the track. A clopping echo emerged from the tunnel and Josey leaned back to see that the gray horse with the black tail, the one from the stall, had been harnessed. The horse threw his head with a snort, and the driver, Eddie, was friendly now and even slowed to shout up to Josey, "You see if you can't get the old man to bring you out to my farm next week: I'll give you a ride in one of these." Josey grinned, Eddie grinned. Then buggy, horse, and driver headed on up the incline Tand onto the track. This gray horse was a real beauty, and as it pulled alongside the black one, anyone could see it was a good deal taller and stronger. Eddie and the other driver were talking and laughing, and Mr. Eddie had to keep reining in his gray horse.

Mr. Garner and the other man were leaning against the fence about thirty yards away. As they waved at the two drivers a robin with a twig in its beak hopped along a branch as if it had placed some side bet.

Each driver gave his horse a snip of the whip and the buggies lurched. Though the gray horse was on the outside it shot ahead of the black one and increased its lead, keeping its head remarkably still, its hooves lifting in that hypnotic trotter fashion. Clip-clop, clop-clop. Clip-clop, clop-clop. All the way until the turn directly across from Josey, the gray legs caressed the ground, the plumy black tail swept the air.

Then moving into the turn things on the track went out of synch and dirt sprayed. Within seconds the gray legs again caught the rhythm and their poise, but Mr. Eddie tilted his horsy cap to show his red forehead. Josey could see him scowl as he and the huge gray horse clopped over the tunnel, even though the second horse was eight lengths back. Mr. Garner and the other man barely nodded when Eddie went by.

"That horse do that tomorrow night, it won't be winning no nothing."

Josey looked up into a face whose blackness glowed. There was a black janitor at school who supposedly went blind or got real sick from the hallway's fluorescent lights, which were then as innovative as civil rights in Kentucky, but besides him, Josey had never been close to a black person. Their skin shone so shiny that he always feared the color would rub off, so some part of him twitched at this man's closeness.

"That's right," the black man said. "I see your head bouncing time with that horse' legs. You see how that horse mess up? That called 'breaking stride.' Fastest trotter in the world don't do you no good if it break stride 'round a turn."

"Josey!" Mr. Garner was motioning Josey back to the stalls.

"Good-bye," Josey told the black man, eyeing the muscles in his forearm.

"Unn-unh," the man sang while he watched the gray horse canter a second lap. He intoned that phrase so close to how Josey's mother sang *Well, shit,* that his voice hung like the echo of a melting star. "Good-bye, child. . . ."

Josey crunched across river rocks then onto grass again. Suddenly the stall door closest to the end burst open and a horse threw its head wildly, yanking the small man holding its lead off the ground. Hooves thumped within feet of Josey, so he jumped, falling then scrambling up. Mr. Garner and the other man ran over to help the groom control the horse. The black man that had been talking to Josey came running with a twitch, which he finally got on the horse's muzzle.

Instead of thanking anyone, the groom, a skinny BB-eyed fellow who stank like soured bedclothes, yelled, "Damned horse oughter be shot. Hit's four times this week now." He put an *h* in front of the word *it* like a lot of Kentucky hillbillies still do and his BB eyes stabbed like they were angry at every bird and twig and leaf in the world. He twisted the twitch until its leather thong distorted the horse's upper lip and nose. The horse neighed a high squeal more like a pig, but moved obediently away.

"He never better do none of Mr. Perez's horses the way he do that one," the black man said. "No wonder that horse try to take his head off."

"You work for Eddie? When'd you start?" Mr. Garner asked.

"Two week ago."

"Well, thanks for your help here. The boy could have been hurt."

"He quick on his feet and skit-jump away. He take care of hisself."

"He's quick all right," the other man said. "Slid right into a fresh pile of horse turds." He pointed to Josey's left pantsleg, stained with greenish-brown horse manure.

"Lord. Your mom will throw a hissy." Mr. Garner spit out snuff he'd probably stolen from Josey's grandmother.

The white man laughed. "Got to be a first time for everyone to step in horseshit, kid; you might as well learn young."

"Better be quick and dirty than be something else," the black man added, raising his eyebrows.

Mr. Garner nodded. "Thanks again for your help. I'll be sure to tell Eddie."

The black man smiled and walked away.

They went home after hosing off Josey's pants and letting them dry in a nearby barbecue house called The Colonel's. One thing Kentucky has never lacked is honorary colonels, most of them hog-fat and never near a war. This one filled the hog-fat part as he slouched against a chrome counter picking his teeth and watching two women. When one of the women got up for the restroom and adjusted her tight tan skirt, he snorted and bumped his belly against the chrome like he'd been tossed a corncob.

Later, Mr. Garner somehow sweet-talked or maybe bribed Josey's grandmother into washing his pants and socks along with the shirt he'd spilled barbecue sauce on. He also talked her into not saying anything to Josey's mother, a bit of a miracle.

The next day, Saturday, Mr. Garner went off by himself to the Trots. On Sunday, he was prancing like a colt and treated the whole family to late lunch at the Campbell House, where they served steaks, something Josey and his mother never had unless it was July Fourth, and a man played a glossy white piano all through the meal, something Josey and his mother never had, period. Mr. Garner kept bragging about how much money he'd won at the Trots until a fat man with a green cigar turned from a near table.

"You hear about Eddie Perez?" he asked.

Mr. Garner said he hadn't.

"He got killed late last night after the trots in a single car wreck on Tates Creek Pike."

Mr. Garner had been slipping bourbon from a silver flask into his coffee since it was Sunday and he couldn't order liquor. He clutched the cup and asked the man if he was sure. The man said yes, and the woman with him said she'd heard it twice on the radio, that he was with his Negro groom and they'd run into a walnut tree.

I tapped Mr. Garner's hand. "Is that the colored man who used the twitch yesterday?"

Mr. Garner barely grunted an "Umm-hmm" yes.

"Well, that's one nigger won't be trying to worm his kids into our schools," the fat man said.

Josey's mother breathed out a "Well, shit," and glared. Her hair was black as a horse's mane and her eyes burst blue as a thunderbolt in a clear summer sky. Mr. Garner started to say something, but just poured more whiskey into his coffee before going to make a phone call.

Josey never can remember the ride home, or much else of the two weeks except Mr. Garner sitting on the single bed in the back room rubbing a buckeye or snapping his suspenders. To tell the truth, Josey never was sure if Mr. Garner went to Mr. Perez's funeral. And he's only sure that Mr. Garner stayed on because he remembers the smell of chewing tobacco and bourbon, and he's only sure he left because the smell's not there now. It's funny what slips away and what stays.

2.

Some decades back, a Quaker named Richard Millhouse Nixon wrote a book entitled *Six Crises.* An opposition psychiatrist was quick to pick up on this title and note that President Nixon saw his life in typically manic-depressive fashion. Psychiatry and politics and religion aside, I suspect many of us perceive our lives just as that past-President did: if not in crises, at least in watersheds where we choose one muddy river path over another; then fall onto or avoid a sunning cottonmouth; where we either sadly stumble over or gladly hop over the mighty snag of regret.

So what did Josey learn from Mr. Garner's visit and those untimely deaths? I'd like to say—my friend, I'd truly like to say—that he absorbed a myriad of lessons. But he's forever been unable to assimilate even a damned comic book moral, much less true epiphany's inspiration. In consequence he views himself not as a higher spiritual being, not even as a genetically select, silken white rat capable of conquering life's mazes, but rather as the world's thinnest fat man, continually stunning crowds below by tossing off some dazzling jewel like, "Well, that's one nigger won't be trying to worm his kids into our schools."

By the way, Mr. Garner did visit again. On one trip he bestowed a keepsake silver dollar, on another a Canadian bill, and on yet another a Hong Kong yen brownly depicting a skull-capped sage with a beard long enough to offer an escape cord to heaven. That beard, those strange Oriental eyes—another mystery for another day. The American dollar Josey spent, the Canadian he lost, but that mysterious yen still travels from billfold to billfold, resting against his haunchbone.

Why this sentiment over an old man's tattered gift? First, the old man's white moustache twitched like nothing Josey's mom or grandmother had. Secondly, he always knew where he was going: to the liquor store for medicine, to the trots to see friends, to the barbershop to chat. Josey could barely bike to Southland Shopping Center without forgetting why he was sent or losing his mother's ten-dollar bill. Most importantly, Old man Garner answered Josey's every question: *Where does rain come from? Where do dogs go when they die? Who is my father?*—Well, nearly every question. Like a lunging thoroughbred, every time Josey even envisioned a male face to accompany that last question, he was jerked to the ground, with a twitch placed around his lips. . . .

3.

Now, when Josey was two-and-twenty and well on his way to being the world's thinnest fat man, Mr. Garner took it in his head to die. From Somerset he sent word that Josey should travel to see him. Josey's mother pushed: Yes, you should go—envisioning, no doubt, the fame, happiness and fortune mothers always envision for their sons, even illegitimate ones. And Josey did actually plan the pilgrimage, imagining his white knight self saddling a Sunset-in-Somerset Suzuki motorcycle, enduring the five or six brief and wise words that might flutter through those hoary moustache hairs, then enjoying Satan's silver dollars tickling his palms by the trillions from a deathbed bequest. Who knows, maybe Josey'd even get an answer to the really big one: *Just who is my dad, anyway?* But before imagination could congeal Josey lost his license from a fourth speeding ticket and had to pasture his Suzuki. It's what happens to single-parent kids. Thank you, Madonna, et. al., for having your baby. Since Greyhound didn't fit Josey's touring image, Mr. Garner died as alone as if he'd head-on'ed a walnut tree on Tates Creek Pike, while the world's thinnest fat man—that's Josey for sure—amused drunks at The Paddock Club by singing for beers then stumbling licenseless home.

Like the black groom said: "He quick on his feet. He take care of hisself."

4.

Trotters still trot and cemetery grass still grows. Just three nights ago, Josey observed the world's thinnest fat man sitting at his dinner table, plucking out his wallet to check his financial standing. Wonder of wonders there were no Hamiltons, no Lincolns, not even a green ol' George. He—the world's thinnest fat man—rummaged until—emerging from a hiding place—the skull-capped sage on the yen tittered at him. The world's thinnest fat man wondered about exchange rates, rare coin dealers.

But what's this? After all those years, a unisex reproduction. Though not a watershed miracle, two congealed bills formerly presumed to be one separated right before his eyes. As usual, the world's thinnest fat man had underestimated a gift.

He felt his moustache twitch as he envisioned Mr. Garner eating peas; then his fingers did something amazing: they began piling green beans on a steak knife. In response, his girlfriend cackled like an angry hen while green beans fell to the floor, where her brown-nosed cat batted them as if sorting a puzzle. Oblivious, the world's thinnest fat man finished the entire crock-pot, more out of inspired cussedness than any attempt at a Guinness Book record.

But listen: despite that they weren't green peas, despite that he's decades and miles from Somerset or Lexington, either one, I swear there's hope yet for this sorry fellow, for he didn't pawn those dual Hong Kong sages. And who knows? Someday their lengthy beards might miraculously bobble to chant, "Butterfly, Butterfly: forget about submerged roots and family vault secrets. Remember only that . . ."

Will the world's thinnest fat man cup his ear and lean? Will both sages cackle, "Man Who Eat Peas on Sharp Knife Is Fool Who Gig Own Throat!"?

Be it so if you will. But also be assured: even that minuscule epiphany will astound him.

My Ode to Sylvia Plath

Daddy. I hadn't even thought this in—what, twenty or more years, and for good damned reason. But at three a.m. two weeks ago I awoke shaking like a revenant of Poe to shout at my walls, *Daddy.* Just like peach blossoms blooming in too early spring, things have a way of popping up when you least expect. Seeming unrelated to my vocal nightmare, an invitation came the next morning to attend Mobile's Joe Cain Day. Over the phone my two friends, Janie and Paul, explained that Joe Cain serves as the modern daddy of Mobile's Mardi Gras, for though an orphan he resurrected the tradition when the Yankees left the city swamped in post-traumatic stress syndrome after the Civil War. Daddy? I asked them. *The* daddy, they averred. An orphan? I asked. An orphan, they confirmed, explaining that he's buried across from their house in a deserted little cemetery off Church Street. Then Janie and Paul cajoled, "Get off your divorced duff, Josey! You remember how you once had fun!" I held the phone from my ear and pictured an orphaned Joe Cain badgering glum Southern faces: "Giddy-up, y'all! Y'all remember how we once had fun! Y'all need t' carry the tradition on!"

Hence, as my authors are fond of writing, hence Mr. Cain's given first name, his orphaned life, and his rag-tag burial site all rang appropriate to that night-haunting word, *Daddy.* And so two weeks *thence* I took time off from publishing cookbooks and tabletop extravaganzas for a leisurely drive down to the Gulf Coast. My publishing house printed *Old South Crockery.* . . . Well, you may not have heard of it, but 50,000 copies sold at 45 bucks a lick. And my line of 'Old South Romances and Mysteries' keeps chugging along too. Sir Walter Scott would be proud. So while I'm not wealthy, I'm certainly not poor. And like every American worth his—or her—salt, I cheat on taxes, so let's leave my income vaguely bracketed as vaguely described. The point is: I could have flown down without stretching the ol' budget, but something urged me to drive.

A mistake, for by the time I reached Mobile I'd played every bluegrass CD I owned, which meant I was good and by-God depressed about my roots—or daddyless lack thereof—and ready for a bottle of red wine, something for the heart, so to speak.

That maudlin depression was to wreak further damage yet on a St. John's Wortless weekend.

"Josey!" my friends exclaimed as I uncorked a sixty-dollar bottle of Haut Medoc, one out of a case. Stinting on airline tickets meant I could upgrade the wine. You know what I mean: Archimedes' principle: If a body of such and such a weight drives down, the price of wine flies up. Hopefully, I'd shout Eureka rather than drown.

My friends and I quaffed the bouquet and toasted to good times. Seconds later I stared out their dining room window towards Joe Cain's grave. A couple stood kissing over it, though "kissing" puts matters mildly: they twined like boa constrictors. I turned away to examine Janie and Paul's house. They'd remodeled the entire shebang themselves, saving it from condemnation. Six coats of wood floor sealant, two refurbished fireplace mantles, a six-burner gas stove with grill and convection oven—you name it. Uh, how about the original property deed from 1838 hanging over the bathroom door? Lest I forget.

Despite the amorous hetero couple outside, part of any modern Joe Cain celebration was a gay crew, the Merry Widows, who would visit Joe Cain's gravesite in drag to strew black orchids, black roses, or whatever dark floral oddity they could ferret, onto Joe's grave. According to my friends, cruising the downtown bars as an eligible bachelor with one of these black ditties sporting your lapel was better than cinnamon aphrodisiac or Spanish fly—or both. Women couldn't resist the challenge.

"And Josey, we know this amazing florist," my friends hinted.

Since I was delving into my second year of post-traumatic stress from an unsought divorcehood, I figured to be game and I raised my wine in a toast.

So we skipped the Saturday night parade and went out. "Joe Cain, that's the parade you need," Janie insisted over flaming dessert. "And we've got a surprise for you tomorrow." I was still game, still thinking she meant pinning me with some odd black flower from the amazing florist, maybe even spritzing me with a hint of ox musk from an equally amazing Mary Kay hostess.

But on awakening mid-morning after a restless night of ghostly banjo licks mixed with not-so-ghostly sirens, I asthmatically wheeze a word that pops me a real surprise: "Daddy." Twice within a fortnight! (*Fortnight* being another word my authors, the romance novelists anyway, tend to favor). And after brunch, when Janie attaches an admittedly stunning black tulip to my shirt with much ado and six straightpins, I wheeze it again. Thrice. I hate odd numbers; they bode ill. My eyes widen, and I hope Janie doesn't hear or understand, for things are twisting with this paternal intrusion.

Then, moving out onto their small front yard and just eleven minutes into the parade, as the third float steers by, a sort of clumsy yellow Chinese worm—well, this happens:

"Daddy!"

I should explain that I'm fatherless. Not literally of course; not even test tube babies are that. But I've never known a biological or familial father of any sort. Janie and Paul look askance at my shout.

As do I.

What I mean is that I'm like truly searching for whoever's mouth spewed that vile word. But that isn't the end of it. A reveler on the Chinese worm float glares with an eye that shows Cyclopean even through his mask; he takes aim, and he clobbers me with a pound of emerald beads joined by masking tape in much the same manner that galaxies are held by muon, gluon, or freon. The bulk catches my temple. As I sway, the reveler lifts his goofball Chinese mask and scowls. In that revelatory moment we both know that what I shouted is true.

Should I repeat that last sentence? I think so: In that revelatory moment we both know that what I shouted is true. I'm not kidding about this.

Daddy.

I grab my wine bottle and hop the picket fence with agility unbelievable for a thirty-something-guy. The reveler dons his mask and turns to toss more beads with frantic abandon. My friends Janie and Paul shout, "Josey! / Josey! What / where are you doing / going?!"

But my blonde moustache tickles and I don't answer. You want to know why? Because Daddy sports one exactly like mine. And he's left-handed, too, like I am. I mean he's side-arming those beads at people in a huge curve. So I don't answer, I run.

I haven't gotten far, say past the street corner and approaching the Mobile Arts Council, when a woman of about twenty-eight (an even, coupled number!) snags my arm, eyeing the black tulip in my lapel, no doubt thinking she might convert a fag.

—Excuse me: convert a gay guy. You can see that my unnatural and unrequested daddyless existence leads to the occasional sexual identity crisis; hence my, um, so recent—as in twenty-eight words ago—Freudian projection of self-hate through name-calling. So I'm a mess. Can I be forgiven? Back to the twenty-eight-year-old:

"Say, don't I know you?"

"I'm from Kentucky," I say. "Two states up."

"I thought so." She grabs my arm.

This woman is determined. I could have been responsive, because she cascades huge, sweet lips; heavy dark brows; a broad face with inviting brown eyes; a pug nose; and such a smile . . . and when I'm able to tear from it and look down . . . tanned cleavage, wide hips, and bare calves lead boundlessly to strapped brown leather sandals and exquisite pearl toenails. It's as if someone has set us up on the ultimate Mac computer date. Kismet.

But from atop the float Daddy glares. He's moved to the rear and is leaning over a makeshift red rail, as if daring me to pursue. I watch him reach for something—a bag of peanuts, it turns out. Not my temple this time, but dead-center amidst my forehead.

"Daddy!" I shout. What else could I yell? *Eloi, Eloi, lama sabachtani*? Daddy, Daddy, why have you forsaken me?

The Joe Cain Parade proper starts at two. Church is over, the communion host served, and it's time for wine, right? So maybe it's two-twenty-one and maybe I've drunk a third of the bottle of Haut Medoc when I get clunked by this bag of peanuts, when the twenty-eight year old beauty lets go my arm. Did you know that Medoc was Edgar Allen Poe's favorite wine? Just thought I'd add that factoid, for misery does love company, and I'm heavily searching for another weirdo to afford such company. Poe works fine. Speaking of peanuts, I could add George Washington Carver, but bless that poor man's black soul, even dead he hears that miracle-vegetable crop crap too much; anyway, his life was evidently rather unweird, despite his being black in a pale society. Besides, he'd make three, an odd number, so let him ride. Poe, Poe—his tintinnabulating alarum bells and silent moldy crypts work just fine. Nevermore Lenore would fit even better, but remember that the twenty-eight year old woman has let go my arm and meandered off to find some other Kentuckian or maybe even a Tennesseean. Or perhaps the crowd separated us? Not kismet, but miss-met?

This particular Mardi Gras season is hot. Mobile does lie coastal deep South, after all. And since Paul, Janie, and I ate sausage, eggs, fried okra, and spicy shrimp gumbo for brunch, sweat is dripping onto my tulip. The woman with the grand smile and the leather straps was sweating too, for her wet grip still clings to my left arm. Undaunted, I take a swig of Medoc, pluck a peanut from my collar to eat, shell and all.

Another woman catches my eye, or do I catch hers? It doesn't matter, for I'm on the daddy trail and have no time, no time. "Daddy!" I yell, pushing through a crowd bending for Moon Pies, beads, and peanut bags.

Now, during Mardi Gras, a push might be ignored, or it might be considered as an infringement upon territorial rights. Since a float has just passed and since its revelers have just tossed a good deal of worthless loot, I'm afraid my push earns a shove plus a garlicky huff from a wiry fifty-genarian who seems ready to fisticuff, just to prove his ability to remain alive.

"Damn, Man, sorry," I say, showing one empty palm and lifting the bottle of Medoc.

This earns me a second shove from the old fart. And that lands me against some black gentleman's easeful side—read *easeful* as in gutted boar hung easefully in a smokehouse—so I get shoved again. Ping-pong not being my favorite sport, I slip through metal barricades onto the street to pursue Daddy.

"Daddy!"

Damned if he doesn't have a walkie-talkie. And damned if he isn't pointing at me and using it . . . to call the cops, I soon learn as one on a motorcycle bumps me. Kawasaki. That's what they ride in Mobile—no throaty Harley roar, which is why the uniformed jerk is able to sneak up and give me a bump.

"You need to get behind the barricade, Mister."

"Put him in cuffs!"

"Jail him!"

"Shoot him!"

The last, I swear, comes from the float, which has stopped for some reason. I have no doubt that my own father shouted the directive, for I recognize his voice, my voice, a grackly hill twang. Crestfallen, I nod at the motorcycle cop, then edge between two barricades. I've crossed to the mostly black side of the street. Not like there's a law, blacks here, whites there, but things have pretty much shifted that way, like oil and vinegar separating. It doesn't matter, since the float starts moving again and I run after it.

"Crazy damned cracker," someone hoots to appreciative laughs. I'm not going to deny the truth of this, but maybe hearing this or maybe running between live oak trees in the two-thirty-one p. m. Deep South sun makes me think, *Phew, this side of the street smells.* Now *that* is a racist and hateful thought, just in case you're waiting for one after my earlier "fag" remark. But as I run and sniff disapprovingly, I realize that these black souls are only laughing, drinking beer, and occasionally hopping for a trinket, whilst I'm running, shouting, and avoiding cops. The body odor, in other words, nudges closer home every moment. A day of revelations. Not only a cracker, but a moldy and stinky one to boot.

When I've drawn within twenty feet of the Chinese worm float, Daddy catches sight of me again. I can see him quivering, and this must stir some womb-memory, for I mimic his quiver. Could we both be re-experiencing the climactic moment of fertilization? His float's slowing to execute a turn, so the two of us pretty much watch one another quiver until I can't hold myself back and again spurt through the barricades. He snaps up his walkie-talkie.

"You're not going to do that to your own son, are you?!" My scream angers the old guy so much that he heaves the walkie-talkie at me. That prize causes a commotion, believe me: a barricade gets knocked over, attracting a marshal on horseback this time. I take advantage of the scramble to run across the street, being pelted by my father the entire way with bags of peanuts, one of which raises lumps. Is he loading them with bird shot?

No sooner am I at the barricaded curb when two women, maybe a duet of hookers, pull me through, eyeing the black tulip pinned to my shirt.

"Thanks," I tell them, catching my breath.

Behind us, a high school band starts the usual racket. I don't mean Vivaldi. A bag of peanuts clips one of the women in the eye. When she begins bleeding, I know it was meant for me, and I know who threw it. Her friend bends for the bag, which is torn despite the surplus duct tape.

"Some son of a bitch has weighted it with pennies," she says, incredulous as the coins roll on the sidewalk.

"Don't insult your sex," I hear myself answer. "Leave out the bitch part. Some self-inserting *prick* weighted it with pennies."

Leaving them with that truth, I flee the band music and run toward Daddy's wormy float. The sun's at my back now. It feels sweet, comforting. I can see Daddy, sweating it out under his Chinese mask. *Fine for you*, I judge.

"Josey!" I think I hear my friend Paul shout my name, but when I turn I can't see him. I feel guilty for leaving him and Janie in the lurch, but surely they'll understand when I get back.

"Josey!" I hear again. It's a female voice, but not Janie's, for she has a strange way of turning the 'J' in my name into a 'Y,' as if she were Cuban, which she certainly isn't, having moved from New York City to attend Springhill College and eventually marry Paul in a first-class Catholic wedding performed by a Jesuit priest.

"Josey!" When I look about I can't see anyone who seems to be paying me particular attention—other than a young black couple twitching their noses at me. So my racist thought from the other side of the street is being met with its counterpart on this side. Well, at least these two have an excuse.

"Sorry," I tell them, discreetly squeezing my armpits unto myself.

Daddy has gotten away from me, but I can make out two revelers on the float holding him, shaking their heads while admonishing him.

"Josey." This hovers over the crowd in an almost red-silk-pillow whisper. I look about, but see nothing, though I do catch sight of one milky leg with a brown leather strap running up its calf. That's what the woman searching for the Kentuckian or Tennesseean wore. Just one calf will never do, though—being an uneven number. God, I think, she did have all ten of her pearly toes, didn't she?

I look up again; now three men are holding Daddy. I run forward, nearly sprinting, if one can ever be said to do that in a Mardi Gras crowd, whether it's Mobile or New Orleans.

"Keep the son of a bitch away from me!" he's shouting.

" 'Keep the son of a *prick* away' is what he means!" I yell back.

At that, Daddy halfway dives off the float, held only by a weightlifter who's joined to make a foursome controlling him. "Joe, get a-hold of yourself," the men cajole.

As if I have to be told his damned name.

Now, I've learned from all the books I publish that you've got to stop once in a while, give the reader a pauser, let him or her smell the roses and watch the honeybees be. So while Daddy dangles off the float, more like a riled yellow jacket than a productive honeybee, let me describe the three buildings that face me from across the street. The building in the center glows a fiery red brick and stands six stories erect. The two buildings on its either side resemble low mosques, for they both have white domes that snuggle alongside the erect middle building. One of the domes seems to pulse; I suppose this is a trick of light from a live oak and its whiskery Spanish moss. Come to think of it, Spanish moss surrounds all three buildings in a most fluffy and pubic fashion. Overhead, a singular, creamy, mid-afternoon cloud floats, as if ejaculating from the tip of the engorged red bricks of the so-erect middle building.—Oh my, oh my, this description isn't turning out right at all. . . . Even Daddy would be dismayed.

Speaking of . . . they've pulled him back into the float, which is twisting crazily now. A motorcycle cop is eyeing me, and I realize that I am leaning, in imitation of Daddy, over a barricade. I straighten and take a sip of Haut Medoc. The cop pulls over; he's thin and wears no-funny-business metallic blue sunglasses that won't let me see his eyes. He pulls out a pad and begins writing a ticket. Instinctively, I put the wine bottle behind me.

"That's not the problem, mister. It's the lewd thoughts."

"Lewd . . . ? I'm not Jimmy Carter," I object.

"Doesn't matter. This is pretty much a Catholic city and you can't go around thinking what you were thinking back there in front of those buildings. You were *indulging*, weren't you? You had all the outward signs." He gives a hard glance to my mid-section and my knees clasp one another in embarrassment.

As a ruse I, give a look to the three buildings.

"Best ignore that trio; otherwise I might be forced to write you a second ticket," the cop warns, asking to see my driver's license. "Ought to tear them down. They're a real occasion of sin."

All this takes four minutes. Then the cop putters off, leaving me to wonder whether there are any female police in Mobile—and whether there are any chthonic buildings clustered about.

Because of Daddy's acrobatic shenanigans, I guess, the parade has stalled. I look up, expecting his smug gloating face because I've gotten a ticket. But I'm taken aback, for they've shifted him into a Frankenstein monster outfit and tied him, by the neck, to the tail section of the Chinese worm. Though he keeps glaring at me, the entire street crowd is hooting at him now; the more he glares, the louder they hoot. Some even toss beads, and several of these ring his arms and neck.

"Josey." This hovers over the crowd in the same sensual fashion it had before, but I'm gun-shy and push it from my mind. I look at the ticket in my hand: the damned thing costs ten dollars more than a bottle of Haut Medoc. I fold it and place it in my pocket, admonishing myself to be careful and not imagine those leather straps and ten instances of pearl toenail polish. I might indulge.

Someone's tugging at my shirtsleeve. I turn, expecting either Paul or Janie, but a huge—I mean seven-foot huge—creature in a glowing white robe stands spraddle-legged looking down at me.

"He wants me to give you something," the creature says, giving a nod toward Daddy. We both turn. Someone has hit Daddy with a raw egg. How appropriate, you spermatozoid prick, I think. And I plan on running to the Stop-n-Go to buy a dozen myself.

The creature tugs again, to push an old revolver into my left hand.

"A .357. It'll get the job done."

I'm still staring at Daddy, who places a green monster of an index finger to his nuts-and-bolts green head, then flicks his thumb in imitation of a trigger, even as another egg spatters his face.

"I'm not that good a shot," I say stupidly. "I couldn't possibly hit him from here."

An ominous chuckle emerges from some spot on the creature. "Hell Son, it's not *him* he wants you to use that bullet on."

Of course. The prick wants me to put myself out of my misery, out of his memory. Daddy. "What, you couldn't tote a gas oven over for me to stick my head in?" I ask this of the tall white creature in my best wisenheimer style.

But the creature is gone, and someone's fondling my black tulip. I see pearl nail polish, ten agile fingers, and I waft perfume sweeter than six tobacco warehouses in fall. Well, I suppose you need to be from Kentucky to appreciate that last metaphor about the tobacco warehouses. I hear her wonderful grin open; then I look at her calves where leather straps cut upward in a most angular whisper. I fidget, worrying about the indulgence police.

"Josey," she interrupts for the sixth time, saving me from another ticket. "Paul and Janie sent me looking for you. My name's Lenore."

Kismet. I look into her brown eyes—let's avoid any more tobacco metaphors—and take a leap not quite Kierkegaardean in intensity— though on second thought, maybe it's Kierkegaard squared or even cubed. No, not cubed, but to the nicely even power of four. "Here," I say, offering her the wine. She takes a sip and gives a sensuous "Umm," closing her eyes.

The revolver's metal cuts into our adjoining hips, so I turn toward Daddy, then look for any male cops: none. Daddy watches, eager. Lenore's eyes are still tightly closed in a Medoc rush, so I put the revolver to my head. Daddy gives a huge Frankenstein monster nod. Another egg splats his droopy left eye. With a banshee's grin I pull the revolver away, flick the chamber open, and unload the single bullet, tossing it idly toward him. Then I drop the gun into a nearby waste can, take Lenore's silky hand with its four sweet fingers, and right before she recovers from the Medoc bouquet I mouth so that Daddy can read my lips even with egg in his Cyclopean eye, *Daddy, Daddy, you prick . . . I'm through.*

A STORY, LIKE ALL OUR STORIES

APPROACHING THE HOLIDAY INN, Josey would glimpse the silhouette of an Interstate, or at least a four-lane highway mounding the distance. Night always, of course, so he couldn't tell where that road led. The Inn itself seemed to boast two stories secreting a myriad of more personal stories inside a white and green façade, but this color scheme was tenuous, for it was always night, as I've said somewhere before. So: a mound in the distance, a parking lot, a possible white and green façade with plenty of possible stories and plots, and an entrance corridor of about twenty feet. Inside that maw, a young woman always checked IDs, though one can hardly imagine why, since the Inn's lounge featured a Bluegrass band. Perhaps she was covertly checking—not upper-case IDs, but lower case ids. Josey had one—an ID—and likely even possessed that lower case Freudian creature also. So with his ID and his id he would pass inward to view the stage that J. D. Crowe et. al. played Bluegrass on, a curving plywood affair whose glaring light countered the glaring night. But behind the band and that light, for all Josey knew, gaped the grisly jaws of Hades, panting to spew eternal damnation. On stage proper, though, Bluegrass reigned, like a country crone handing out bright nuggets of homespun wisdom. Capital B Bluegrass: does not even the name itself offer a fine paradox: blue . . . *grass*?

Things like this concerned Josey since he was molding an ego and superego to accompany his id: a lengthy and rugged process that went far to explain his moral quest at the twangy feet of Bluegrass.

There were various people besides the band members who would help enlighten him: lanky Joe Willett and squat Chris Whatshisname, the assistant manager of that illustrious clothing chain where Josey bought threadbare suits and limp ties, that illustrious chain whose illustrious name Josey also forgets. Whats*its*name? No, wait. Josey hasn't forgotten; it was Robert Hall. And Whats*his*name's last name was North. Chris—North—was transferred south; Robert Hall hauled itself away. See? Even if slouching on morals, this Josey's a swell mnemonic genius. But let's cut the word game fat: North's girlfriend was what every young man ever and aye dreamed of, for she owned a fully connected WD-40 hip-swivel and a chest that never ended. Moreover, an eternal Yes tingled her frost-glossed lips and sparkling blue eyes. *Procreate, blindly procreate*, she chanted in primal plainsong. *The birds, the bees, the beasts, and even some trees do it. And not a one of them needs Bluegrass or even Genesis to teach them how to hew it. . . .*

What other Buddha haunted those reclaimed horse pastures to guide Josey? Harry Daniels, another Bluegrass aficionado. Both Harry and Josey shored up their entire moral system with Bluegrass, much as one imagines ancient Greek children lying on hillside goat pastures to achieve with Aesop's fables—that is, those Greek children who weren't abandoned as infants to lie on those hillsides and die.

Who else, oh muse, haunted the Kentucky pastures? Well, sing of Josey's wife of the time, his brother-in-law of the time, and his brother-in-law's hotshot musician friend from California, which meant that likely Tara, Josey's sister-in-law, was there, though she blurs in a most Einsteinian way. Einstein, while he wasn't there, does remain a convenient chap with his relevancy, irrelevancy, so we should at least honor him with a small black hole gravitating behind the stage or out in the parking lot, ready to suck in unwary sojourners. Harry's girl was there too. She was Josey's ex-girl, though the trio pretended that game never happened. Or maybe they pretended to dwell amidst some Bluegrass song like "The Long Black Veil." Or maybe they were patiently awaiting a Bluegrass moral just like in the Greek fable, "Two Plough Mules and the Nightingale."

Up on the curving plywood stage J. D. strutted as the listed star, but Josey talked with Tony Rice, since those two were closer in age and since Josey also played guitar, though his real pretended vocation was writer deluxe—Homer, Samuel Johnson, Ichabod Crane, Arnold the Duck. When Josey wasn't pondering his scrivening career, he wondered how anyone could be as hot on a guitar as Tony Rice was, at his age. Maybe late twenties then. Licks upon amazing licks. Shit, all Josey was writing for his intended authorial vocation was *Billygoat come, Billygoat go*, on bumpety, typewritten lines. Not being Greek, he typically tossed some stone fences built by slaves, or a wizened tobacco stick into all his fables to provide local Kentucky color:

The Wizened Tobacco Stick

There was an Athenian lad who daily peripitated a grassy hillside in ancient times. Along that hillside, as far as any eye could see, stretched picturesque stone fences that needed no mortar, for their stones interlocked like puzzles. Local folk claimed that helots had pieced them generations back, but the lad wondered: Did ancient gods or a race of giants really fabricate this work? And if so, did the pattern of the interlocking stones hold the key to Veracity? One peripatetic day he chanced upon a thoroughbred mare giving foal. Wheezing in the summer sun, this mare appeared to have given up the battle, for though her foal lay nearby, a heavy caul still surrounded its barely twitching body, while a thick umbilical cord twisted about the mare's leg. The charitable Athenian lad hopped the stone fence and ran to the mare, but cord and caul were too thick for him to tear with bare hands. He looked backwards, spying the fence's thin stones. He ran to find one that had been chipped into a near knife blade so as to snuggle between two comrades, and he tugged this stone loose. With it he sliced through the caul and severed the umbilical cord. The colt wheezed and stood unsteadily. The Athenian lad pulled the afterbirth free of the mare, some forty pounds of greasy, bloody mass; then he lay down in exhaustion to watch the mare stand and lick its foal. Thirty minutes later mare and colt were frisking and eating grass, and the Athenian lad wiped his hand on the grass and sat up to watch Phoebus guiding his fiery chariot through the sky. He—the Athenian lad—waved and could almost swear that Phoebus—or some godlike avatar—waved back. The knifelike stone pressed the lad's calf, so he returned it to its origin in the fence, pushing and jiggling until it once more interlocked. When he stood back to admire his work, he heard the glorious thump of hooves behind. Yes, he sighed, these fences, like all of terra firma, surely offer an eschatological pattern designed by purposeful gods intent on assisting Man, Beast, Beauty, and Nature in a most veracious manner. Why hadn't this been clear to him all along?

MY FRIEND, LOOK AT THAT clingy-clumsy clunky-clanky rhetorical moral, not to mention the poor tobacco stick protruding from the title, never to appear again in the actual story. And *veracious*? Where did Josey, our erstwhile author, dig up that word—from under the stone fencing alongside a dung beetle he sniffed out? Couldn't he at least have made the Athenian kid a cripple who pre- or post-figured Oedipus by employing that eyesore wizened tobacco stick as a cane? I mean, if the damned sticks are strong enough to hold over a hundredweight of tobacco leaves in barn lofts during curing, one could easily support a blind Greek gimp who lacked the vitamins to sprout as tall as we moderns. But, no, we hear nothing more of the wizened stick; instead we get Phoebus and some stonemason giants. It's a flat Kentucky wonder that Phoebus didn't toss down a bowl of sushi or grits as he waved, the images run on so mish-mash. . . .

There was also—up on the plywood stage, to resume our scene—a chuffy guy who played acoustic bass and occasional fiddle, the latter to much applause. Analyzing through the lens of time, I suspect the audience was happy for any change from a shrill mandolin and banjo, so they enthusiastically encouraged his opening a black case and plucking out that fiddle. I mean, really now: let's not get carried away and attribute Kentucky hill-folk with sudden sophisticated urges to hear Itzhak Perlman render Sibelius. In fact, the audience invariably celebrated that black case's click-clack with hog calls of "Soo-**wee**! Soo-**wee**!" (Josey? Was that you?) Tony Rice's younger brother, who played mandolin, he was also on stage. Waitresses, who, if Josey'd had any hog sense—*Procreate, will you please?*—would have riveted his attention, slipped about carrying drinks on trays while wearing aery dresses. After all, they too strutted on the plywood stage in a manner, or at least fluttered before it.

So have we been dead wrong in assigning an id to the poor Kentucky lad? Perhaps. Perhaps not. Perhaps the child was so perplexed and muddled by his monomaniacal intent to acquire a superego at the feet of Bluegrass that his id became suppressed in a surprise Freudian flip-flop. *Say what?* Well hell, *something* happened.

Through all this, the plywood stage's dark, flat black backdrop never seemed to worry a soul. Still, someone must have wondered: *Does that dreary backstage exit connect to the four-lane and escape? Does a Dempster Dumpster lying behind teem with body parts? Are* they *what Einstein and his black hole were gravitationally attracting? Or does a starving Grecian orphan keep beat to the Bluegrass by thumping a chain link fence with a wizened tobacco stick? Or maybe does . . .*

While awaiting an answer, let's sift some individual Bluegrass moments:

Moment 1: Josey laughs at the lyric "He was raised up in Milwaukee, though he never was that famous." And Tony Rice—this may prove to be Josey's lifetime claim to fame—laughs in response. They laugh because a piss-tasting beer named Old Milwaukee was using that phrase in its ad campaign: "The beer that made Milwaukee Famous." But the Bluegrass lyrics surrounding the phrase were so sad, with the character in the song dying on the side of a road near Boulder Dam, Colorado, if I remember correctly, in ten-degree cold, growing ever colder, because no mother's child would pick him up as he hitch-hiked toward Milwaukee. Was Josey's laughter a nervous premonition? It may be, for just such abandonment seized him in West Palm Beach years later—except for the cold, that is—as he hog-wallowed alongside a sandy road. Soo-**wee**!

Moment 2: God, this is embarrassing, because surely Josey went to the Holiday Inn twenty or more times, but Moment 2 might be the last moment he remembers about the place. And guess what? This moment consists of pre-Holiday Inn memories, nothing within the green-and-white edifice itself. So is the story over? Time to flick on the TV and view a real plot with high-speed action? Sure, but while the popcorn's popping let's move ahead to Josey's brother-in-law of the time—the most complete, perfected asshole of brother-in-laws. This perfected asshole brother-in-law was a musician who'd moved to California. Of course. Now he was back visiting the hill folk, chomping corn on the cob and breaded pork chops. In Josey's redneck two-bedroom trailer Josey told this perfected brother-in-law how good J. D. Crowe and Tony Rice were on banjo and guitar. The brother-in-law commented to his California friend, "You hearing this?" Meaning, Are you hearing this Kentucky redneck who can't tell the note of C-flat from J-sharp? . . . Well, dear hearts, where's Kenny Pumpkinface now? That's all Josey ever wants to ask stridently. And Josey doesn't mean Kenny Rogers.

Ah. Can you see the *real* point of Moment 2? Josey, the bitter. And the real point of Moment 1 was . . . ?

Moment 3: Lynette, Josey's wife then, always drank a Tom Collins with two cherries, please. Josey drank whatever the waitress brought. She didn't even like Bluegrass—Lynette, I mean, though likely the waitresses didn't either. Lynette could, however, tie a cherry stem into a knot with her tongue, and this struck Josey as something of a moral feat.

Moment 4: J. D. Crowe playing banjo so stiffly under his sandy hair that it was clear nothing else in the world mattered to him, though Josey much later heard a rumor that J. D. became a postal clerk who complained that, "No one listens to bluegrass." He should never have said that. He should have capitalized "Bluegrass." He should have just kept quiet and plunked his banjo. He should have gone postal. I mean, you can't disparage people's entire moral systems in public.

Moment 5: Josey really ought to remember something about his first wife, Lynette. Really. I'm sorry for him, I'm sorry for her, I'm sorry for all of us—because he doesn't. Did she like Bluegrass? He can't even remember the answer to that from eleven lines back. What would embrace sufficient galactic punishment for his callow laxity? Friedrich Nietzsche coined the myth of the Eternal Return. Perhaps that chore would suffice. Other than the mythos of this never-ending return, Nietzsche gave us the death of God and composed piano concertos. Given the right *zeitgeist*, Friedrich might have been a Bluegrass aficionado, camping onstage at Holiday Inn and composing "The Eternal Milk Run," "The Hermit's Last Words," or "God's Little Rosewood Casket."

Oh yeah, the concept of resentment—Nietzsche bears responsibility for that too. What song might Friedrich have written to illustrate resentment? "Siccin' Them Coon Dogs on My Too Musical Brother-in-law"?

Moment 6: This moment really isn't a moment, it's now. Well, I guess that's a moment, though "now" never seems to be. Now, Josey is listening to Tony Rice on a CD singing, "What Have They Done to the Old Home Place?" Being a Socratically wise Bluegrass musician, Tony offers no answers; he fills his song only with rhetorical questions.

Moment 7: Let me step in here, since I can remember something for Josey, something he told me inside an I-75 truck stop over burnt coffee and wet pancakes. He remembered playing a Bluegrass cassette of J. D. Crowe for his mom when she was alive. This was when he'd been living in Florida, pretending to enjoy the heavy sun down there, though how he could feel it from the confines of roadside ditches escapes me. Anyway, hearing the cassette, Josey's mother thought that maybe Josey'd been in Kentucky longer than he'd admitted to, that he hadn't dropped in to fulfill his filial duties right away. "No, Mom, Bluegrass is popular everywhere now." / "Why?" she asked. "All that sad hillbilly horseshit. Why?"/ As if working a tobacco allotment with a mule, Josey stared at the table and its thick coat of varnish his mother'd plopped on two years before. Noise and laughter were blaring on TV, for his mother, you should know, was a devotee of TV; and a crossword puzzle lay prostrate before her, halfway completed, on that table's ridiculous furrowed glaze, for she was also a devotee of crosswords.

LISTEN. Maybe your mom never uses the word "horseshit." Maybe she never works a crossword as if mining for runes, stopping to gaze at you with steel-cold hillside eyes. Maybe, just maybe, you could have come up with a veracious response to her one-word refutation of an entire Bluegrass moral system. Maybe you could have inserted a sturdy tobacco stick to stave up both local color and galactic eschatology. But Josey couldn't.

And neither can I.

A Perfect Stranger

The Florida beer joint Tom and I haunted in Land O' Lakes employed an Australian barmaid who pulsed every American redblood's hemoglobic dream. She and I, countrymen of sorts, shared a Pavlovian joke: whenever I made entrance, she'd place a finger to her temple and trigger her thumb with an imaginary pistol shot. In canine salivary response I'd lap one beer, another, another . . . to the point of not so imaginary canine suicide. If she strolled off to other business, I'd whisper to Tom in what passed for wisdom and insight, "You just never know when and where you'll find true love—even with a perfect stranger."

"Ha. You should direct movies," was Tom's comeback.

And he was right, because Cupid took French leave from the land of Mickey Mouse.

"She's gone!" I wailed on not spotting her red Nissan as we pulled into the parking lot. Despite my oceanic sadness, Tom coaxed me out of the car with my own platitude, "You just never know when and where, Josey . . ."

"Fellas!" came a shout as the bar's pine door yanked my shirt. I looked toward the bar to see glacially glistening teeth and crooked arms. *Glacial Teeth?* All I can say is that while I freed my shirt from the damned door something set me uneasy, like bare electrical wires beside a full bath. I mean, this bartender looked as if he was intent on piloting a fighter plane to dive and strafe refugees.

"Give me a Bud Lite," Tom said.

"Give me a draft," I said.

Discord. And so soon. Where was true love, even true friendship, to be found? The presumed new bartender—he with the glacial teeth—fetched our beers.

Other than the absence of the Aussie barmaid other decorating changes struck me: an enlarged B+W photo of eight airmen posing on a tarmac before a bomber; another photo—in color—of yet another bomber flying high, plus a Magic-Markered sign reading "Strategic Air Command." I leaned. Yes, one of the brave airmen resembled . . . the new bartender. The new owner? "Tell you," this bartender/owner said, thunking our beers to test the bar's post-Colonial knotty pine craftsmanship. "Tell, you: somethin's gotta be done. There's kids in grade school stealin' and takin' drugs. What kind of school system's that?"

I turned, thinking he was finishing a conversation with someone returning from the bathroom. Nope. When I looked back—Whoa! Not only were those glacial teeth glinting, but the bomber on the tarmac was shimmying, as anxious to take off as the front door had been.

Uh, pardon me. Didn't I just walk in a perfect stranger?

I sniffed my draft for a submerged whiskey boilermaker or hallucinogen, then looked to the rotating ceiling fan. *A perfect stranger . . . love*, it whickered, just as it had with the Aussie barmaid. Was it possible that this glint-toothed dervish and I were about to become in-laws? Was his daughter back in the storage room shuffling beer cases? Outside planting petunias? You never can tell when or where you'll find true love, right? So instead of a political tirade, were the bartender's words a promise of future friendly Sundays nudging me about school children and bambinos while I filled myself with chicken-gizzards and pawed his daughter, the blushing twenty-three-year-old bride? But before I could go search for her in the storage room, Tom laughed.

"Ha. Yeah," he answered, being a true sport about truncated conversations and not being one to get lost in romantic petunia byways. "The school system's something, all right."

Oh yeah, the school system. Well, it consumed our first beer. But

Der Führer, as we came to label our strange friend, had other problems freighting down his mind, too. For one, he thought that the nig—well, our darker brethren—were driving up the prices of everything. Did we know that the wholesale cost of kegs had already increased and he'd owned the bar only a week? And there was this too: he wanted to install chessboards and backgammon—deliver the working folk of Land O' Lakes, Florida, some friendly, challenging sophistication.

"Yeah," I said, gaining ground to aid Tom's wide-eyed slack. "Chess'd go great in here."

Chess? Listen: the edge of cigar-making Tampa lay twenty miles south. Six miles east sprawled a cow farm where leathery cowboys rode roped and branded 'em with horses and dogs. In a swamp eight miles west burbled J.R.'s Hog Shop, "hog" meaning either Harley Davidson or Hefty Ogres & Grunts. Five miles north, a nudist colony was always getting busted for drugs. Between and all about, acres of house trailers stacked brittle retirees around and about golf courses, each golf green flapping a starched American flag. A red-blooded American flag, since we began on that hemoglobic subject. And to retain the subject, how's this for a topper: just one mile north, a ten-year-old girl's blood had been drained in satanic ritual. Chess?

My finger nudged an ashtray of butts. Check. . . . *eh, Mate*? I wept, I wept, I wept for the missing Aussie barmaid.

"And if that don't work," Der Führer continued as if he'd read my mind via micro-implants in the barstool (whereon my mind mostly resided), "If that don't work, I told the wife I'd turn this place into the biggest redneck joint you'd ever seen."

Not much magic needed there, Merlin.

Der Führer unloaded more freight from his troubled boxcar brain: "Last night two kids was in here—I mean they was drinking age and all, but kids. Cussin' and usin' all the four-letter words. The F-word too. Afterwards, I drove home thinking how glad I was the wife wasn't here. Tell you, I thought about pulling my Glock machine pistol from under the bar and warning them to keep a clean mouth . . . or else."

Holy Sh—oot.

"Yeah?" Tom began to watch Der Führer's hands. If they suddenly were to reach under the bar . . . well . . .

"I'm gonna get me a girl in here, something you guys can look at. One's starting today, soon."

Good move, Adolph. Then you can R & R to back acreage and excavate mass graves instead of planting petun—Be nice, Josey, I amended. After all, you never know when or where you're going to find love, even with a perfect stranger. So say something positive. "Yeah, the gal who worked here, the Aussie, she brought in a lot of guys. Ha. She brought me in like . . . like a worm playin' a bass," I finished brightly, proud of my tactic.

The owner cleared his throat with patriotic spittle: "She did . . . things in here that weren't right. Bad . . . things I can't talk about."

Bad.

Things.

Let's skim the possibilities: 1.) She snickered at Der Führer? 2.) Told dirty jokes about mothers and/or apple pies? 3,4,5.) Gave away a draft to pad her tip, burned the Freedom Fries, made out with a customer? 6.) Forgot to salute the new bombers?

"'Course, you had no way of knowing something like that."

"Thass right," Tom said, tipping his empty bottle. "We just talked to her over this bar." He gave the pine an honest, Colonial thud.

Tom, saving Josey from the Death Squad. Giving up on true love or any new true friendship, I called for another beer, hoping Der Führer's mounting profits wouldn't sponsor too many hollow-point bullets.

In strolled this blonde I'd seen haunting Wal-Mart, shop-carting up and down. She always posed a real test for my theorem about love being just around the corner, almost as much of one as this crook-armed owner did. I mean, every time I walked into Wal-Mart, she was there, a perfect stranger. But where was love? Melting amid chocolate-covered cherries? Burbling by the tropical fish and gerbils? But let me give her credit, for she likely thought the same: *Look at that bozo: every time I'm here, he's drooling over hardware. Doesn't he have anything to fondle but power tools?*

So in she strolled, I say, wearing a pink polka dot blouse, and around the bar she jounced, and down she plopped a heart-shaped, genuine purple leatherette purse. Under the fan's whip-whop, her eyes spattered like diamonelles. *Love, you never know when and . . .* Discreetly, I put a finger to my temple and pulled the trigger, thinking how a Glock would finish things nicely for me.

Though standing closer to us than she was, Der Führer handed her our second round of beers. "They go to them," he said with a backward nod, disseminating a CIA directive. I mean, with a stretch he could have served us, while it took two steps to reach her. And I mean, who the hell else *would* they go to? The bombardiers hanging on the wall?

Giving a diamonelle blink, she scooted us the beers and got them reversed. Der Führer chided as if she were a moron headed for the state euthanasia program, "No, no, no—just the opposite. Just the opposite.

"Fellas . . ." he continued, handing our money to the new barmaid. He watched as she rang up the bill. He watched as she counted our change. The black-and-white bomber—the one on the tarmac— revved all twenty jet engines. World peace hinged on her calculating everything right.

Praise the Lord, she did.

"Fellas," Der Führer said again, after sending the poor gal and her polka dots to polish scratched tables.

"Fellas," he said a magical third time, his eyes shifting when she was out of earshot. "I'm banding together a group of people who think America's gone far enough. Friends, that's what we'll be. Friends who get things done."

Like a rag doll, the barmaid dropped over the farthest table to flop face-up on the floor. Her mouth sprawled, as did her eyes. Gaping polka dots revealed three bullet holes, but the blood was gore-blood, dried and blackened. How . . .

". . . it's not political, though, we're just going to . . ."

The door to the men's room burst with a Whack! Three codgers on a lime-green golf cart puttered out, grim-faced, balancing bolt-action rifles from some dark, ancient war on their thighs. Atop their cart a tiny American flag flapped wildly, though there was no discernible breeze. Behind the cart two tied, teenaged boys were being dragged through chairs and tables to be slammed into a far pinball machine, which flashed this message: "Just Say No!" One codger hopped off and ungagged a boy. "You son of a bitch!" the kid shouted. A second oldster, relinquishing cart seat and rifle, slipped a golf iron from a green and white bag. "We'll teach you not to curse," he muttered. Straddling the boy, he began battering the kid's mouth and skull. The sounds turned liquid, sickening.

". . . at first, I thought we'd meet just once a week and talk over things we'd seen on TV and read in the newspapers—what can you trust from those liberal sons-of-guns? We oughta take their printing presses and dump them in the Gulf. . . ."

A thin, balding man jumped through the back door, both pate and pastel blue sports coat spattered with mustard, moldy cottage cheese, green peas, and torn Kleenex from some Dempster Dumpster. He glanced wildly for a place to hide. Too late. A rushing mob wedged him against the bar's far end. With their every shove, his body vibrated knotty pine against my elbows. Then two fat, red-faced men held his right hand on the counter while a sunk-cheeked woman slammed down a hatchet. One finger flipped like a Freedom fry. "Now type s'more of yore damned lies!" Her high Kentucky hill voice left him sucking air and spattering blood, holding his hand upward like Lady Liberty sporting her torch.

". . . you guys look like good fellas, and even though we were perfect strangers fifteen minutes ago, I know you like old friends. You don't have to tell me now. I'll just leave this pamphlet with you to think over. Here, let me buy you a couple of beers. There's a game on ESPN, isn't there?" He gave us two beers and winked, then turned on the TV.

On cue, the front door opened and a happy crowd of six bounded in. They had to stoop, for on their shoulders they were carrying someone who wore an old-fashioned checkered hat. My gosh, it's Paul Bear Bryant! *Whether a life-size dummy or the man's actual preserved corpse, I couldn't tell. They propped him atop a table and ordered beers and Freedom fries. His hat fell and a woman scrambled, jumping once, twice, to replace it amid cheers. "Blood makes the grass grow! Kill them, kill them!" they shouted, shaking the Bear until—I swear— he smiled.*

A cheer went up from the television.

Again the door clunked open, and three men struggling with something—a seven-foot white pole, ah a miniature goal post and— I'll be damned—the third man, a black guy, he wasn't helping—he was stripped nude and hanging by the neck from the post. "We was wondering what was taking you so long," the woman who'd fetched the Bear's hat joked. Her face was a swollen summer tomato and any minute I knew she'd belch. "We got hung up," one man cackled. They teetered so hard in laughing that the goal post threatened to knock over Bear Bryant, but their friends lurched to stabilize things. Once they had, I couldn't help but notice that what people say about dead hung men and erections isn't true. Either that or this black guy had been hanging so long that blood had settled past that part into his feet and calves.

The group, restless for Freedom fries, began chanting, "Hup, hup, hup!"

"You ready to go?" I asked Tom as we slugged down our beers.

"Yeah bo'," he answered, grinding his bottle on Der Führer's pamphlet.

"Fellas," Der Führer insisted, giving us a grand smile from the kitchen's deep fryer some ten feet away, where grease beaded his forehead in ghostly splotches. "Fellas. Come back real soon. Us Americans need to stick together. You just never know when and where you'll find a true friend, even with a perfect stranger."

Six Weeks Ago

"She's Greek. You know how I know?"

I take my eyes off her hair, as dark as desire, look at my Armenian friend Henry's heavy jowl, and I shrug.

"Thick ankles," he replies to his own question. "All Greek women have thick ankles. That and a puckered mouth with no sense of humor."

"She's laughing."

"Wait 'til you got her home. Sha-wham! Dried olives, hard bread, stinking goat cheese, lousy retsina wine—and no more laughing. The wine, only if you're lucky. That's why they got thick ankles: everything drains to their feet from all that salty puckering. You've eaten a Greek olive, right?"

The bartender and a regular customer laugh at our conversation. We all four give a last look at the woman, who's sitting in a booth so that we can get a clear view of her legs and those ankles, though not her face.

"Uh, Jeff, I'd better get that other cognac for . . . you-know-who," I tell the bartender, raising my eyebrows. He and the customer and Henry shake their heads. They're all in on the story and can barely believe it. . . .

That was six weeks plus ago. Henry no longer works here. Five months before that though, Henry and I started work at the Gray Nag Pub on the same day. The management had decided to class up the joint and go all-male at night. Let women serve burgers and iced tea, guys New York strips and cabernet. Fine with me. It's hard, you see, whenever you accidentally get flip-flopped atop the oppressee/oppressor cycle, to remain politically correct. If you haven't yet found that out . . . with any luck, you will. So instead of sympathy marching for feminism I double-timed to and from the server's station to my tables—double-timed to beat a busboy to my tips.

And Henry? Armenian with that name? I was present at neither conception nor christening, so I can only report his side of the tale: yes, Henry; yes, Armenian, though second-generation. There's stranger than that, though, because Henry was a licensed jeweler who'd worked in the American Virgin Islands and made bucks—bucks enough that he gave me a Seiko watch just for drill. And just as strange was our meat-cutting chef who was at that very moment six weeks plus ago—and is at this very moment tonight—trying his—ahem—hand as Casanova with a knockout rich blonde out in the parking lot. As if his burnt-crisp version of black-and-blue steak wasn't bad enough. Me? I'm prancing around the floor as a philosopher-waiter—something akin to a singing gorilla, though nowhere as rare, at least in the sunshine state of Florida, where philosophical waiters/waitresses complete with tuxedo rent out for . . . say about ten-fifty a dozen.

So anyway, six weeks plus one day or one week ago, in-between Jean Paul Sartre's *Being and Nothingness,* in-between odd velvet pouches of diamond chips that Henry produced from who knows where, and in-between watching with drop-jawed gorilla amazement as our pimply, twenty-two year old chef diddled a Palm Beach socialite in the parking lot while her cotton-haired husband sat inside drinking Martell cognac—six weeks plus ago, I say, Henry and I once more hit the party circuit, which is considerable in West Palm, for that city allows drinking until five in the a.m. And if you're *really* thirsty and tip *really* well, you can drink at most bars for free until six, when regular hours resume. This likely represents a bargain the city politicos made with the devil their own six weeks before—or maybe with the Vanderbilts, Posts, and Kennedys, sixty years before. *Keep your hoi polloi across the intercoastal, keep 'em caged, slouching, liquored and oblivious, and we'll* . . . I have no idea what Palm Beach's aristocracy promised West Palm's politicos: senators' souls, a dozen savings and loans—something equitable, no doubt. Maybe indenturing Florida's entire working class for fifteen years.

Henry and I, twin pinnacles of *hoi polloi*, sat out that one-hour wait several times. One night at Ed's—an a.m. spot for waitresses, waiters, and other omni-sexual denizens . . . there, you see? I *can* show sympathy when I'm flopping downside with the oppressees—one late night Henry wrenched his Toyota's steering wheel to the left, then stomped the accelerator. Did that black sports car ever hop. Making donuts, the local boys called it. A local boy in blue sauntered over. "Son, if you even sit in this little car before daylight, I'll drop you in jail. Let a friend drive." Me, the friend. But some great or Greek god or goddess occasionally does protect drunks and idiots, so off we drove for beer and steaks, to return at dawn. No policeman, no wreck, no hangover.

Despite what I just glibbed out, not a damned thing in this world comes really free. I suppose people learn that at differing ages—most well before I ever caught a glimmer.

The beginning of my education imposed itself exactly six weeks ago when Henry and I were getting the Gray Nag ready for dinner, polishing silver, folding napkins, filling condiments—hoi-polloi stuff that would no doubt rend Jean Paul Sartre into the lower depths of Nothingness, like a prime French sow boiled to tallow. I was hustling— plip-plop, plip-plop, tossing down silverware—but Henry wasn't pulling his load. This wasn't normal: what was normal was for him and me to have a couple of drinks and glow cheerfully while awaiting socialite hordes to trip (tip!) in and be amused by our *hoi polloi* grins. Double check. . . . More than not pulling his load, Henry looked like— to borrow a phrase from my Kentucky past—horse hockey.

"I don't feel so hot."

Thirty-year-old Henry was rubbing his heart.

I drove him to the emergency room. By the time we reached the hospital he had to be taken in on a stretcher. Some asshole nurse yelled at me for not getting him there sooner. Fuck her, what'd I look like, a slick-haired medic racing an ambulance on prime TV?

A doctor collared me next morning when I came to visit: "Does your friend drink a lot?"

"I uh don't know, some—" I counted the booze we always matched—"about ten drinks a night." I figured I better stop with the first double digit I encountered.

The doctor watched my fingers twitching, then nodded. What we had was an understanding on one side: *See you in here soon, son. How about that corner bed over there, the one with all the pretty monitors and coiling tubes, will it suit you?*

On visiting Henry he was laughing, ticking a morbid list off his own fingers: "Kidney failure, liver failure, gall bladder failure, and a heart attack. The doc says I gotta stop drinking."

Henry had a genuinely happy laugh—rich, deep, and perfectly timed. I always wanted to fly to Armenia after hearing it. He even laughed as he said, "stop drinking," and I laughed too, looking down while he limply held his wrist as if the weight of the hospital's green plastic I.D. was overpowering.—*Yeah, stop drinking and decamp to Armenia to ride steeds, Bud-o'-mine. Let's blow this sterile popstand and these white-starched bitches who expect . . .* but when I looked at his pallid face, what we had was an understanding on one side: *Good god, I'm his age and I drink elbow for elbow, guzzle for guzzle. He pees, I pee. He drinks, I drink.*

Henry was young, so he was back to work in a week. We went out after work, of course, and he did try not to drink:

"Look," I finally said, tiring of his pasty face staring blankly across the bars and their fluorescent lighting. "You know you can't go cold turkey. Why don't you just order something like Kahlua and cream?"

It's a good thing that damned nurse wasn't hovering by the beer taps. If she hadn't been happy with my ambulance service, what would she think of my medical advice? But Henry had a unique solution that by-stepped both me and the medical profession. He got on heroin. Dime-bagging the dirty brown stuff and shooting up.

Two things happened here: Henry began running with another

waiter who shared his chemical viewpoint, and Henry's wife and two-year-old daughter drifted down from New York City. Wife and daughter? Yes, I vaguely remembered his mentioning their sitting patiently in some skylight apartment up in the Big Apple. But seeing them, staring them in the eyes, was, as Jean-Paul often points out in his grand tome, quite another matter.

I wasn't no damned ambulance driver, I wasn't no damned doctor, and I wasn't no damned marriage counselor. Still, drinking liquor with me had to be infinitely better than shooting up smack with the infamous Cal, our other waiter. So I toddled over to Henry's apartment, ostensibly wanting him to help me check the compression on the vintage 1950 Ford I'd bought, hoping I could also coax him out for a few beers and a heart-to-heart.

Ding-dong.

"Come on in, Josey. This is my wife, Dora."

"Hi, Dora."

Nothing.

The woman, despite her dark beauty, had just reinvented the ice age, and I was a fluff of prehistoric pollen, quick-frozen in her glacier.

Henry and I soon—very soon—retreated outside into the Florida heat to take the Ford's compression. Dora watched from concrete steps on the second flight. We passed a car with a bashed-in side and Henry elbowed me to snicker: "Downers, she was drinking vodka on top of downers two nights ago." The *she* certainly wasn't Dora. Dora was too viper-angry to drink anything without a vinegar base. I looked back and saw icicles calf from her folded arms, plunge from the balcony, and stab the blacktop, despite Florida's heat. Then I did a double-take on the bright blue car. It belonged to Theresa. My god, Theresa from Down Under, the blonde, laughing bartender who Henry had . . .

"Don't say anything to Dora about her living here."

No kidding.

106, 108, 112, 102, 95—40.

Yeah, well, that's about what I expected for a compression reading, a bum cylinder for a bum philosophical waiter. I sighed and glanced up: glaciers were now heaving the blacktop, creeping toward us.

"Want to go out for a beer?" I asked, watching Dora fold and refold her arms.

"No way." Henry wouldn't even look at the balcony. He laughed briefly, giving a sort of facial crack that made me want to fly to Armenia once more, but not for the same reason as before. This time I wanted to fly anywhere, anyplace where I wouldn't have to watch him grow thinner as he and Cal tied knots in their arms, as he and Dora tied knots in their guts.

A week later in my puttering Ford, I passed Henry and Cal in a car heading oppositely. We were supposed to meet, but they clearly weren't going to show. The heroin, working its geographical magic with SST velocity.

As I said earlier, Henry quit the Gray Nag. He landed a job as a jeweler. But a week after that he was again a waiter, somewhere else. I went to visit and he tried to talk me into changing jobs and coming over. He even slipped me a French wine opener and a free artichoke appetizer. I didn't protest, though his thick black eyebrows shifted, which made me wonder about his recent week's interlude as a jeweler. I wondered about his wife Dora, too, as I left the restaurant. I wondered about her and the kid stranded in New York City, about her standing on that Florida balcony like a bull glacier—then it dawned on me. Thick ankles, she had incredibly thick ankles. So she was Greek. Dried olives, crusty bread, goat cheese, lousy retsina, and Dora.

It was worth a chuckle, all worth a chuckle. Dora was a Greek calving glaciers; Henry an Armenian kicking alcohol with heroin; I a Southerner reading *Being and Nothingness* to overcome loneliness in West Palm; the Grey Nag's owners were Northerners relegating women who'd worked for them six, seven, and ten years to lunchtime burgers and fries; and Henry's little international daughter . . . better to leave that sadness alone. And the magnate from Palm Beach—you remember him from the beginning of the story, don't you?—Even now he still totes his young blonde wife in at least once a week to eat burnt black-and-blue steaks while he drinks cognac shamefacedly and she trots outside with our twenty-two-year-old chef to check the backseat springs of his green Dodge.

Here's how that little madness came about: Six weeks plus ago she'd insisted I take her to the kitchen to meet this chef of all chefs, since his steaks were so juicy. *Juicy.* She puckered that word with her Paris lips, drooling a steamy trail on our faux-silk napkins as her pale Palm Beach husband gripped the table with manicured fingernails. I didn't know it then, but this was a parade he'd likely watched many times. She wiggled out from the table and I had to blink not to pay too much attention to her short skirt. I led her back and was dismissed with, "I think *he* needs another cognac." *He* meaning her husband, of course.

"Hey, Tim, you got somethin' salty puckering the side of your mouth," I told our young chef of chefs as he shambled back inside half an hour later. She was still outside—re-arranging herself, I presumed. I'd been doing my best to keep the old Palm Beach guy in cognac.

"Really?" Tim gave a quick, guilty wipe and I gave a quick, cynical grin.

That was six weeks ago, thereabouts.

Tonight, I go through it all again, minus Henry: Martell cognac, Jeff the bartender and our faithful regular shaking their heads as I carry it away, and the guy's fingernails—polished with a clear fingernail polish that I notice for the first time—wearing a groove in the booth's wood.

So I think, Why not try the joke once more? Everyone else seems to be.

"Hey Tim, you got something on the side of your face." I make a motion with my finger when he walks in the door twenty minutes later.

"Really?"

And it turns out that really, he really does. Really. But hey, relax. We all do, every father-mother's son and daughter of us. And whether we're slithering down the oppressee/oppressor cycle or clambering up, it'll take a sight longer than any six weeks to clear it away. Really.

Judas

I ONLY MET HER ONCE more after that fall afternoon, and the meeting came around Christmas. She stood across the room with her back to the fireplace, looking out a window at snow falling in the nighttime, illuminated by a barn's safety light. It wasn't much of a snow, and it seemed that she had deteriorated since the fall afternoon when I first met her, for she had to lean against the windowsill to support her body. After that night she disappeared, as people are wont to do. I hope she's still alive, that maybe she's become a handicap rights lawyer piling litigation against idiots worldwide. Both times I saw her, I was visiting with my Aunt Lena, who wasn't really my aunt, but maintained the honorary title through some nebulous connection to my mother. On the fall afternoon I first mentioned, though only eleven, I was already perfecting my world's thinnest fat man act, being peacock-proud of a buckeye I'd found because it had a white blemish resembling an airplane. Here's what I now imagine about her on that afternoon. . . .

AFTER SCHOOL SHE WOULD PLAY ALONE behind the barn, picking up buckeyes in fall and four-leaf clovers in spring. Sometimes she wandered ahead from the space that was now for her, from the space where the straight line of black fencing reached with its creosote planks and stared with its knot-hole eyes. In that space that her mother couldn't see she would drop to the bluegrass and imagine countless peacocks, just like her own Judas, mounting countless fence posts to spread their plumage. But then those feathery eyes would stare too, those beaks would open in a peacock scream like they do, though no sound would come. The eyes, the posts, and the beaks stretched as far as she could see. A lead peacock would lift its right foot like a rooster lifting its spur; it would teeter on a post, ready to jump, and all the other peacocks would lift their right feet and teeter too. When she imagined this, she would cross her eyes until her nose intruded upon the dream. She knew it was her nose because it was ugly.

Then on Saturday came pies. It was the day when she got to scrape a bowl of sugared, half-cooked fruit, and chew strips of gummy dough. (God sakes, Leslie, stop! Don't eat anymore—it'll swell your belly. / She knows when to stop, it's instinctive with children. / Instinctive? Can you look at her and say *instinctive*? Tell me that one thing, will you, George? Someone has to watch her every minute. Don't lecture me about instinct, I'm her mother. / Stop it! / Well, look at her. / Come over here, Leslie, honey. Your mama really loves you. And me too. She—we didn't mean to yell. Come here and let Daddy wipe your pie-face.)

This Saturday was different. Daddy was at work and Aunt Lena was visiting with one of her boys or maybe with someone she babysat. It wasn't the one who wasn't afraid of the fence, the one who used to let her ride piggyback as he ran along the row. (The fence won't hurt you when I'm around. Touch it. See?) That one never came anymore. Aunt Lena said he got married. (Bill's wife thinks she is p-r-e-g-n-a-n-t. They've been fixing up their second room. / That's wonderful, Lena. We'll give them Leslie's old crib. / No! . . . I mean, Bill's father is making one already. You know how he likes to do things like that.)

It wasn't that one. It was a short and skinny one who somehow managed to have fat cheeks. Leslie could see him through the car's front window as Aunt Lena twirled his curly blonde hair with one hand while she pointed to Leslie with the other. The boy turned to stare big-eyed; then he rubbed his head against Aunt Lena's hand, just like he was a dog. Leslie had been talking to Judas, but the car had scared the peacock away. Aunt Lena got out and took the boy's hand.

"Josey, I want you and Leslie to play together while Alice and I talk. Leslie, why don't you show Josey your peafowl?"

"Peacock," Leslie whispered, because peafowl were tiny chickens. As soon as Aunt Lena walked away, Leslie drooled at the boy, hanging her tongue out one side. He didn't pay any attention, though. He just kept staring at the brace on her leg. When he bent to see how it ran up the huge oversize khaki shorts her mother'd bought, Leslie walked toward Judas. Between clomping steps she listened to hear whether the boy was following. She didn't think he was, so she turned. He pretended to look at something in his hand, though she knew he'd been still staring at her brace. She moved her hands to her hips, like she'd seen her mother do, and the brace let out a loud squeak like it sometimes did.

"Do you want to see Judas?"

He jerked, maybe because her voice sounded like an oompah horn, one of those fat German ones people blew when they ate sauerkraut. It reminded her of the box factory's whistle, which was supposed to sound at noon, but usually howled at five after instead. She hated the whistle, and during the summer she would sit in the barn in a stall and scream when it shrieked.

"I said, 'Do you want to see the buuuuurd?'" She hooted the last word. The boy only stared, squeezing his hand open and closed. So he really did have something there. Leslie slung her leg forward.

He didn't move until she tried to grab his hand; then he spun quickly and looked to the back door where Aunt Lena had disappeared.

"Do you want to see Judas or not?"

He nodded with his nearly white hair, which caught the sunlight.

"Let me see what's in your hand first." Leslie held her open palm in front of his face. He looked from it to her then stuck out his own open palm. It held a buckeye with a white splotch running down one side.

"I found it in the street yesterday."

Leslie had seen plenty of buckeyes behind the barn but never one with a white spot like this one. It looked like an airplane. She watched him put it to his nose. At first she thought he was going to eat it and decided she'd let him, even though buckeyes were poison, but changed her mind.

"Don't! They're bad for you!"

He laughed and held it out to her. She fingered it and shifted her weight.

"It's pretty." She started to rub it against her nose too, but she saw the boy again staring at her leg brace, so she flung the buckeye at the barn.

The boy's face puckered and she could see he was going to cry. She remembered the family dog shaking her black-and-white teddy bear, tossing it all over the living room rug. The dog had bitten into her bear when she tried to take it away, shaking it hard then leaving it on the floor to stare at her with two button eyes and a blue-gray tuft of lint pushing from its broken plastic nose. She'd hit the dog's skull with a book, sending it howling like the factory whistle. Like her. She hated the dog. Her mother had walked in while she was trying to re-stuff the bear's nose. (God help me! Sometimes I could just slap the living daylights out of you. If you were only—go to your room, just go to your room. Go!)

Giving a sniffle, the boy put a fist to his eye.

"Come on. I was only teasing. It's right over there near the barn. I can find it."

He followed.

The grass was tall. Leslie cocked her body at the spot where she thought she'd thrown the buckeye, and the boy peered down too. They walked circles around one another until the peacock strutted beside the barn to shrill loudly. The boy slid behind Leslie then.

"He won't hurt you." Leslie took dried corn from her pocket and threw some at Judas, who began pecking as soon as it hit the ground.

"See? That's just Judas. He doesn't do anything but eat and show off his tail feathers. It's because he's so pretty."

The boy remained behind Leslie until the bird found the last kernel and began dipping his head at Leslie.

"Do it, Judas. Show Josey."

The bird blinked its grey eyelids and wobbled its head; Leslie reached into her pocket and waited. When Judas shifted his weight and looked to the boy, Leslie rattled the kernels in her pocket. At last, the peacock spread its tail.

"See! See! I taught him that." Leslie started to throw more corn, but handed it to the boy instead. Josey took it and held his palm open for the bird.

"No! Not like that! He'll peck your hand miserable. You can't trust him. That's how he got his name in the first place." Leslie made a motion for the boy to throw the corn, and they stood watching after he did. The boy must have thought something, she thought.

"Do you know who Judas was?"

"A bird."

Leslie rolled her eyes at the peacock as if pleading for intelligent company.

"Do you want to see where buckeyes come from?"

The boy stared blankly.

"The thing you had in your hand. It was a buckeye. Do you want to see more?"

He nodded and they began walking to the other side of the barn.

"My mother said it was a chestnut."

"It's a buckeye. We have a whole tree of them in the back. They fall over the fence this time of year. I get as many as I want. They look like chestnuts, but you can't eat them like chestnuts. Chestnuts don't grow much in America anymore. Buckeyes are poison."

"Cree-ew!"

The boy jumped but Leslie reassured him: "That's only Judas. He's following us for more corn. I sound loud like him, but I don't eat corn." She watched the boy for a response, but he only stared at the ground. She looked at Judas, but the peacock wasn't laughing at her joke either.

The heat of October's Indian summer reflected off the black barn onto Leslie's face, and that must have reminded her of the fire her parents would sometimes start late at night when they were watching TV. If she was real quiet she could sneak from her room and watch too. She always tried not to laugh at the TV or at the things her parents did.

But she hadn't done that in a while. (I don't want her in a home.

She belongs here with us. / *With* us? She's not *with* us and never will be. Something else is wrong with her besides that leg and her voice. She's my flesh and blood, but you know what I say is true. What did her teacher tell you, the one that's so tall and blonde and has such a thing for you? / Not tonight, I don't want to talk about it anymore tonight. / We'll have to talk about it some night. I warn you, George, I'll not raise a normal infant alongside her. I don't know that I could even have a child now: I look at her and think I'm a biological failure.) Leslie touched her hand to the dried, black, creosoted wood of the barn. Josey did the same. They looked to the sun, then to Judas, three steps behind them.

"Can I give him more corn?"

"Wait till we get to the tree."

They turned the corner, Leslie banged on the barn's drainpipe with a stick she'd picked up, heard Josey bang on it behind her with his fist, and heard Judas peck it one time with its beak. She stopped where the shadow of the barn creeped toward the fencerow and its spiny planks and posts. Josey tumbled into her.

When Leslie first learned to walk with her brace, her mother had warned her about climbing the fence. The fence's planks were devil lips that gobbled up any little slow girl who came near. Once when Leslie showed for supper late and out of breath from playing behind the barn, her mother told her the fence circled the farm around dark, looking for anything stray to eat. After that, Leslie would memorize certain planks before she went inside for the evening, then check each morning to see whether they were out of place. Most of the time the fence returned to exactly where it had started. Sometimes not. Those were the nights, she decided, that the fence had found something to eat. She told her father. (What God-awful horror stories have you been telling this child? / I had to keep her away somehow, George. What if she crosses it and gets lost? Or falls so that she can't get back up? / How do you expect her to climb a fence with that damned brace? The doctors say she's lucky to walk. / There's my point, George, exactly my point.)

The planks today looked like they always did, except they were in the barn's shadow. She hadn't really seen them move for nearly a year now, so she hardly checked anymore. (See the tree way over there, Leslie? Bill kindly asked. Bill was just the type to play army with the stupid boy even though Bill was ten years older. That's a persimmon, Bill said. Come this fall and we'll go get some. Right over the fence. Go ahead, you can touch it while I'm here. But then he'd gotten married.)

She started looking for buckeyes. Josey pulled her arm and pointed to Judas pecking at something beneath a drainpipe.

"Okay, but throw them. Remember what I told you."

Josey took the kernels and sifted them from hand to hand. Leslie rattled the remainder in her pocket and Judas spread his tail.

"Throw them now."

Josey threw the kernels then stared at the pecking bird. Leslie began searching the yard's collection of prickly shells, the ones that she had been busting open for the last week and a half. At last she spotted one that had fallen recently and still contained a buckeye.

"Cre-ew!"

"Go away, Judas! We want to play know. Come over here, Josey." Leslie stepped on the full shell she'd found, covering it with her ugly brown and white shoe. Then she picked up a halved one she'd emptied days before. "These have buckeyes in them when they're full. Some have neat white patterns like what you had. All we have to do is look."

"Will we find another one with an airplane on it?"

She crinkled her brows. "If we look hard enough."

Josey circled Leslie, kicking through shells she'd already opened during the week. She moved her foot when Josey came near.

"There's one!" he shouted, pointing to the buckeye she'd stood on.

She showed him how to crack the outer shell with a rock.

"It doesn't have a plane. It doesn't even have a white spot at all."

They kept searching the yard, but Leslie had picked over the shells too carefully in the last week. Josey finally wandered toward the fence and stuck his head through its planks.

"I bet we could find an airplane and all kinds of things on the ones over there." He placed his foot on the bottom plank. "Look at all the shells."

Leslie began coughing, staring at the boy who was bumped over like a frog ready to hop. She studied the fence around him, its planks reassuringly in the same place they'd been for the past year, a knothole still spying from the middle board, the lower board still curving upward like a troll's belly. But when the boy-frog Josey bounced on that lower board, it didn't even seem to care, much less burp. And then he was on the second, and the knothole didn't even seem to blink.

"Wait for me!" Leslie swung her leg forward as the boy reached the top to straddle the post and look down at her. She reached to touch the middle plank, carefully avoiding its spying-eye knothole.

"It's just like walking up stairs, but you use your arms to pull too. See?" Josey backed down two rungs to demonstrate.

"I know how!"

She did as he suggested on the first rung, which was easy. She did the same on the next then looked to where her foot with the brace was: balanced right over the knothole. Josey was already climbing down the other side, so using one hand to hold on, Leslie used the other to help lift her brace over the top board. When she straddled that board she looked up to the sky, and when she did that, her insides stretched with cool air.

She heard a noise from the barn and turned to see Judas still pecking beneath the drainpipe near the corner timbering. She flapped her elbows at him and turned away, crossing her eyes until she could see the tip of her nose. Keeping it in focus she aimed it along the fencerow, lifting her face as the posts stretched into the distance. Her skin tingled with the sun's warmth. But she was cool and light and in the air. As she looked down the row, she realized it wasn't straight like she'd always thought, but that it wavered in and out with each post, like she walked, to finally disappear over the small hill before the road. She imagined hopping from one post to another until she too reached the road. She saw herself skipping to the neighbor's fence and continuing her trip until she reached the state highway. There'd be other fences too, that would lead to other highways.

"Come on! They're all over the place!"

Leslie worked her way down the three planks to the ground. Then she and Josey scoured the grass for the unopened, prickly buckeye shells, placing their grey-green husks on a flat fieldstone and slapping them with another feldstone. They tossed the empty shells to make a mound by a fence post, and soon the buckeyes themselves left their pockets bulging.

There weren't any airplanes, but they did find one white spot that looked like South America, one that looked like a three-pointed star, and one that Josey said looked like his art teacher.

"A round fat face with no ears. She's mean, too. She made me stand in a corner for making noise." Josey squeezed his palm underneath his armpit and flapped his arm to demonstrate the noise.

"Well, she should have made you stay after school. That's disgusting. My teacher made me stay after school."

"She said she would the next time I did it." Josey fingered a buckeye and looked at Leslie. "Why'd your teacher do that?"

"Because I beat up three boys and two girls."

"By yourself? Why'd you do that?"

"Come on, let's go look for more buckeyes."

"Tell me."

"I'll tell you the next time you come. We'll be friends then."

"Promise?"

"Promise."

They kicked their way through more shells, but then Judas started crying out, his screams echoing off the barn.

"Why won't he stop? It hurts my ears."

Leslie walked to the fence, and Judas headed for her. She shook her pants pockets, but they were too full of buckeyes to let the dried corn rattle. "Hush, Judas, hush, or they'll wonder what's going on."

"Aunt Lena would spank me if she knew I was over here."

"Well, what makes you think my mom wouldn't?" Leslie picked up a buckeye shell and threw it at the peacock. It hopped backward and was quiet for a moment. "And if she's really your aunt, then you'd have to be my brother, because my mom only has her for a sister." Judas started his cry again. Leslie and Josey both threw shells, bouncing one off the bird's neck and sending him loping.

They returned to gathering shells, soon just leaving them in their husks, stacking up cannonballs for the fort to use against Apache, then heaving them as chunkers against blackbirds in a nearby black cherry tree, finally counting the husks as pirate's gold ingots.

"What if they're dragon's teeth instead?"

"Leslie! Josey!"

Suddenly Leslie imagined her mother perched in the hayloft spying on her, since the shout seemed to fall from the sky like hard hail. She wanted to run into the woods with Josey and hide forever, eating persimmons and wild cherries, sowing dragon's teeth to keep people away.

"Aren't you going to answer?" Josey whispered.

"We're here!"

"You and Josey come on. It's time for pie."

The two scrambled for the fence.

"Race over!"

"Race!"

Josey was on the ground on the other side while Leslie was still trying to swing her brace over the top rung. Her pants pockets full of buckeyes squeezed tight. Suddenly the back of her leg was scraping against a splintering plank and when she grabbed the top board its black creosote mashed into her nose. She hung there, smelling pitch. Her eyes began to hurt, and then her leg, and then she began to cry. Josey held his breath and pushed her leg with the brace, boosting her up until she finally straddled the top plank. But she was shaking, and the back of her leg burned. She could feel blood trickling down and looked to her hands shivering and trying to clasp the fencepost. She expected the black planks would open their mouths and their teeth would lash at her. But beneath was only Josey, staring at her bleeding leg and the brace.

"I touched your brace."

"You can't catch what I have."

"You aren't really my sister."

"You can't catch what I have."

"Are you okay?"

"Yes, okay." She climbed down and they walked to the house together.

"You tore your brace. And there's blood."

Leslie looked around for Judas, but couldn't find him.

"What are you going to tell your mother?"

"Just that I fell behind the barn, that's all."

Aunt Lena met them at the back door. "Child, what have you done to your leg?" she asked in her high voice.

Leslie heard a pan clatter in the kitchen. "I fell behind the barn and cut it a little bit. That's all."

Looking behind Aunt Lena, she saw her mother run through the kitchen doorway, through the dark living room toward her.

"That's all! My God, what were you doing?" Her mother was pulling at one shoe and trying to unzip her pants at the same time.

"Momma! I'm okay!" Leslie fell against the wall to avoid her mother's grip. She saw the wide, staring eyes of Josey as her pink panties were exposed.

"Hold still!"

"Momma, I'm okay!"

"You're not okay. You've torn your brace to shreds! God knows what you've done to this damned leg!"

"What were you two doing, young man?" Aunt Lena asked.

"For God's sakes, Leslie! Quit tugging your pants back up and let me see that leg!"

"Momma-uh! Momma-uh!"

"She told me it was all right to climb the fence. She told me she did it all the time. She said if I didn't go with her, she'd hit me until I screamed like her."

Leslie thought of the twelve o'clock horn, how it echoed hate across the country all the way from town. She thought of Judas screaming, children yelling. She slapped her mother's hand away and pulled at her pocket to hurl the buckeyes, then the remaining corn, at everything moving in front of her.

From her room she heard the car start. She stared at the window and saw her nose reflected. Closing her eyes she knelt to lay her head on the sill by the open window. (I'm sorry, Lena. I don't know what to do with her. She's as sweet as corn pudding, and then she's a fury. She's a little Judas. Josey, she didn't hurt you, did she? / No ma'am. / Lena, I can't say how— / That' all right. It's a burden the whole family has to bear with you. I just thank God for Bill and boys like Josey. I just thank God.) Leslie wandered ahead to the space that wasn't allowed her. She saw rows of black fences staring with their knothole eyes. Teetering on the posts were peacocks just like Judas. They perched with their plumage spread, their feathery eyes all staring at her. Their mouths opened in a scream like they do.

"A-aaaa-uh!" She opened her eyes and saw her nose. She knew it was her nose.

The Odds Against Going to Heaven

Tuesday, May 20th

ON THE RADIO, WE HEAR that Reverend Nathaniel Hart of Graceville, Florida, has predicted the world will end in "fire and conflagration" on July 4th because God has "sickened with the United States and its peoples." He (Reverend Hart) has convinced 24 parishioners to travel with him to Mount Rushmore, where they will pray to God for America and Americans.

"What about the rest of the world?" I quip. But quietly I rearrange my Independence Day plans: Do something near water.

"Forget that mental trash." Jeff glances at my perspiring brow and punches the truck's cassette player. He laughs his two-beat laugh: rat-tat. "Just listen to the song, man, just listen."

We're going down a Florida road, the kind that usually arrows into a bull's eye of nothingness, though today we have a job at road's end. Jeff is driving—breakneck, of course. Six-point-five miles back, he had suggested that I "jump Cindy's bones." After that advice, say four-point-nine miles back, I'd insisted on recounting a recurrent dream: There's a room (a tomb?) surrounded by stained glass windows; inside it, me cold (old?); And booming through it, a godlike voice nudging me (judging me?) as I search for a passageway out.

Jeff had rolled his eyes.

Exactly two-point-zero miles ago, the news about the Reverend came on. And now, at the Zero Moment of Zen, Jeff is playing his favorite song, an early sixties hit called "A Walk on the Wild Side."

"Listen," he says.

I always do, though I don't suppose he ever really does, for the song jazzily exhorts sinners to shuck their evil ways and ease their bodies off that wicked side of the street.

> "One day of prayin' and six nights of havin' fun
> *The odds against going to heaven, six to one."*

"Six to one, you hear? Grab what you can. This is the nineties, man. Hippies and gurus are kaput. You keep 'getting your act together,' as you call it, and some screwball roofer with tar under his nails is going to snake you out of one fine woman. I mean Cindy, Bozo, in case you've forgotten her name. Hey, I'm surprised you don't want to take time off and climb Mount Rushmore with the good reverend. I'm sure he's getting his act together too."

I bridle, tapping my head against the truck's window. How can he have known me less than a year and hit every sore spot I have in twenty seconds?

"Hey, Josey, who was that hotshot philosopher you said made a bet about heaven?" He asks this as the song ends. At the same time, he snaps his finger to point out the glove compartment. I blindly grab for another casette.

The only one who hits the sore spots more often is me. I'm not sure how I ever saw the light to work instead of kow-towing for my M.A. in philosophy. An M.A. in philosophy and a roll of toilet paper will get you . . . go figure. And I'm doubly not sure how I ever managed to impress Cindy. A fine woman and a quarter will get you . . . well, I'm still trying to figure.

"Pascal," I say, returning to Jeff while fighting the jumble in the glove compartment.

"Yeah, Pascal. Your boy Pascal just didn't get a close enough look at *The Daily Racing Form*, you know?" Jeff rat-tats this out in the same smooth manner that he does everything, and I react by staring stupidly at the Tammy Wynette cassette in my hand: *Yeah, not a close enough look, all right.*

Later, after we've arrived at the job, poured concrete in some fool's launchway of a driveway, brushed it rough so Momma Fool won't slip in a summer thunderstorm, dinked our "company" initials in the mortar like high schoolers professing love—after all this and getting the check, of course—we stop at a run-and-go for beer.

Beer in hand, I, college graduate plus, try to explain to G.E.D.less bumpkin Jeff about moral fiber, America and the Third World. I'm taking up good Reverend Hart's argument, at least in spirit. "That's right," I intone, "even here in our own fine land, things aren't as swell as they seem. Case in hand—" I tap the truck's window as we pass Florida condos pretending that the scummy canal before them is the vast, clean Atlantic. "A fine job of zoning and sanitation," I comment, leaning to check the odometer. "We've travelled 25.9 tax-deductible miles," I add.

"You counting the stop for beer, Reverend?"

My brows gather as I scribble in an honest 24.7 instead. Then I babble about Afghanistan, Libya, Lebanon, Israel, about whatever politico scene is topical. "That's only the beginning," I intone, using my best post-baccalaureate cant. "Or rather, the ass-end of humanity's glorious history."

Oh yes, I'm a thinker, all right.

"What you need is some here-and-now grain cereal," Jeff says. He pops me a beer with one hand, and drives with the other.

What are we doing? Eighty? I lean to look at the speedometer. Fifty-eight.

Thursday, May 22

Two days on down and we are talking in a bar with Cindy, a woman who makes light shine even inside dark, Florida sarcophagi. But what to do about her and all that light? Marry? Join the Condo-ites in a barbecue before the scummy canal? Buy a BMW?

It's forty-three days until America's Boomday-Birthday. And yes, I'm canting again. I decide to play my ace card with Jeff, the non-believer. It's the card I evilly hope will stymie his no-stop life, for it's the *pons asinorum* that keeps kicking me with the angry hooves of a meat-headed jackass.

"Listen," I say. "If what you say is true, if we sneeze and slobber on this planet . . ." I zest my case with some Sam Beckett humor for Cindy's sake; after all, we recently drove 98.7 miles to Miami to see *Waiting for Godot.* "If we sneeze and slobber on this miry planet for sixty-seven odd years, seventy-one if we're female . . ." I nod to Cindy. "If we sneeze and slobber, then one bang morning we just flat disappear under gummy clay or wet sugar sand—well, what if we'd spent those average sixty-nine years fighting a single, crafty shoelace? What if we'd spent our time tying and then re-tying it, you know, and it just never broke, and what if the undertaker fancies this prize shoelace and he tosses it to his child or grandchild, who takes it outside and ties it to the leg of a June bug—and the damned shoelace still doesn't break? Don't you see? All that time. No soul, like you say, so we're dead as a stiff hen, but the shoelace waves on, supple in the sun. Beaten by a damned shoelace. KO'ed in 69th round. I give you Shoe-lace-a, the incontestable champ-een over humanity." I pause, out of breath. "That's if what you say is true. Can you really buy into that?"

I wait for a reaction.

"I'll have another Chivas, barkeep."

That is what he says. I'll have another scotch. Ah Truth, who wants your lies?

Cindy plops a lovely, tanned leg on our table and points to a mint-green shoelace interwoven with lemon striping. It's come undone. "Josey. Is this the one?" She looks at me and smiles. I return her smile and nod. She yanks, and the shoelace breaks. We give a cheer.

Jeff shakes his head. "You two, Pluto and Plato." His finger is starting upwards to tap his forehead, to indicate that we both think too much. Instead, his eyes set in a glimmer. "Damn, would you look at that honeybun who just walked in? Cindy, do you know her? Please say yes. I dream of women like that and me marooned on a sandy island. Sheday and me."

Hormones, I think, my shoulders falling. Freud was right. Hormones rule this precious green earth: the only archetypal thoughts we squeeze out in dreams are Buildings, Caves, and Bedroom Eyes. But when I dream of running away to a hot sandy shore where my feet can shift in the tide and my gullet can gullet all-day beer and my eyeballs can eyeball long, so-long legs . . . well, from nowhere, I mean from flat nowhere, I suddenly spot Jesus traipsing down said tropical shore and gently slipping my hands inside his five slim but jagged wounds, one bloody wound at a time, one at a winceless time. Or if I'm in an agnostic mood, it won't be Jesus, but Nietzsche descending Bald Mountain with his eagle, slogging to the shoreline, there pleading humbly, numbly, sadly, madly on syphilitic knees for the drayman to whip him rather than the poor mule carting Sno-cones about. So the sandy shore and the icy beer and the honey that just walked in the door and the cleansing tide—all disappear as my pea brain blisters with some philosophico-religico-armtwister-gutbuster racing mental trash through my head.

Friday, May 30

MEANWHILE, WHAT DAY IS IT? I know. I can't help but know. Memorial Day, the ticking away of the millennium, wherein years are growing, time diminishing. It's 5:32:04, :05 p.m. . . . . :06 p.m. Mental trash.

We are alone. I don't mean in the Universe . . . or maybe I do. No, what I mean is that Cindy's gone. She's over at the bar where she works. It's after our Friday job, and my man Jeff has cashed the check and is lifting his leg like a dog kicking grass that it's wet, and he's not really caring about the eschatology of the cue ball he just hit—he's caring if the sweet potato brunette standing nearby noticed his grin. And honey, she did. Click!

One atomic blast would prove both him and the sweet potato wrong. Or would that be me proved wrong, honored Epicurus? Should I do as Jeff says? Grab Cindy before Armageddon? The brunette catches Jeff's leg as he leans to make some ridiculous bank shot. He jiggles, she scratches, then he scratches. I mean, both crotch and cue ball. So, the game's mine if I play everything right, isn't it?

They both giggle.

Saturday, June 7th

I WATCH JEFF STRAP A MOTORCYCLE to 110. Not in a death-wish sort of way, but to squeeze miles into that moment.

"Lord!" he yelps when he gets off the bike. Somehow he's managed to drop an extra rat-tat laugh into the middle of that one word, to explode it about ground zero.

"You want to try this horse?" he asks.

I gear it to 70, and for a minute the goddamned air on my face makes me think that I've finally gotten hold of something, that I've finally seen a Zen flash and that things will be better ever after: Honda Satori. Then I look wide-eyed at the climbing speedometer and back off. This Japanese dragon could flip over a wad of chewing gum and spatter my American brains across two roads. Both wider than any *pons asinorum*.

Zen says that after Enlightenment, the air smells like air once more and the roads stretch ahead of you like roads stretching ahead of you. Me, I thought the air smelled *good* when I was doing 70. Thinking, that was my mistake. Mental trash.

"She's something, ain't she?"

"Sure is." I get off the war chariot. Jeff one-wheels it to behind the house, then re-appears with two beers.

"Let's go," he says.

Go. That words reigns. Heraclitus would have appreciated this American. A simple *go* that's fascinated with life. I mean the every goddamned second fascination of people who refuse to ponder, because when they ponder, they're reflecting, dwelling, dawdling—and that's time gone, baby, gone. Like the river and Heraclitus, like Jack Kerouac.

I tried to get Jeff to read the Beat King once; not that Kerouac is exactly the heavy hitter of the philosophy department, but I figured that Kerouac would get Jeff started. "What's that he says?" Jeff asked after several pages. "He's says never to yawn, because life's too exciting. You think you gotta read to know that?" Jeff had nudged the yellow book back to me like it was soured pizza dough.

"Go," he says now, angry that he's had to repeat the obvious.

And me, the New Wave workingman's Marx, gets into the truck to consult . . . my crystals? My telepathic Cro-Magnon? Nietzsche?

Kant? Buddha? The Amway Plan?

We drive. *Go.* He's taking in the palmettos lining the road; I know he can see each separate one, while I see only a gray-green blur. *Palmetto-ness. Will I ever truly know it?*

"They say some son-of-a-bitch hermit used to live back in there the early part of the century," he says, sipping his beer. "The story goes that he had two daughters and wouldn't let them out because he thought the invention of the car signaled the Second Coming. He kept those two girls clean out of the world. Made them weird and unnatural. Story goes that they were raven-haired and wild-eyed, that they could confront a hunter face-to-face and make him turn his own gun on himself. They'd find dead hunters back there with pages of the Bible pinned to their jackets. People always thought the girls were trying to leave some big message. . . . Sort of like you, you know? But by the time anyone got to the hunters they were just skeletons, their jackets rotted, and those big-message pages were bleached whiter than sugar sand." He takes another sip of beer and gives the wheel a jerk that bolts me upright.

"You think Cindy will be working tonight?" he asks.

Cindy? Who is . . .

I'd seized on that story of the old man and his daughters with the fierceness of an archaeologist eyeing a half-buried tomb, hoping it would reveal the cornerstone of the temple, which would reveal the cornerstone of the urban sixth layer, which would reveal the cornerstone of subsequent city-state layers, which would reveal the cornerstone . . . of all global civilization. I envisioned two blazing Amazonian sisters with their right breasts neatly removed; I envisioned them delicately toting the egg of life on a purple, silken litter. Behind then strutted worlds fighting one another: Persians against Greeks, Greeks against Romans, Romans against Christians, great Industrial monsters clashing with icons of the Sacred Heart. And behind those swaggering mechanical Cadillacs, another noise already nipped at Detroit's rusting tailpipe: the newborn Taoist-Marxist God. In that story of the old man and his two daughters I envisioned the ruthless circles of history.

Come down, come down . . . *Is Cindy working tonight?*

"I don't know. Why do you ask?"

"Why? You ought to be staking your territory, that's why. She likes you. You like her. Women need the smell of a man. For that matter, men need the smell of women. We're all just too stupid to admit it. Listen to the song, Josey, listen to the song. *Walk on the wild side.*"

What the hell is he saying? I feel like an astrophysicist debating a freshwater game warden.

"What about the girls?" I ask.

"What girls?"

"The ones in the woods who could make hunters kill themselves."

He sips his beer. As we drive along, Australian pines overtake the palmetto scrub and cypress. He taps his head at me and turns on the radio. I look out the window to *pine-ness*. I press against the glass and listen for its secret atman-breath. . . .

—Are you girls out there?

They laugh at my question and their dark eyes scan me.

—I'm here hunting pig and got separated from my friend. I think he's over that way. I point. You know, it's dangerous out here for two girls (no, too condescending) it's dangerous out here without a gun.

They smile and motion me to follow. The scrub changes to tall oaks and darkly clinging vines that drip downward like spinal cords. I smell the wet of a long rain. Suddenly a cave opens before me, a cyclopean eye. As they walk into it their gowns glow with a lapis lazuli hardness. I recognize that they are the handmaidens of wisdom. "Sophia!" I shout. "Sophia!" But they've already disappeared into the cave. I plunge in and behind a huge boulder they wait, smiling. Dead hunters are spiked to the walls like salted pig, their stiff, hog heads facing the rear of the cave. There I discern a glow emanating from a golden book. I look to the handmaidens and see only bare, sharp teeth.

Jeff's yelling at some guy seven cars away, asking him if Cindy's working tonight. We've pulled into the parking lot of the famed Black Forest.

"Ya, ya, Cindy ist vorking tonacht."

It's a joke. Every moron who goes to the Black Forest comes out after two beers talking like a burgher. We try to grin as we get out of the truck.

When you enter the Black Forest Bar, you immediately know you are in the presence of tastelessness. Before you, in a hallway and hanging over a lintel, are two imported deer heads, imported from somewhere where real deer roam, not Florida puppy-dog deer. A picture of the Alps separates those two deer as surely as God separated body and soul. The picture itself is lit by a Budweiser bottle happily skiing down a virgin slope.

Jeff likes it. He reaches up and brushes one of the deers' necks every time he enters. A different one each time, he declares. It's the closest he's come to admitting either cosmology or eschatology. And what, I always ask, about the picture of the Alps lit by a skiing bottle of Bud? What inspiration does that bring besides Onan's orgy?

He rubs the left deer's head and laughs. . . . Yeah, it *was* the right deer he rubbed last time we were in, so maybe he really does . . . I look at the deer and think of Jeff as the hunter encountering the two waifs:

—You two must be snipe-hunting out here. They giggle. No? I could have sworn so, because you don't need a gun to snipe-hunt. But I should've known, because it takes a man and a woman—or women— to hunt snipe. And he reaches into his backpack and somehow pulls out three icy cold beers. Let's go, he says. And they say, Yeah. The first word they've spoken since their father hid them in these wretched lonely swamps: Yeah. The old world has crumbled. Long live the new.

All the beer in the Black Forest gets served to 'Mug Club members' in county fair German mugs that depict a man in relief holding a county Fair German mug midair in a toast—all to the everlasting admiration of his woman, who is also holding a county fair German mug midair in a toast. If you look closely, you can see the scene repeating midget progeny, *ad infinitum*, like Banquo's descendents in *MacBeth*. How could Germany ever produce great thinkers, I wonder while gripping my mug. Then I reconsider: how could any country *besides* Germany produce great thinkers, its burghers being glazed eternally between the laughter of birth and the tragedy of death, the lightning of war and the gangrene of defeat. Fraulein Oprah conducting Wagner's *Flying Dutchman*, Herr Hiraldo Revera blasting on a farting oompah tuba.

Where else could a sane German turn except philosophy?

Cindy walks up in her *jungfrau* outfit. Is she my Margaret? I, her Faust? Then Jeff would be Mephistopheles? I watch him order a beer—the same, I tell Cindy—I watch him, his eyes darting the room, graciously scanning Cindy's tanned legs, never looking to the mirror behind the bar. Why not? Is he among the undead? I search for his face behind the bottles lined against the wall mirror. I see only my own and immediately scowl.

—Our poppa says we shouldn't talk with strangers. —Why's that? Jeff the hunter asks, not really awaiting an answer. I'll tell you why. He's afraid of losing two good-looking gals like you. What would he stare at if you two left? His whiskers? Say, isn't your momma enough for the old man?. . .Go ahead, honey, and knock that beer on down, there's plenty more. She does, then speaks: —Our momma died three years ago. She woke up one day alive then went to sleep dead. The silent one (who looks like Cindy with those long legs and that silky blonde hair), it's her turn to speak now: —Our poppa says that the end is coming soon, that those in the city will go first and hardest. He says that automobiles are the handcraft of the Devil. Jeff takes her in his arms, her body coupling with his like an electrical socket. —No, my sweet child, Jeff says. The Devil could never make anything that moves so fast. Automobiles are the work of the Lord. Life, don't you see, moves too fast for there to be a Devil. Life stays one footstep ahead of any devil. That's why you should never slow down.

Cindy stands before the jukebox. Jeff smiles, I smile, we know what she will play. An elbow blasts my ribs like God must have blasted Adam.

"What are you thinking, Man? Always thinking." He points to my beer.

"Listen to the song," I say.

"You got it. Listen to the song." He lifts his mug in a toast. I try not to look at the eternal line of burghers and frauleins.

I know what he hears. But I keep envisioning some damned intruding philosopher who glares in warning, if not of heaven and hell, then at least of some final balance sheet that sets everyone's life in a minutely detailed frieze—maybe not as looming as Mount Rushmore, but as large as individual morality, responsibility, integrity and death.

You walk on the wild side; you better cross over.

Jeff smiles a Buddha smile, all the while swaying to the saxophone beat.

"What you need, man—"

I wait. What I need is not to wait, not to think, but to do, to scatter rice seedlings in the paddy at planting, to swim with the tadpoles of God.

"What you need is a woman." He snaps his fingers toward Cindy, who has waved her pearl nails at us in a jazz riff. "To keep your head from burning."

Mephistopheles.

"I had a French friend who said only Americans are naive enough to take Freud seriously—his sublimation-frustration bit, she meant." I tell this to Jeff.

"France and Freud. Neither one's the big F you need."

And while Jeff proceeds to tell me just what big F I need, I think of Descartes, the Frenchman who proved beyond any logical doubt not only that he himself existed, but that there could be no such phenomenon as a vacuum. It's crystal clear, he argued, for not only does nature abhor a vacuum, but the existence of a vacuum would indicate a trifle of space, however minuscule, that could never participate in God's omnipotent, omnipresent will. Ergo, the existence of a vacuum would indicate . . . the non-existence of God.

The palmettos are scratching me mercilessly as I struggle through the swamp and its scummy canal. I see a cave, opening like a womb. Plato's Cave of Wisdom? Come, child, come. Out of the city. *She is walking toward the cave also, her dress torn to reveal tanned, brown, animal legs, but I reach the mouth first. Its rock walls seem smooth after the stinging palmetto tips and the fireants. Its inner shade caresses my back and head. Farther inside, on an altar, sits a book, its writing holographing many languages.* Come, child, come. Learn Sophia's secrets, enjoy Sophia's shade. *A hand covers mine. Soft, yet it burns with sunshine's vigor. I cannot help myself; I look from the book and turn to her wild eyes, her tangled black hair.*

"A woman would slow me down," I stupidly tell Jeff.

"Slow? You? You're a caterpillar at most. Look at those legs over there and tell me they would slow *you* down." He nods towards Cindy, who struts around the end of the bar. "You know what slows you down? His nod dips like a tipped-over metronome. "*That* slows you down." He points to my head. "Mental trash. You think life's a dream and you're some kind of butterfly."

A modern Faust, am I to ignore the second part of the tragedy, the revitalization of the canal? Am I to sway about the Black Forest, that dank dungeon, amuck, amuck? *Daylight is coming! Daylight is coming! Is it? Is it?*

Now behind the bar, Cindy stops in front of me. Jeff knees me. I look at her, but to her right I notice a clock. It has somehow passed midnight. So it's June 8. Twenty-six more days.

"Say, Cindy, what are you doing for July 4th?"

She gives a laugh and shrugs. Jeff's beating my knee with his own.

"I don't know, Josey. Why?"

"I just wondered if you'd like to go snorkeling or fishing. Something on or near water."

She raises her eyebrows to Jeff for confirmation. He drinks his beer and grins.

"Sure, why not? I don't wanna be pushy, Josey, but are we allowed to do something in-between now and then, too?"

In-between? A word whose existence I'd forgotten.

On the jukebox, the chorus sings one last time. *One day of praying and six nights of havin' fun. The odds against going to heaven, six to one.*

We all three listen, each of us hearing what we must.

Chewing Tobacco and Other Splendid Inventions

WHEN I IMAGINE UNDERTAKERS trying to fit *moi*, the world's thinnest fat man, into a coffin, I have to laugh: *"On the count of three twist hard, guys; it's the mouth that's giving us the problem. Alive, a mouth like this'd mush your ears to cabbage. Heave! Ho! Heave! Ho! Heave! . . ."*

But I'm working on a dual invention to prevent this scenario, for while many people insist they don't care what happens to their dead corpus, I look upon mine—if not as a temple—at least as a portable freezer chocked with fine worm casserole and delectable fluid vital for nourishing the ecosystem.

Why a dual invention, you ask? Because its purposes encompass not only said eco-system, but our fragile society. Briefly, my dual invention is an insert to be placed in my mouth—or any mouth that suffers embarrassing hyper-extension—to re-hinge and tighten jaw muscles upon receipt of a stressor code from the mastoid gland (the mastoid being seated just over the brain stem, wherefrom it secretes anger, angst, frustration, idiocy, hormone or alcohol imbalance.) If any such phenomenon should prod mastoid secretions past a determined point, say ZipNull-squared, my dual invention's bio-electronics will tighten the jaw muscles and thereby impede, if not downright prevent, unwanted, insipid, or ungainly speech. If I'd been born with such a device—or at least had one implanted at birth—I'd never have needed to undertake (no pun intended) the dreadful occupation of being the world's thinnest fat man. There's no changing that, however. But it goes beyond me, so I ask with a plenitude of societal concern: Just how many others wish I'd had a similar device inserted at birth? Indeed, how many others wish they themselves had had such a device inserted at birth?

So I work night and day, day and night, over my invention, for just as the enormity of my mouth's self-absorption is bound to invite trouble even in the casket facing death, it continually does so in the open air during life. This has posed no minor problem for me, and also I confess, for the eco-system itself. All that hot air, I mean: more plenteous than cumulus clouds absorbing cow farts to poison the atmosphere with methane.

& & &.

Upon becoming aware of the mastoid, I experimented with wads of processed chewing tobacco, hoping they might impede or at least render indecipherable any rash words. Useless, useless, for not only did my tongue jabber directly through the tobacco—whether in compressed or flake form—but a brown spittle continually dribbled from my mouth upon chance delicate violets and all my best pink shirts. With an uncharacteristic surge of gregarity after examining a speckled shirt one night, I became convinced that the resultant viral mosaics might be useful to biological science, but when I shipped them to an esteemed state institute I was treated most indecorously in reply. To top the insult of an Alabama state trooper at my door, there was a sizable monetary fine for sending biohazardous material through the P. O. In pure fact, I was nearly over my chewing tobacco phase anyway, for I'd come to suspect that the sugars laced in processed tobacco exacerbated rather than inhibited my rash comments. Nonetheless, sugar intolerance be damned, I herewith aver that I was neither baying nor barking, as the trooper testified in county court. . . .

& & &.

Surely, my dual invention will work better than chewing tobacco, since my invention contains no sugars, fats, carbohydrates, or dog bones. Here I must tell you that though the opening vision of my burial and those squalid undertakers inspired my invention's creation, and though eco-concern has prodded it along, it was the eschatology of finality that imbued it with a capping significance. For my invention will set in motion, upon rigor mortis (whose onset mimics mastoidal over-stimulation), an endless-loop mini-cassette recorded with my favorite epithets and scatological comments, and played at a decibelage loud enough to forestall grave robbers, Pentecostal preachers, or crematorium-minded undertakers until my body fluids can melt into the good earth to feed tomatoes, fresh air, corn, and fried okra. Again, note my concern for the eco-system! So while, as I insist, my invention will accomplish all this upon death, its hinges will also serve as a handy prophylactic while I live. Again, note my concern for society! Not only that state trooper but endless others have misjudged me.

But here, let's look in on a hypothetical funeral home for proof:

"Watch where you put your damned pudgy fingers," my invention will intone as rigor mortis triggers it. "Because this jerk purposefully contracted AIDS to demonstrate his third world solidarity." Can you imagine the mortician's look? And what of his young assistant, that gal who just graduated from Tupelo School of Mortuary Science?

Though I don't reside in a lightning-tossed castle wherein I can refine my invention, a metal lawnmower shed with its wasps and mice has served well. For six weeks after envisioning those lousy undertakers, I worked ass-iduously, logging my grandest witticisms, epithets, and slurs to the sound of vibrating wings and munching mouths. I made sixteen trips to Wal-Mart for blank mini-cassettes, the expensive long-lasting kind, and I spent sweaty nights in that shed recording my past gems. Herein follow a select duo:

"That's your sister's **bridal** *bouquet? Serious? I thought it was a water-logged hornet's nest."* (Said to a previous acquaintance.)

"I'm not trying to hurt your feelings, but do you really think you're bright enough to matriculate into law school?" (Said to a favorite student.)

& & &.

SOMETHING STRANGE HAPPENED while I was recording those raw

gems: after my dozenth trip, Wal-Mart's staff were no longer avoiding but were actually magnetically drawn to me. Had wasp-sting venom from the shed mellowed my mastoid? Had furry mice nibbling my toes improved my mood? No matter, for the shed will soon be passé. My dual invention is almost finished. A week more, tops. Meanwhile, I'm calling the Patent Bureau in Washington D.C., to get this thing registered. There are people out there who need it desperately! Again, note my rush of gregarious—dare I even say amphibious—charity.

"United States Patent Office. May I help you?"

"Yes, this is Josey, the World's Thinnest Fat Man, calling from Alabama."

"Did you say Kentucky?"

"No, I've moved to Alabama."

A thud, as if the phone's been dropped, then a muffled voice saying "That figures," and then other lines picking up. Click, click; click, click. . . . Hundreds! Even bureaucrats over in the Library of Congress must be listening in.

So my reputation has proceeded me.

"Yes, go ahead, ma'am—I mean sir."

"That's all right, a lot of people mistake me for a lady because of the beard."

"The beard?"

I rub it on the telephone's mouthpiece with a scritch.

"Just a little joke. Listen, why I've called is to let you know that I've invented something revolutionary—something that can work on both the living and the dead, on a dead or living mastoid gland."

"A mastoid—what?"

"Gland. I discovered its existence as a teenager—me as a teen, not the mastoid as one, that is. Ha. That's a little joke, too. Anyway, the mastoid's that part of the brain that teenage hormones incite most, along with pimples, pubic hair, and musk."

Though I'm trying to describe the mastoid *clinically*, I hear snickers and snorts. That's all right: idiocy among minions I'm prepared for.

"Since my invention will key into the mastoid," I continue, "it will revolutionize social interaction—especially for the inept." Like a sharpshooter aiming and pulling the trigger, I carefully blast the two-syllable word *in-ept* through those wires at whoever dared to laugh. War is swell, as Sherman taught us.

"So I'd like you to go ahead and fax me a patent number right away, as my machine is almost ready and people await it."

"Sir, we can't just give out registration numbers over the phone. We have to physically see a working model of the invention."

"A working—but my invention works only when I'm saying something farcical or drunken—surely you can't expect me to perform in front of total strangers, can you?" Immediately, I realize the farcicality of my very statement, for my machine has been necessitated by a myriad of just such performances:

"Marian, can you imagine us entwining and growing old like those two trees along the bank? Ah, love." Then I overturned the canoe into moccasin-plagued waters. It was our last date. Marian, was that her name? Marla?

Here's a bonus: *"Whadya mean I've had enough to drink?"* Um, was that before or after I put Tabasco in my schnapps?

"Sir? Sir?"

It's the woman on the Patent Office line. I nearly forgot, having become so immersed in past vocal transgressions before other perfect strangers.

"I'm still here." I sigh as a sign of my still here-ness. As I do, a familiar tingling stirs my temples, rotating from the base of my skull. *The mastoid cometh.* I inhale deeply, for on occasion oxygen can quell a mastoidal onset. Letting out the tiniest burp, I speak in falsetto, then with perfect calm, intone: *"And naturally*, the other part of my invention only works after I'm dead and rigor mortis has set in. You see, the body is a temple of ecological food that shouldn't be destroyed by formaldehyde. By that I mean that our blood is a sacred nutrient that mustn't be drained by fraudulent undertakers to be cast into sewers and water reclamation systems. You wouldn't do it to eyeball fluid, right?"

Distant receivers clunk. Well, the truth must out. The woman herself remains silent. From the quality of her silence, I ascertain that she's lovely in the extreme.

"Listen, I know you're busy and have lots of silly bureaucratic rules that you as a beautiful, thinking feminine person aren't particularly responsible for, but this here is important. Can't you just make one exception and issue a registration number over the phone?"

"Sir, sir, I'm sorry, but my other line is ringing. Can you hold?"

"Surely, but this *is* long distance."

"Maybe you'd rather call back. . . ."

"No, no, I'll hold." Do I detect a laugh, or is it a muffled scream?

To entertain myself and drown the militant Muzak that the Patent Office broadcasts to torture callers, I press the playback button on my invention. My nasal voice and the following gems override an especially insipid rendition of "Raindrops Keep Fallin' on My Head":

"The only good child is a mummified child." Now when did I say that? I don't remember addressing the La Leche League.

"I can't believe you're eating all those French fries. Aren't you concerned about becoming even fatter?" Oh yes, I remember her. She told me she was going to the ladies' room then called a cab.

"Jesus Frig. H. Christ. Even a Roman Catholic would have more class than to eat this tuna salad.—Oh dear, you are? Well, some of my best friends—"

"Sir? Are you still holding?"

I look at my watch; it's been ten minutes. "Yes, yes I am, thank you."

An ineffable noise trips through the telephone wire. A weep? A sigh? A chipped tooth?

"You have a hard job, I'm sure," I say to the silence. "I didn't mean to upset you with my talk of eyeballs and spilt blood, but you must understand their importance to my invention. And vice-versa, for my invention will be the downfall of the undertaking industry and we will hitherto bury *au naturel.* Just imagine what my invention will do for the breathing world's ecology, not to mention the global peace it will promote. What's your name, by the way, darling?"

"Ms. Griswald. Darling."

"Griswald. That's a lovely name. Do you have a first name?"

"Yes."

I press my ear to the receiver, awaiting impassioned breath from the lovely lady at the Patent Office named Ms. Griswald. But neither breath nor words forthwith or forthcome.

"Do you?" I ask again, hoping she's misunderstood and isn't playing recalcitrant.

"Indeed, I do. As does nearly everyone."

"Well?" I almost add, *drool it on out*, but keep quiet to again wait.

In the face of mounting silence, something rises in my throat and I panic, for I know the danger signals. I certainly don't want to bollix matters when they're going so famously between this Grisell woman and me, so I attach my invention to the base of my skull near my mastoid, for its first public test. I push the button. Nothing. My mastoid continues tingling, enlarging, growling.

My god, the batteries. I've solipsistically looped the tape so many times that I've run the batteries down. My throat itches; I feel mastoidal onset.

"Listen, Ms. Grisell," I say, singing her lovely name. "Are you doing anything tonight? I've got a Gold MasterCard. I could fly up and show you my invention and we could go out for dinner. Or something." Have I over-reached? Have I insulted her? "I'm sorry, I've . . . I mean, we don't know one another all that well, but I just felt this electrical pulse over the ph—"

"No problem. I know exactly what you mean. I felt it when I first heard your voice. It'd be great to go out. I know a cozy little Russian restaurant directly across from the National Rifle Association's headquarters. Oh, just one thing, though, Josey. I can call you Josey, can't I?"

My god. I've become a golden throat. NEVER MORE will I fear my mastoid gland over-reaching propriety; NEVER MORE will I call myself the World's Thinnest Fat Man. "Sure, sure," I say. "Sure, Ms. Grisell."

"That's Gris*wald*."

"Oh, sorry, Ms. Griswald. Whatever you ask. *Anything*," I add to show my compliance and liberality. After all, she's a D. C. bureaucrat.

"Well then, Jo-sey, you said you're flying up from Al-a-BAM-a with your GOLD card to show me your invention. . . ."

"Yes, yes," I say, excited, feeling my skull and other parts tingle.

"And you said your invention can work on a person who's dead or alive. . . ."

"Yes, yes." I'm panting now, bending into the phone.

"Well I'd just love to see it working on you dead."

A thousand clicks; all of Washington D.C. just hung up. My mastoid shrivels as I cradle the receiver in my teeth. And we were getting along so splendidly. If only I'd hooked up my invention to monitor my mastoid before I called, I could be making plane reservations and savoring upcoming Russian caviar with Ms. Gristle. Instead, I'm once more The World's Thinnest Fat Man, squatting on my tan-gray couch, prodding its intricate weave for benign life forms such as lice eggs.

& & &.

AFTER A MOMENT OF MEDITATION I jingle my car keys, thinking, *Wal-Mart*. Batteries, batteries, I'll stock a shelf load of Energizers in case Ms. Grist takes pity and calls back. She may, who can tell?

People have done stranger things.

Joe Taylor has stories published in over ninety literary magazines. His storynovel, *Oldcat & Ms. Puss: A Book of Days for You and Me*, was published by Black Belt Press. His previous story collection, *Some Heroes, Some Heroines, Some Others*, came out from Swallow's Tale Press. Along with Tina Jones, he edited *Belles' Letters: Contemporary Fiction by Alabama Women*. He is presently working on a story collection, *Child's Play*, plus a novel in verse entitled *Paradise Muzzled.*